D1231570

the Edge of Summer

The Edge of Summer

ERICA GEORGE

POPPY
LITTLE, BROWN AND COMPANY
New York Boston

Poppy
Hachette Book Group
1290 Avenue of the Americas, New York, NY 10104
Visit us at LBYR.com

First Edition: June 2022

Poppy is an imprint of Little, Brown and Company.
The Poppy name and logo are trademarks of Hachette Book Group, Inc.

The publisher is not responsible for websites (or their content) that are not owned by the publisher.

Library of Congress Cataloging-in-Publication Data
Names: George, Erica, author.
Title: The edge of summer / Erica George.
Description: First edition. | New York ; Boston : Little, Brown and Company, 2022. | Audience: Ages 14 & up. | Summary: Eighteen-year-old Cor Cabot navigates first love and the loss of her best friend, all while working on her summer internship to save whales on Cape Cod.
Identifiers: LCCN 2021031461 | ISBN 9780316496766 (hardcover) | ISBN 9780316496728 (ebook)
Subjects: CYAC: Whales—Fiction. | Internship programs—Fiction. | Dating (Social customs)—Fiction. | Guilt—Fiction. | Cape Cod (Mass.)—Fiction. | LCGFT: Novels.
Classification: LCC PZ7.1.G47188 Ed 2022 | DDC [Fic]—dc23
LC record available at https://lccn.loc.gov/2021031461

ISBNs: 978-0-316-49676-6 (hardcover), 978-0-316-49672-8 (ebook)

Printed in the United States of America

LSC-C

Printing 1, 2022

To all the whales of Cape Cod who swim in my heart: Lightning, Pepper, Salt, Venom, Appaloosa, Apostrophe, Wolverine, Dragon, and especially Spinnaker. Your stories matter. We'll keep working to be worthy of sharing this planet with you.

There may come a time when, in some remote, moonlit ocean glade, deserted of humanity, the last call of a humpback whale will start, and spread out, and then vanish, until those who heard it last will only wonder if they heard it at all.

—Roger Payne, *Among Whales*

Chapter One

It's been 314 days since I last felt the rush of the sea clawing up the sand, weaving between smooth pebbles, grasping for my toes, my heels, my ankles. Now that I'm here, I don't know why I stayed away so long.

I knew that whenever I returned, if I returned, the only memory the ocean would hold was the expression on her face just before I turned away. That look of utter disgust, like she didn't even know me. Like we hadn't spent the past ten years of our friendship attached at the hip, secretly passing notes between classes, sharing jokes with punch lines only we knew. That look that made me feel like a stranger. Maybe I was a stranger to the ocean, too. After all, the ocean is what took her from me. Where she must still be, considering they never found her body. It must be hard to find a body in the North Atlantic.

The waves that batter Cape Cod's shoreline, the murky blue-green sea.

What's weird is that now that I'm here, ankle-deep in ice-cold water despite the sweltering June sun beating down on my pale, freckled shoulders, this is the only place I feel like myself. This is the only place that makes sense.

Carefully, I unfold the crumpled page of notebook paper I've been carrying with me since last September, since I went back to school without her. We made a list years ago. A comprehensive list of all the things we'd both accomplish before we went off to college. She knew she wanted to go to Stanford, and my dream school is Boston, and we'd at least be together until then. But the list feels so empty now, littered with half-filled goals.

1. Internship at Marine Research and Conservation Alliance on Cape Cod.
2. Whale tattoos.
3. See Harry Styles in concert.
4. Wear elaborate ball gowns to prom.
5. Real boyfriends. Not crushes.
6. Complete the pebble collection.

I cross the first two off. I got a whale tattoo in February, and I'm here now. I'm doing the internship. Even if I am by myself.

I lift my gaze from our scribbled words and back out to sea, almost willing her to tell me what it's going to take to make things right. Or maybe to confirm that I'm going to feel like a piece of shit for the rest of my life. I'd take either at this point.

I turn from the ocean, and I pace to where I parked the Jeep on the side of the sandy, almost-paved road. The beach house we always stayed in is to my right. It looks empty, waiting, like my voice would echo if I chose to speak within its walls.

The dunes of Truro surround me. When I get to the top of the hill, I catch a peek of Pilgrim Monument in Provincetown in the distance.

In the back pocket of my jean shorts, my phone buzzes. "Uncle Jack," I answer. "I'm maybe ten minutes away."

"You should be here by now!"

"I'll be there by noon. Love you."

"Coriander!" he yelps, but I hang up in the middle of it. I can't talk to him yet. Definitely not in the right headspace.

I sit in the driver's seat of the Jeep, staring out at the thin line of blue that I can still distinguish as the ocean. I need some time to change my mindset. Push myself far away from girls lost in a swirling sea. This is my first day on Cape Cod. The first day of exactly seventy-seven that I'll be spending in Uncle Jack's house in Wellfleet.

I turn the key in the ignition and then shove the Jeep into drive, heading back toward Route 6 and then south. I pass little seafood shacks on either side, buildings that serve as a deli and a liquor store all in one, sided with cedar shake shingles, and the occasional advertisement for my uncle's business: John Michael Sutton Realty. He prides himself on picking the most decrepit, pathetic houses on the Cape and then flipping them into million-dollar getaways. His name is synonymous with fancy.

I pull into his seashell driveway, catching a glimpse of a little cobblestone patio that rests against the side of the house, surrounded by blooming tangerine tiger lilies and bright blue hydrangeas, and shaded from the sun by an umbrella that matches the shutters.

"There you are," says my uncle when he sees me heading up the driveway, burdened with my multiple pieces of luggage. He lounges under the umbrella, his legs crossed, a teacup and saucer in his hand. Across from him sits another man with dark, curly hair, but I don't recognize him.

Jumping to assist me, Uncle Jack is the epitome of New England elegance, dressed in khaki pants and a loose-fitting white button-down shirt. His blond hair is short and shiny.

"What took you so long?" he asks, hugging me so tightly that I drop my bags. He smells like clean laundry with a hint of sandalwood.

"The traffic," I manage to get out when my lungs are free to expand to their full capacity. I don't feel like saying much more than that. Not yet, at least.

Uncle Jack clucks his tongue, willing to accept my response. "And it's only beginning," he says, bending down and lifting one of my duffel bags. "Before you know it, we'll be inundated with tourists."

I won't take this personally, because I know he doesn't mean me. I'm working my way through this summer like a local at the Marine Research and Conservation Alliance. Cleaning up beaches and saving whales. I follow Uncle Jack back toward the patio, where his companion waits for us.

"Cor, come here and meet my friend, Chad."

"Chad, huh?" I reply. I lower my voice. "You know that anyone named Chad is inevitably a tool."

"Watch your mouth," Uncle Jack whispers harshly. "Oh, Chad!" he calls, waving his free hand.

We round the hydrangeas to the patio, and Chad stands.

"Cute," I whisper.

"I know," returns Uncle Jack. "Chad, I'd like you to meet my niece, Coriander."

I cringe at the use of my full name. I can't miss that Chad has practically the same reaction. Which I'm used to, of course. It's been almost eighteen years of the same response when people hear my name. I try to pretend that it's no big deal, but it takes a certain kind of person to go through life explaining to people why they're named after a spice, and I'm not sure it's me. I'd love it if just once, someone wouldn't have any kind of reaction at all. I could take indifference.

"What a unique name," croons Chad. He's very English. "Is there a story behind it?"

"My sister is a bit of a free spirit," Uncle Jack supplies. "When Cor was born, she said she wanted to name her something clean and fresh, but with bite, so Coriander was her choice."

"You can call me Cor, though. Everyone does."

Chad smiles and lifts his teacup to his mouth, taking a sip. Awkward silence ensues.

"Well, I'm going to help Cor get settled in her room, and I'll be right back down," says Uncle Jack.

He leads me in through a pair of French doors, and the air conditioning is refreshing after multiple hours driving in the sweltering summer sun.

"So, what do you think?" asks Uncle Jack.

"Of Chad?" I pinch the front of my shirt and flutter it back and forth in an effort to get some cool air up there.

He laughs. "No, of the house. It's still a work in progress, but I think it's coming along. I'd had my eye on it for such a long time."

"When was it built?"

"It's hard to say," he replies. We begin to climb a narrow staircase hidden behind a door in the corner of a nautically themed parlor. "Legend has it that a famous whaling captain stayed in this house but went back to sea unexpectedly, leaving his fiancée here. He had promised to marry her, but he was killed by an enraged whale."

That's what you get for harpooning whales. "What happened to his fiancée?" I ask.

At the top of the stairs, we turn a sharp corner down a tiny hallway. It's not wide enough for my uncle to walk with my bag at his side, so it trails behind him.

"She married his cousin, though she mourned her beloved for the rest of her life." He finds another staircase behind a door. "Of course, I don't know if the story's true or not."

"Where are we going?" I ask, maybe a little too quickly. I don't like dwelling on this topic, this feeling of being left behind.

"The attic."

I stop. "I'm sleeping in the attic?"

"It's a finished attic," he says as he opens my bedroom door. "You'll like it."

I cross the wide-planked floors to the wall of windows. We're high enough that I'm supplied with a hint of a view of Cape Cod Bay. The sun glimmers off the surface of the waves. Turning around, I flop onto the fluffy pillows piled on my bed under a canopy of gauzy white muslin.

Uncle Jack reaches out and then retracts his hand. He covers his mouth. "Maybe," he starts. "Maybe you could shower before you lie down on the bed? Because you're sweaty? And I just made it? It's so fresh." Then he considers. "But you can't use the one down the hall. I'm renovating it, so you'll have to go downstairs."

"Okay, I'll go shower."

"Oh, good." He grins. "Listen, I have some houses to show this afternoon, so you have the place to yourself. Want to meet me in P-town for dinner later?"

"Sure," I reply.

"Great! We'll go to the Sea Ghost. It's my new place."

"Okay, text me the address." I usher him to the door. "And go back downstairs and sit with your new boyfriend."

"Well, I wouldn't quite say boyfriend," says Uncle Jack. "These things take *finesse*, you know."

"Then go *finesse* your new boyfriend. I'll be, like, twenty minutes."

He pauses in the doorway. "That's it?"

"Go away!"

He laughs down the stairs as he leaves. Leaning against the door after I close it, I reach into my pocket and pull my phone out. I search my contacts until I find Brent, my brain struggling to convince itself that it's a perfectly healthy thing to text a guy who liked hooking up with you but never took you on actual dates.

We parted ways in May, unceremoniously. He said he didn't want to keep whatever it was we had going considering he was off to college. I said I didn't want to keep it going, period. But my thumb still hovers over his name in my contact list.

You wouldn't really text him, would you? Ella asks me.

She lounges on the oversize chair in the corner, watching me as I deliberate whether or not I'm pathetic for even contemplating the act.

You know he doesn't count as completing that part of our list. You might have gone out with him, but he wasn't good enough to be your boyfriend. Or anyone's boyfriend, really. Not when he's so in love with himself.

I skip Brent Tompkins and scroll back up to Ella Ridgewood.

If I just sent her a text message, sometimes I think—I hope—she'd still be at the other end, on the edge of replying. I could ask her where she went. If there are whales in the afterlife. If she can swim with them.

I send her the text I always send her. The one she's never read.

Cor (12:43 PM): I miss you. I'm sorry.

Provincetown hunches itself on the tip of the Cape, curling out into the bay and around the harbor. I crest the highest hill on Shore Road, and I push myself up as much as physically possible while still maintaining a firm grip on the steering wheel. The Jeep veers a little to the left.

I cruise down Commercial Street, passing the tourist traps, the T-shirt shops, the bakeries advertising their Portuguese fried dough, and practically every rainbow flag ever made. The colors of this town swirl around me, somehow combining with the scents of fried seafood and the salty breeze coming in from the pier.

I wonder where I'm supposed to park as I leave behind the buzz of downtown Commercial Street and begin passing little cottages tucked neatly into the corners of their fenced-in lawns, their porches hugged by huge, blooming hydrangea bushes.

On my left, I see the sign for the Sea Ghost, and the building doesn't look like a restaurant. It looks like someone's seaside retreat. Across the street, their lot is completely full, but I catch Uncle Jack, locking up the BMW, and I roll down my window.

"Want my spot?" he asks, placing his hand on the door.

"No, I'll find something."

Uncle Jack pauses to take in the Jeep. "Good lord, this thing is grotesque. Where the hell did you get it?"

"It's Rhett's," I say. "But he's on some kind of road trip with his roommates all summer, so I, you know, borrowed it."

"Does your brother know you borrowed it?"

I clear my throat and dab at a mascara smudge under my eye in the rearview mirror. "What he doesn't know won't hurt him."

"Living life on the edge, I see." He cranes his neck. "Go back the way you came, and there's a lot on the right. You'll have to pay." He shoves a twenty into my hand. Summers with Uncle Jack are wonderful.

I park in the lot Uncle Jack referred to and then cross toward the street, holding my key high in the air to lock the Jeep, but the car doesn't respond. "Dammit," I mumble. I keep backing up, my hand over my head, trying to lock the car from every angle imaginable.

I step on an unseen foot behind me and ram into someone's chest.

"Here, let me try," says the owner of the foot and the chest, grabbing the keys from my hand.

"Hey!"

I glare up, and he grins down at me, holding the key higher than I ever could, and the Jeep beeps in response. He's rather disarming, and I can feel the animosity melt from my face.

"There you go."

I take a step back because I'm suddenly aware of our extremely close proximity. He drops the key into my waiting hand.

"Thanks," I say.

"Anytime."

My mouth parts because I want to keep talking to him. Maybe I can think of something ingenious to charm him with.

"Well, see you around," I say, and keep walking. I grimace internally. See you around? I couldn't flirt my way out of a hole.

"Something I said?" He has this ease to his presence, to everything he says, that makes me feel like I should answer.

I turn and examine him: his blue-green eyes squinting because of his shit-eating grin, his sandy-brown hair, golden at the tips, and his nose slightly sunburned.

"No," I reply. Then I thumb toward the street. "I'm meeting someone, though." I back up, like I'm really busy and I can't waste any time.

He shoves his hands in the pockets of his dark gray shorts and takes a few steps forward. "Lucky someone."

As it turns out, he's not repulsed by my lack of flirtation. Intrigued, perhaps? Or is this weird.

We walk side by side in amiable silence, until finally I need to know. "Are you following me?"

"Nope," he replies.

"Because we're heading in the same direction."

"Looks that way." He stares down at me, his amusement hardly contained.

"Sure does," I reply. He's next to me, hands still secure in his pockets. I try to assess how old he is. Maybe my age. Maybe slightly older.

"I'm a little nervous," he says quietly.

Fine, I'm hooked. "What are you nervous about?"

"New job," he says.

"I'm sorry." I don't know what else to say to a stranger (a cute stranger) who's nervous about his new job and feels the need to confide in me. "I'm starting a new job, too."

"Right now? Because that would be a coincidence."

"No, this week."

The Sea Ghost comes into view, and Uncle Jack stands at the end of the sidewalk, waiting for me.

"Here's where I get off," says my companion, turning down a side street.

"Oh." I stop in the middle of the road and watch as he ambles past two Volvo SUVs parallel parked.

He gives me a little wave and then disappears around the side of a building.

"Who was that?" Uncle Jack asks once I arrive.

"I dunno, some guy from the parking lot. He needed to get some stress off his chest." We head into the restaurant.

"I won't even ask."

We enter through what appears to be a front door and into a little sitting area, complete with a fireplace. After a turn down a snug hallway, the dining room opens up before us. Huge windows line the back wall, and the bay laps at the sandy shore.

"I want to sit there," I tell Uncle Jack.

"Beautiful, isn't it? Let me order my drink, and they'll bring us to my table. I even have my own bartender. His name is Terry, and he makes my martini *just* right." He ambles over to the shiny oak bar and taps the top. "Barkeep!" he calls.

I lift myself onto one of the stools and rest my elbows on the bar. A big man who I assume is Terry comes out and grins when he sees Uncle Jack. They exchange pleasantries, and Uncle Jack orders his martini.

"There you go," says Terry once he's done shaking. He pushes the frosted martini glass over to Uncle Jack, then looks back at me. "Are you gonna sit at the bar, or do you want a table?"

"My table, please," Uncle Jack says. "By the windows."

"Sure thing." He grabs two menus and leads us to a table for two in the corner of the room. From here, we have a perfect view of the harbor, and farther out, the bay. A few ferries pull into their spots near the dock, and past the breakwater, a sailboat floats by.

Around us, groups of friends, couples, all enjoy cocktails and appetizers.

Uncle Jack settles into the seat across from me. "So update me," he says.

I scan the menu. "Update you on what?" I ask without looking up.

"How's the family?"

I chuckle a little to myself. Uncle Jack and my mom talk on the phone at least twice a week. Whatever updates he needs, he gets them from her.

"Everyone's fine," I say, closing my menu and pushing it away from me. Out of the corner of my eye, I notice Terry talking to someone, but I can't get a good glimpse of who. When he finally turns the corner, I see the guy from the parking lot, tall and tan from the sun. He wraps an apron around his waist. This must be his new job. I quickly divert my attention back to my uncle.

"What is it?" Uncle Jack asks.

"Nothing."

"It's something."

"Just the guy from the parking lot obviously works here, and I think he was trying to flirt with me, but I'm bad at being cute when I can't plan in advance, so now I'm embarrassed."

Uncle Jack cranes his neck to see him better.

"Stop it!" I whisper, slapping his hand. He settles back down in his seat. "Ignore him. Keep talking."

"All right, all right." Turning back to me, Uncle Jack asks, "How's the boyfriend?"

I blink. "Really? That's how you change the conversation?"

"I'm doing my best, Coriander!"

I lean back, raking my fingers through my hair. "I don't know if he was ever really my boyfriend, officially. But he's going to college, and I'm busy, so yeah. We're done now."

Uncle Jack nods knowingly. "Well," he says, leaning forward. "Then this is perfect, isn't it? You have a whole summer to put you first. Your internship, your whales, your passion, your fun. It's the summer of Coriander."

Close, but I don't feel like correcting him. He might be weirded out by the truth. That I have this list of all the things my best friend and I would have done before going to college, and I only have one year left. Doing this internship and spending my summer with the whales is at the top of that list. I'm not ready to be that open, even with Uncle Jack.

"I'm going to run to the restroom real quick," he says, standing. "Be right back."

I pull my braid over my shoulder, noticing how being in the sun makes the loose ends more coppery than my usual red, and pretend to study the menu, even though I already know what I want. The thing is, the guy from the parking lot is now across the room from me, spraying down empty tables and then wiping them clean with a white cloth.

I browse through appetizers, scallops wrapped in bacon, Caesar salad, clam chowder, oysters from the raw bar. I even make a study of the wine menu. But he's at the table right next to mine, and if Uncle Jack were here, he'd be blocking this guy, and I wouldn't have to think so hard about him or how well that T-shirt fits across his shoulders.

Finally, he finishes, and I lift the menu, now doing a thorough reading of the multiple ways the Sea Ghost prepares lobster. As he passes my table, he taps the top of the menu, leaving behind a folded piece of paper that looks like it's been ripped from something bigger. I catch a glimpse of him, and he offers me an amused grin over his shoulder as he heads back to the bar.

Opening the scrap of paper, I see that there's just a social media handle that reads @maybemannix.

Uncle Jack plops down in front of me again, and I jump.

"Oh, sorry," he says. He lifts his martini and takes a sip. "I thought you saw me coming."

"It's okay, I was reading something." I fold the piece of paper back up and I almost push it away, thinking of leaving it on the table. This summer isn't about boys from parking lots. It's about Ella because last summer wasn't.

I glance back at the bar, watching him chat with a few patrons. Slowly, I inch my hand toward the paper near the salt and pepper. I lean forward, slipping it into my back pocket.

Chapter Two

I spend more time than I'd like to admit sitting in the oversize chair by the window in my bedroom browsing his Instagram. Apparently, Mannix Reilly is also a lifeguard in Wellfleet. He looks remarkably good in red board shorts, and at Christmas, he wore an ugly sweater of a gaudy tree with flashing bulbs, then topped off the ensemble with a jingling reindeer antlers headband.

He laughs a lot, and his eyes squint up real tight when he does.

I almost put my phone away except that I notice he recently posted something from this morning. A picture of a few other lifeguards drinking coffee in a parking lot overlooking the ocean. Definitely not the parking lot for Cahoon Hollow, otherwise the Beachcomber restaurant would be in the background.

Feels like the wrong shape for Newcomb Hollow. It might be White Crest. Before I can think logically about my decision, I launch from the chair, shove a towel, sunblock, and a book into my beach bag, and trot down the back stairs and into the kitchen.

"Going to the beach, gotta run before the lot fills up," I say, my hand on the doorknob.

"Not so fast," says Uncle Jack.

I knew he wouldn't let me leave that easily.

"Aren't you going to eat something?" he asks from his spot by the stove. He stands over a frying pan of bacon.

"This is fine," I say as I grab a banana and an apple from the basket on the island. I shove them into my beach tote and retrieve my keys from the bottom.

"Unless you're Carmen Miranda, it's not fine. You need a well-rounded breakfast; you're a growing teenager."

Pushing my sunglasses up past my forehead, I give him the death stare. "I'm missing peak beach time, you know."

Uncle Jack transfers the crispy bacon onto a plate piled high with scrambled eggs. "I made breakfast. The least you can do is sit for five minutes and eat it."

"You are definitely my mom's brother."

"That's what the records say." He pulls two plates from the upper cabinets and places them on the island. "Now, eat up. I even squeezed some orange juice for us."

I pour a glass from the pitcher and begin stuffing my mouth. "Mom doesn't make bacon," I say between bites.

"She's always been a little crunchy." He butters a piece of toast. "But, as you're my guest for the next two months, get used to it." Adding a dollop of half-and-half to his coffee cup, he turns on the stool beside me. "When does the internship begin?"

"Tomorrow," I reply. I try to cover my mouth, but it's too late. Bits of egg splatter across his forearm. "Sorry."

He clears his throat and grabs a dish towel. Gently dabbing at his arm, he replies, "Never a problem."

"I start tomorrow," I say again once I've swallowed.

"And today?"

"Just the beach."

"Which one?"

"White Crest," I reply, shoveling a final forkful into my mouth. I swig my orange juice, stand, and pull the legs of my shorts down a bit.

"You are a pithy girl, Cor, do you know that?"

"It's an art."

Uncle Jack is quiet for a moment. He sips his coffee and makes a pleased face, allowing his eyes to rove the length of the island and settle on my wrist. "Is that a tattoo?"

I look down at what he's referencing. Like I wasn't there holding back my baby tears as the tattoo artist permanently branded me with the black-and-white whale's tail, the whale with the half fluke, one frosty February night in Philadelphia.

It was my older sister Peyton's twenty-fourth birthday, and she invited me to come out with her and her friends, told me I was getting morbid and depressing and I needed a night out to shake me from my funk. I was the only one who couldn't drink, so by the time we arrived at the tattoo parlor that never checked IDs, I was abhorrently sober and their sacrifice for the sake of entertainment.

"You like it?" I ask Uncle Jack.

He frowns. "Does your mother know?"

"I live with her, so I hope she noticed it by now."

Nodding, he takes another sip of coffee. "It's, um. Very artsy."

Uncle Jack's euphemism for *no thank you*.

But I'm not unhappy with my whale. I've loved this whale with the half fluke from the moment Ella and I picked her out of the adoption pamphlet.

"Okay, I'm full," I assure him, pushing away from the island and grabbing my tote.

"Be safe!" calls Uncle Jack as I exit the kitchen. "Wear sunscreen! Watch out for sharks!"

"It's their ocean!" I call back.

Crossing the cobblestone patio, I pull my phone out, squinting at the screen in the midmorning sun. Once again, I'm contemplating texting Brent, which brings about a swell of mixed emotions. A burdened kind of recognition. I wouldn't know what to say to him, anyway. This is why we couldn't be together. Because we don't have anything in common. We never did. I slip my phone back into the side pocket of my bag and pretend the fleeting moment of weakness never even occurred. I hop in the Jeep and drive toward the ocean.

When I turn off Route 6, I follow the road, sheltered by wild trees, as it winds through the forest, then turn right onto Ocean View Drive. The name's not a liar. Through the scrub pine and the cedar shake houses, the North Atlantic glimmers beneath the cliffs of Wellfleet. The lot for White Crest isn't full yet, but I have to park far on the end.

Pulling my phone from my bag, I click on @maybemannix's Instagram one more time. Same-shaped parking lot. Same purple flag with the image of a great white warning beachgoers that there's always a threat if you go swimming. I crane my neck to see if I can spot the whiteboard, but it's too far to read clearly.

I look back down at my phone, knowing this is the last time I can check my messages before my service disappears with every step I take to the beach. Tossing it back into my bag, I slip out of the driver's seat and lock the car. I can't be distracted now; the sea is calling. And possibly a flirty lifeguard.

Before even stepping onto the sand, I study the whiteboard the lifeguards put up each morning. The water is a bracing sixty-seven degrees, the air temperature is seventy-eight, and there haven't been any sharks spotted (yet). Lifeguards on duty: Kelsey, Nick, and, oh yes, Mannix. No maybe about it. I stand up a little straighter, fluff my hair, adjust my crop top so that the wide, ripped collar slips off my shoulders, revealing the straps of my blue-and-white-striped bikini. Sunglasses on, flip-flops discarded and tucked into my bag. I'm ready.

The path to the beach is somewhat steep, and going down is infinitely easier than it will be to get back up. At the bottom, the beach stretches to the water in a flat expanse dotted with beach blankets and umbrellas, and in the middle, the lifeguard stand.

Amid the roar of the waves, and then the quiet hush once they hit the sand and trickle back out, sea gulls swoop and soar above me, occasionally landing to pick up a scrap or two abandoned by the countless people on the beach. I make sure not to appear too interested in the lifeguard stand as I pass, searching for an open area away from the crowd.

When I'm sufficiently distanced from my fellow humans, I shake my blanket out a few times and then lay it down on the hot sand. I pull off my T-shirt and shorts, lather on the sunscreen, and attach myself via earbuds to my phone. Now that I'm sufficiently immersed in my beachgoing experience, I scan the lifeguards at the stand. One's a girl, so not Mannix. One's super short with curly blond hair, also not Mannix. Is there a possibility that there's another Mannix on duty today? That doesn't sound probable at all.

I turn my attention back to the water. I haven't been swimming since Ella died. I can't tell if it's been purposeful or not, only that water has been restricted to drinking and showering. Part of me was afraid that maybe I'd never swim in the ocean again. All those vacations on Cape Cod, winter breaks visiting Grandma in Jupiter, Florida, and splashing in her pool, or floating down the Delaware in the midsummer haze. All lost.

But maybe it's now or never.

Because I'm spending the whole summer working at a nonprofit that is literally about the ocean and everything in it. Because if I fall off a boat, I should be able to maintain some semblance of calm. I should start by stepping into the ocean now.

I pull my earbuds out of my ears and place them and my phone in a zippered pocket in my bag. I walk to the edge of the water.

The ocean is cold, the breaking waves leaving trails of foam at my feet. I wade in. Wave after wave rolls past me, knocking me in the knees, but I keep going. The water creeps up to my waist. Gulls fly above me, whisked away by the updraft of the wind, and before me, the Atlantic stretches to the east. I clench my eyes shut, take a deep breath, and dive under the next incoming wave.

The sea roars in my ears, sand skidding past my skin as I kneel on the seafloor. I'm safe, I tell myself. I'm in control. I made conscious decisions. I'm swimming near lifeguards. I'm not swimming at dawn or dusk. I haven't been drinking. I'm not too deep. I know what to do when there's a rip current.

And the sensation of being underwater is alarmingly calming. The feeling of being close to Ella again is strange and nostalgic, and when I'm here she doesn't feel so far away, or like she only exists in my imagination.

The sudden sensation of someone's arm hooked over my shoulders and heaving me upward is startling, and when I break the surface, I suck in a sharp breath and struggle to get out of their grip.

"Let go," I say, but it's quiet from my surprise, not the loud, serious scream I intended.

When they don't, I start to struggle, free my elbow from being pinned against my torso, and lodge it directly in their stomach. I'm released, and I swerve to confront my companion.

"What the fuck?" says Mannix. "Are you okay?" He grips his stomach and backs away from me.

"I'm fine, what the hell are you doing?" I push my wet hair away from my face.

"I was rescuing you!"

"I didn't need rescuing!"

"Well, I know that now." He stands there for a minute, taking deep breaths in the waist-high water. "What were you doing?"

"I just dove down and..." I try to think of how to explain it to him, but I can't. He would never get it. "I'm fine. I was swimming."

"That wasn't swimming."

"I know what swimming is."

"And I'm trained to rescue people in distress. You disappeared under the water for way too long."

"Were you watching me?"

He motions behind him at the ATV parked beside my blanket. "I was patrolling the beach, and I saw you go in."

"You knew it was me."

He places a hand on his hip and runs the other down his face, flicking off the water. He's annoyed with me. "Your red hair is kind of a dead giveaway."

I pull it over my shoulder and twist it into a thick rope.

"Besides, after our riveting conversation yesterday, I had to come back for more."

This makes me smile, despite everything. He grins.

"Thanks," I reply.

"No problem." He clears his throat, becoming suddenly serious and crossing his arms high over his chest.

"Are you okay?" I ask.

"Yeah, totally fine. But, you know."

"Know what?"

"You know..." He trails off, looking up to the sky. "Maybe readjust."

I glance down at myself and see that my bikini top has slipped from its normal location. "Holy shit. What the hell?"

"I tried to be polite!" he says, meeting my eyes.

"Well, don't look!" I motion for him to avert his eyes while I slip my boob back into my bathing suit.

"I'm sorry, I'm sorry. I thought you'd notice on your own. I was trying to be polite." He turns so his back is facing me, only for a wave to sneak up behind me and shove me into him. He's a lot faster than I give him credit for. His hand juts out, grabs my forearm, and keeps me from any further embarrassment. "You good?" he asks without looking at me. I'm able to right myself quickly.

"Absolutely freaking great," I reply. "I'm going to go sit on my blanket and pretend today never happened."

"Too late," he says when I stand beside him. "I witnessed it all. Literally everything."

I glance up at him, and he has this teasingly soft smile that's the most beguiling thing I've ever experienced in my entire life.

"Come on," he says. "I'll take you back up the beach."

I shake my head as we wade through the water together. "No, thanks. I think I'll read here for a little while."

He walks me to my blanket, though. "You here for the summer or vacation?"

"The summer," I tell him. "I'm doing an internship at the Marine Research and Conservation Alliance."

"Cool," he says. He still stands there, and I don't mind, I so desperately want to relieve this tight sense of awkwardness that's camped out between us. "So did you follow me on Instagram?" he asks me.

"Oh, you know what? I didn't get to it yet." This is not technically a lie. I didn't follow him. I just stalked the shit out of him.

He grins a little lopsidedly, playing along with my lie. "Just happened to be headed to White Crest today?"

"Definitely my favorite beach," I reply with a nod. "My uncle lives on the other side of Six, but I don't like the bay beaches as much. Waves aren't big enough."

"Yeah, definitely." He scratches the back of his head and thumbs back toward the lifeguard stand. "I should get back."

"Of course," I say with a nod, grabbing my towel and blotting my face. "Thanks for almost saving me."

"It's my job."

Before he can turn to leave, a call goes up among the beachgoers in the distance. Lifeguards grab their binoculars, families launch from their beach chairs and head to the edge of the water. Beside me, Mannix steps into the surf, shading his eyes as the others begin to cheer and clap.

At first, I think it must be a shark. But this reaction is different. It could only be a whale.

Whales have this effect on people like no other animal. When one appears, normal, rational humans transform into cheering, excitable messes. I remember my first whale watch with Ella. A humpback and her calf swam alongside our boat, and every so often, the calf would break from the water, breaching, his long pectoral fins extended into the air. And Ella turned to me and said, "Cor, I'm crying. Why am I crying?"

Because that's what happens. Because whales always remind you of how small you are. How insignificant you really are. And that even when you're fifty feet long and forty tons, possessing a physical power no human has ever had, you can still lead the gentlest of lives. It's why whales are worth dedicating my life to.

Now, at the edge of the Atlantic, I stand on my tiptoes and wonder how many of these whales I've seen. Two spouts flare into the hazy sky, and from the shape of them and the time of year, these can only be humpbacks. As they pass us, we applaud and cheer as though they were saints.

After spending a few minutes at the surface, their signature "hump" appears as they begin to dive, and then finally, a glimpse of their magnificent flukes. Streams of water drip from the first whale, and the second only has a fluke and a half. The right side is missing an entire section. I pace away from Mannix, hoping to follow along the shoreline in the direction they're going.

Our whale. The whale Ella and I adopted when we were eleven. I stare down at my wrist, her tail permanently tattooed on my body. I asked for a sign. I asked for something that would matter, and I'm a logical person, I like facts and figures, but this whale feels like something I can't explain. Like she was answering my call.

A few minutes pass, but they don't return. They're probably far out at sea now.

I return to my blanket, trying to appear unaffected. I try to convince myself that the waters off Cape Cod are filled with whales, and these whales return year after year. Only not many of them are missing a piece of their fluke, and the chances of that whale being here, now...I can't wrap my head around it.

"I saw a whale!" says a little boy with a beach ball. He trots up to Mannix, tossing his toy into his hands.

"Yeah, they were awesome, right?" Mannix replies.

The boy looks like he might be in kindergarten, and he sports reflective blue sunglasses and swim shorts covered in sharks. "So awesome," he agrees.

"Jackson," says Mannix, putting his arm around the kid's shoulders. "I'd like you to meet this girl I didn't save from the ocean whose name I still don't know."

Jackson waves like this is a totally normal introduction.

"Jackson is my neighbor's nephew," Mannix continues, poking Jackson playfully. "He's staying on the Cape for the summer, too."

26

"Hey, buddy." I put my hands on my hips and look down at him. "Do you like whales?"

He nods, digging his toe into the sand and making shapes. "Yeah, I like whales. I like spiders, too."

"Spiders are pretty cool." That's basically a lie.

He grabs his beach ball from Mannix and gallops back to his family.

I stand for a moment, trying to come up with a way to introduce myself to someone who's actually seen more of me than most people. Finally, I say, "My name's Coriander."

"Coriander," Mannix repeats.

I brace for the inevitable comment.

"That's pretty."

My shoulders relax.

He extends his hand. "Mannix Reilly."

I smile and shake it. "Coriander Cabot."

Turning from me but still smiling over his shoulder, he ambles back to his ATV, repeating quietly to himself, "Coriander Cabot."

Chapter Three

The Nature Center is a huge, modern building with massive glass windows overlooking a pond and shares a parking lot with an ocean beach. It's full today, with beachgoers and the Marine Research and Conservation Alliance summer volunteers who all have to attend an orientation. Volunteers like me.

I'm right on time as I pull into a parking spot in the middle of the lot, and as I walk into the foyer of the building, I'm greeted with the sound of quiet murmurings and people gathering. There's a folding table covered in name tags, and a man with both arms covered in sleeves of intricate ocean-themed tattoos and bleached-blond hair pulled back into a bun. His name tag hangs around his neck: JUSTIN BURKE (HE/HIM), ORLEANS, MASSACHUSETTS.

"What's good? I'm Justin," he says, extending his hand.

"Coriander Cabot." I take his hand. He has an intense handshake.

"Coriander, Coriander," he says, searching through the layout of name tags. "Who could forget that name, right?"

"Not me." I smile and tuck a loose strand of hair behind my ear.

"Here we go." He lifts my name tag and presents it to me: CORIANDER CABOT (SHE/HER), DUSK HOLLOW, NEW JERSEY. My existence reduced to one laminated name tag. "Glad to have you with us this summer, Coriander."

"Me, too." I smile, draping it around my neck.

"Here's some paperwork we're going to have you fill out. Any allergies, emergency contacts, you know the drill." He hands me a clicky pen and points across the foyer. Two people my age stand near the open staircase that leads upward, clutching their paperwork and clipboards and glancing around. "Over there you'll find Kyle and Mia, your volunteer colleagues this summer. Go mingle, make friends!"

I do as I'm told, trying not to make eye contact too overeagerly, but still wanting them to accept me because this is the worst, and I'm sure they feel the same way. The first day of anything is the worst. You're always inevitably alone, you have to extend yourself when making new acquaintances, and then conjure forced small talk. But I take a deep breath, envisioning the knot in my stomach slowly unraveling.

"Hi," I say when I arrive.

"Hello." Name tag: MIA CHO (SHE/HER), FALLS CHURCH, VIRGINIA.

"Hey." Name tag: KYLE SONNEVELD (THEY/THEM), RHINEBECK, NEW YORK.

I notice they're both busy staring at my name tag, too, and

I might as well save them the awkwardness. "Coriander," I say. "Like the spice, but if ever you need my attention, and you feel weird yelling Coriander across a room, I usually go by Cor."

"I like that, though," says Mia. She bounces on her feet. "It's nice to meet you." Mia's long, thick black hair is held back with a headband, and she has the most genuine smile I've ever seen on another person.

"It's nice to meet both of you."

"Kyle," they say, extending their hand. Kyle is well over six feet tall, and Mia must be close to a foot shorter than that. I'm pleasantly in the middle, and I already like them both. I didn't anticipate making friends at this internship, but it gives me butterflies to think it might end up that way. "Did you fill out your paperwork yet?"

"Just started."

Mia sighs. "I need to text my mom and see if she knows my blood type offhand."

I study the paperwork in my hands. "They're thorough here."

"I'm surprised we don't need a physical," says Kyle, tossing their long brown hair over their shoulder.

"I'd have a physical if it meant securing this internship," says Mia. "I've been counting down the days until this summer."

I touch her elbow. "Me, too."

"So where are we all staying?" Kyle asks. "Nearby? Maybe we can carpool. I would love to carpool and get coffee together in the morning."

"My family rented a cottage in Truro for the summer," Mia replies. "Has a nice view of a pond, and an outdoor shower."

"That sounds lovely," says Kyle.

"That's the only shower." She smiles up at them. "It's um... sparse."

Kyle nods. "Oh, I see. Like a real *Thoreau* experience."

"Something like that. What about you?" Mia asks them.

"I'm staying in my cousin's little apartment in Province-town. I have a pullout couch and an outlet for my phone, and that's all I need."

"How about you, Cor?" Mia asks. I like Mia's cute sundress, and her flip-flops with the big daisies at the toe.

"I'm staying with my uncle in Wellfleet. He lives there."

"Is he, like, a cool uncle?" Kyle asks. "Or an annoying suf-focating uncle who doesn't respect your autonomy?"

"No, he's the best," I reply with absolute confidence.

The crowd around us begins to stream into a separate room with a whiteboard in the front and posters of the Cape's wild birds. Kyle, Mia, and I find three seats in the second row, right at the end. But just as I'm getting comfortable, situating my clip-board on my lap so that I can continue to fill out my paperwork while the presenter speaks, a tall Black woman kneels down beside Kyle.

"Hey, group," she says. She has long coils pulled back from her face in a high bun on the top of her head and wears a MRCA T-shirt, khaki shorts, and gleaming white sneakers. "I'm Lottie."

I stare at her name tag: DR. CHARLOTTE RICHARDS (SHE/HER), TRURO, MASSACHUSETTS. She's living my dream.

"This presentation isn't for you. More like for the people who are volunteering to clean up after our rehabilitating ani-mals or answer phones." She nods toward the door and stands. "Come with me."

She leads us out of the conference room, back through the

foyer, where she stops and says something to Justin, then out the glass doors to a little picnic area under the shade of several trees. The air here is sharp with pine and salt. I breathe in as deeply as my lungs will allow.

"Take a seat, take a seat," says Lottie as she straddles the bench on the opposite side of the table. "Finish your paperwork, relax. Let's talk about what your summer is going to look like. I want to answer any questions you have."

I hope it's going to look like getting out on the water. Taking skin samples from whales, tagging great white sharks, pulling into the harbor at sunset, and sleeping soundly because you've had a full day on the high seas.

"I am at my very *best*," Kyle begins, folding their hands in front of them, "when I am interacting with the general public. Spreading the good word about conservation, making allies for our cause. Give me a podium, and I'll be your politician."

Lottie leans back and giggles quietly. "You'll be doing plenty of community outreach," she says. "Lots of time on the beach, some manning of the merch shack on MacMillan Pier in P-town, some paperwork from time to time."

I'm getting a little panicky that I haven't heard the word *boat* yet.

"We do beach cleanups, and fundraisers." She keeps going.

"And maybe some time out on the water?" I ask hopefully.

Lottie shrugs. "Sometimes. We'll need someone to assist the naturalists on the whale watches, take pictures of the whales we find while we're out there."

"I've taken some photography classes at school," says Mia. "I've even attended a few after-school sessions at our local community college."

"Oh, that's great," says Lottie. "You can teach us a lot, I bet."

Mia smiles down at her lap and shrugs.

"Do you think we'll take part in disentangling?" I ask.

"Take part in?" Lottie appears astonished, and I didn't realize that my question was so outlandish. "No, never."

My mouth opens, but I can't think of anything to say.

"Professionals have died disentangling whales," she continues, leaning back and crossing her arms over her chest. "It takes training and knowledge. There's no way we'd ever send a kid out there to deal with a terrified and agitated whale. Nope."

I feel the surprising sting of tears at the back of my eyes, and I hate that. I hate that her response makes me feel bad. Like I'm thoughtless. Like I should have known better than to have asked such a dumb question.

We sit there for a little while longer, Kyle and Mia still asking questions, but I want to curl in on myself and disappear. I pretend to take copious notes to appear engaged. The sound of an ice cream truck pulling into the parking lot lifts me from my notebook.

"So there are a lot of things you'll be participating in this summer," Lottie says. "Definitely something for three college-bound students who love the ocean, right?"

Kyle and Mia nod, and I follow along.

"Did you both spend summers on Cape Cod before this?" Mia asks, glancing between me and Kyle.

"Almost every summer," says Kyle.

"Me, too," I reply.

Mia agrees. "Same."

"What got you all interested in applying?" Lottie asks.

I don't even listen to Mia's and Kyle's responses. I can't. My brain is thrumming with the quiet hum of my elementary school library, the buzz of the tired HVAC system, how Mrs. Hanson would murmur lyrics to old songs while she put books back on shelves, and Ella would almost whisper the words to whatever book on whales we shared. Our safe space and the little prayer we offered between us. The only place I ever felt I belonged.

A space that became increasingly too small the older we got, and I was afraid I'd outgrow it and never fit in anywhere else.

But always the whales. Always their songs that would drown out the sound of our classmates distantly on the playground.

"Coriander?" Lottie asks.

I glance up. "Yes?"

"Why did you apply for the internship?" She looks genuinely intrigued. Mia and Kyle, too.

Tell them, Ella says. *Tell them about the whales. Tell them how you know each species by the shape of their flukes. Tell them how their eyes are humanlike, and you told our fourth-grade teacher that whales had souls. Tell them how we planned for this internship since we were twelve. Tell them how you dream about the whales, and in your dreams they're always right at the shoreline, so close you could reach out and touch them. Tell them, Cor.*

I press my lips together, shaking the image of Ella, and her voice, from my mind. Not yet. "I mean, I'm good at science. I took honors bio. I want to major in marine biology, and I guess an internship looks good on college applications, right?"

Lottie's mouth is slightly parted and her eyes narrow at my response. "Right."

Mia laughs nervously.

"Why don't you all take a break and grab something from

the ice cream truck?" Lottie suggests, standing from the picnic table and stretching. "You have one mandatory presentation this afternoon, and then we can reconvene tomorrow morning at headquarters in P-town." She collects our paperwork and clips them together.

"Thank you," says Mia.

Kyle waves. "See you tomorrow."

I remember to shake myself from my embarrassment. "Bye, thanks."

Lottie makes her way back into the Nature Center, taking a moment to glance over her shoulder at me and then disappearing behind the glass doors.

"I'm getting a Choco Taco," says Kyle. They swing their legs over the bench and stride out to the parking lot.

I'm a little slower.

"You coming?" Mia asks. She tilts her head to the side and waits for me to join them.

"Yeah, ice cream sounds good," I reply, even though my stomach is a little bubbly from our discussion. I follow them across the parking lot to where the truck waits to take our orders.

As I pull into the driveway, my phone dings. It's Uncle Jack.

Uncle Jack (4:48 PM): Meet me for dinner later at Sea Ghost. Been here with clients all afternoon.

I love a free meal. At least that's what I tell myself. Free meals are a great excuse to go to the restaurant Mannix works at, and

Mannix is perhaps the most perfect distraction from everything boiling up inside me today.

It's considerably easier to find a parking spot this evening than it was last week. I hop out of the Jeep, and suddenly, I'm second-guessing everything, from my choice of shoes to my earrings, and I try to wave my jitters away. Mannix works here, at a restaurant that my uncle frequents. He won't read my presence as anything out of the ordinary, so I should attempt to be a little more casual than I feel. As the sun sets and casts a golden glow across the lavender sky, I travel the cobblestone sidewalk up to the front door. Inside, the host, an adorable guy dressed in tight jeans and a white oxford with thick-rimmed black glasses, smiles at me.

"Table for one?" he asks, clutching his menus to his chest.

"No, I'm meeting someone." I peer over his shoulder and see Uncle Jack at a table with an attractive young couple. "I see him."

The host smiles and gestures for me to go ahead.

I can't plop down next to Uncle Jack while he's discussing real estate with prospective buyers, so I slip onto a barstool, waiting for my moment to let him know I've arrived.

"Come here often?" A cocktail napkin slides into view.

I smile and steady my sweaty palms on my thighs. "I guess I do."

Mannix grins at me, his meticulously messy hair glowing in the low light of the bar. "What can I get you?"

"I dunno. Um, water, I guess."

He contemplates for a moment, leaning on the bar. "What about tomato juice?"

Tomato juice is one of those things I don't enjoy but feel it necessary to consume for my overall health. As I've absorbed mostly Diet Coke and ice cream all day, I agree to it. "Okay, let's try it."

He slaps the bar with his palm and begins rummaging for the ingredients. "You'll like this, I swear."

"How long has my uncle been here?" I ask, taking a sip of the ice water Mannix gets me before my drink arrives.

"All afternoon, one client after another. He's a popular guy."

The doors to the deck are open, and the gentle lapping of the bay on the shore soothes me. The breeze swirls around, flickering the candle flame in the votive near my hand. "He texted earlier. Said he wanted to grab dinner. I guess his meeting is going longer than he thought."

Mannix pours the tomato juice into a highball glass. He adds a few ingredients, like he's making a Bloody Mary minus the vodka. "You know what would help you avoid this situation? Wondering if your uncle was finished with his meetings and all that?"

I arch my eyebrow. "What?"

Smirking, Mannix replies, "If I had texted you to let you know. But, you know..." He wipes down the bar and pushes my tomato juice toward me. "I'd need your number for that."

I grab my drink and take a swig. It's a little salty and the perfect antidote for my high-sugar afternoon. "You *would* need my number for that," I agree.

He waggles his eyebrows at me.

"What?" I ask.

"Nothing." He shoves a stalk of celery into my glass. "We're in agreement."

"Of how texting works? Yes, we are."

I feel Uncle Jack plant a kiss on top of my head. "Glad you got my message," he says. He squeezes my arm and then acknowledges Mannix. "A refill of my usual, good sir."

Mannix salutes him.

"Sorry that took so long," Uncle Jack continues. "But I think I just sold *the* house to that couple."

"Oh yeah?"

"Oh yeah. It's right off Shore Road in Truro, overlooking the bay. It's been completely renovated, and they want to rent it when they're not staying in it. It's a gold mine."

"Cheers," I say, and clink my glass to his almost-empty martini.

"What are you drinking?" he asks.

"Tomato juice," I reply, and then pluck the celery out to examine. "With celery." I take a peek around the side of the glass. "And green olives. And one of those spicy peppers."

"Peperoncini," he clarifies.

"Mm-hmm." I take a bite, immediately regretting my enthusiasm when the heat hits my tongue.

"So, tell me about your first day."

I sigh, which is probably not what my uncle wants to hear after the first day of my internship. "It was good. I filled out a lot of paperwork, and there was a lot of talking. But maybe tomorrow we'll actually start working."

"Are there other interns there your age?" asks Uncle Jack as Mannix places his fresh drink in front of him. His phone buzzes on the bar before I can reply, and he stares at it for a moment. "Damn, that's my contractor." He lifts the phone and swipes right. "Hello?"

I ignore the conversation in general, focusing instead on Mannix making drinks.

"Who's on the phone?" he asks, drying his hands on a towel.

Somehow, when he asks, it doesn't feel intrusive.

"His contractor," I whisper. "His house is being renovated."

Uncle Jack's face drops. "But Merritt, we're so close to finishing!"

Then silence.

"You're just going to leave me in the middle of this? Without an upstairs bathroom?" Uncle Jack removes the phone from his ear and stares incredulously at the screen. He clicks it off.

"Yikes," says Mannix, folding his dishcloth.

"Well, he's not getting the rest of the money I owe him," Uncle Jack mumbles, dropping the phone on the bar. He sips his drink and then covers his face with his hands. "What am I going to do now?"

Mannix steps back and places his hands on his hips. "You need someone to finish a bathroom?"

"Yes," Uncle Jack moans.

"I can do it," says Mannix.

"You?" asks Uncle Jack.

"Sure." His self-assurance is astounding.

Before Uncle Jack can ask him any more questions, Mannix is flagged by a couple at the opposite end of the bar. The two men must know him, maybe they're regulars, too, and he makes them laugh.

Pretty charming, says Ella. She's camped out in the corner of the room, watching Mannix. *Everyone likes him. Clearly you like him. But I get why you're hesitant.*

She's persistent today, and I veer my attention back to Mannix once he stands in front of us again.

"Do you have any experience with renovations?" Uncle Jack asks.

Mannix leans on the counter with both hands, his shirt cuffed up to his elbows. "Plenty. My uncle's a contractor, and I help when I can."

"But bathrooms, specifically?"

Mannix reaches into his back pocket and pulls out his phone. After swiping through a few pictures, he slides it over to Uncle Jack. "This is one I did down in Eastham."

Uncle Jack studies the screen for a moment. "Come by tomorrow, and see what you're in for. Then we'll discuss price."

Mannix extends his hand, and they shake.

"Let's exchange numbers," suggests Uncle Jack. "Mannix what?"

"Reilly," he replies, and then supplies Uncle Jack with his cell number. "Be there around eight tomorrow morning?"

"Perfect," says Uncle Jack.

Delightful, says Ella.

I pretend to be preoccupied with the floating olive in my drink. I can feel Mannix waiting for a response, and finally, when I glance up, he wiggles his eyebrows at me again.

And no matter how hard I fight it, I blush down at the bar.

Chapter Four

The playground I used to frequent after lunch each weekday at Lafayette Elementary School was bright blue and green, and the monkey bars were my favorite location. One day, I hung from the monkey bars with an inadequate grip and then fell to the ground, my skirt up around my waist, flashing the entire second grade my *My Little Pony* panties. From that point forward, I transformed into a social pariah. As though the red hair and freckles weren't enough.

I started sitting on the wooden beams that lined the wood-chipped playground, watching my classmates from afar. That was when a half-eaten apple landed at my feet. I looked up to find a gang leader looming over me. Carleen. She even blotted out the sun.

"Look," she said, pointing at the apple with her foot. "That's you."

By her sneer, I knew that wasn't supposed to be a compliment. "What?"

"That's you. It's an apple core. A brown, wormy apple core. You're a core, Cor!"

Hair. Panties. Name. All the stars aligned.

To avoid having them notice my tears, I slunk away to one of the lunch aides and asked if I could go to the bathroom. Wish granted, I trudged inside, but not before the apple core hit the back of my head. I found solace in the foyer between the doors and hallway, where I had myself a good cry, then escaped to the bathroom and washed my face with cool water like Mom always did.

Feeling somewhat refreshed, I stared up at the clock over the pink door. There were still twelve infernal minutes left to recess, and the only place I felt safe was within the confines of an elementary school bathroom.

I tiptoed as slowly and quietly as possible past the library. I poked my head in when I noticed my classmate Ella Ridgewood curled up in the corner nearest the door, her nose glued to whatever she was reading.

She must have sensed me. "What do you want?" She squinted her eyes.

I had never been mean to Ella. But I had never bothered to talk to her, either. She was kinda weird. Even weirder than me, apparently, because she had never even tried to go out on the playground. She knew better.

I took a step forward. "What are you reading?"

"A magazine article about humpback whales by Dr. Roger Payne. He was the first to discover that male humpbacks sing songs."

She didn't talk like the other second graders. Maybe she could be trusted.

"Oh," I said stupidly. I began to back out of the door.

"Wait!" Ella cried, holding up a hand. "Do you want to learn about them? I can tell you anything you want to know about whales."

"Anything?" I asked.

"Anything."

I glanced over at the media specialist, Mrs. Hanson, and while she knew I was there, she didn't make any motion to stop me from coming in. Crouching down beside Ella, I allowed her to lead me, gently, into the quiet world of the whales.

Sitting here now, in Uncle Jack's kitchen with my binder of whale flukes and my flash drive of photos taken on recent excursions, I think about how Ella would have thrived with this task. She would have loved being surrounded by the whales on the water, and she would have risen to the challenge of identifying the whales we saw by the flukes of the whales that frequent Stellwagen Bank each summer.

The more I think about her, the less I can concentrate on my homework. Lottie asked me to identify twenty-six individual humpback whales on my day off, and with Uncle Jack showing houses all day, I figured I could knock it out, easy.

But Chad has decided to stop by and monopolize the kitchen island with Tupperware reorganization.

"You know, he never lets me near the pantry when he's home," Chad says over his shoulder. He's behind me, sorting through Uncle Jack's lids and bowls.

I try to contort my body language to read "frustrated worker attempting concentration," but Chad is far too focused on his own chore this morning to notice my demeanor.

"So the moment he told me he'd be in Chatham all day, I knew I had to sneak in here, and lucky me! I get your company, too, Coriander."

"I'm sorry I'm not more fun." I'm trying to make it sound like I'm the one who's being annoying. Maybe he'll keep his organizing to a one-man job that doesn't require conversation. I even glance apologetically down at my massive binder of flukes. I woke up at seven and came downstairs to get a head start.

"Oh, never you mind," Chad insists. "I'll hardly be a bother. So what are you up to?"

I sigh, staring across the kitchen and out the window over the sink. It's breezy this morning, and Uncle Jack left the air conditioning off and the windows wide open. The scent of the rosebushes that border the side of the house, mixed with earthy pine and the hint of salt, coasts in on a lazy gust. Followed by someone shouting, "Jesus Christ!"

"Oh," says Chad in surprise, placing a hand over his heart. "My, my. Someone's morning isn't going well."

"There isn't anyone close by that we should be able to hear except Mrs. Mackenzie."

"Maybe she has a gentleman caller."

I cross the kitchen and stand on my tiptoes to see more clearly out the window. Mannix stands in the backyard, hunched over and ushering something small on its way.

"He seems a little young for Mrs. Mackenzie," says Chad, standing behind me.

"He's not here for Mrs. Mackenzie," I assure him.

"Is he here for you? Because then I want to fix your hair." His arms crossed over his chest, he examines my coppery locks. "A little flat, but not bad."

"Chad, he's here to renovate the upstairs bathroom."

He grimaces. "Then what's he doing outside with that turtle?"

"I think he needs help."

"The boy or the turtle?"

"Both."

"He's struggling, Coriander. And breathtaking. Go help him."

"I see you have an altruism-for-hunks-only policy," I mutter, pushing my stool away from the kitchen island and trudging over to the door.

"You'll thank me someday." Chad ushers me out to the patio.

The broad, leafy branches of a maple tree shelter me from the bright morning sun. Across the lawn, Mannix hovers over what looks to be a box turtle, his hands on his hips as he tries to verbally coax it toward Uncle Jack's man-made koi pond.

"Whatcha doing?" I ask.

He turns to observe me and points to the turtle. "Trying to get this jackass to safety."

"He's not a jackass," I say, crossing the green slope down to the pond. "He's a box turtle."

Mannix tilts his head to the side.

"Get it? He's not a jackass, a donkey, he's a box tur—? Never mind. Where did you find him?"

Pointing to the end of the driveway, he replies, "He was in

45

the middle of the road when I pulled up. So I hopped out of the truck and tried to bring him back to a safe place."

"Which way was he heading?"

"The other side of the street."

"Well, there's our problem." I crouch down and lift the turtle with two hands and pace across the lawn and down the length of the driveway. Mannix follows. "If you're going to help a turtle cross the road, make sure you bring it wherever it was headed. Box turtles can get stressed if they're moved too far from where they live."

I skip down the little hill on the side of the road and leave the turtle in the safety of the underbrush. He shuffles along on his way.

"Where'd you learn that?" Mannix asks, watching the turtle disappear behind a wall of green foliage.

"Books mostly." I look up at him. "Working on the bathroom today?"

He thumbs over to his truck. "Just have to get my tools out of the back."

"Meet you inside." Then I add, "Want some coffee? I'm about to make a fresh pot."

Mannix grins. "Wouldn't want to wield any power tools without caffeine."

"Please don't." I shove my hands in the pockets of my shorts and smile over my shoulder at him. He stands beside his truck, watching me walk back up to the house.

"Did you save the turtle?" Chad asks once I'm back in the kitchen. "Did you save the boy?"

"Both are doing quite well and thriving due to my intervention, thank you for your inquiry." I stand in front of the coffeemaker and begin measuring heaping scoops of ground Colombian blend into the tan filter.

"He's coming inside," Chad whispers, like Mannix will hear him from the patio.

"All the better to renovate the upstairs bathroom."

"Hey," says Mannix, coming through the back door. He puts his equipment on the floor and looks at Chad. "Oh, hi. I didn't know someone else would be here."

"I'm Chad, and I'm charmed." He extends his hand to shake Mannix's.

"Chad is Uncle Jack's partner, and he's here organizing while Uncle Jack shows houses today."

"I won't be in your way," Chad assures him, turning back to the pantry and tossing the Tupperware he doesn't like.

"I'll bring up your coffee once it's ready," I say.

"Thanks, I'd like that." Mannix lifts his things and heads to the back staircase, then pauses again. He doesn't say anything for a minute, almost like he's trying to think of something witty but comes up short. "So I'll be up there all day."

"Mm-hmm."

"If you need anything, I'd get it now."

I glance from side to side, taking inventory of my surroundings. "I should be good. Got my laptop, coffee soon. Probably gonna make a smoothie once you start."

"Good," says Mannix. "Great." He smiles over at Chad. "I guess I'll get to it, then."

"Lovely meeting you, Mannix," says Chad.

"You, too." He climbs the stairs and disappears around the corner at the top.

I tap the granite countertop of the island once and then

search through the cabinet next to the sink for Uncle Jack's blender. A nutritious, protein-filled fruit smoothie and a massive cup of coffee is just the way to start off my day.

Chad watches me as I clang around. "You want one, too?" I ask. "I've got some fresh strawberries and yogurt, so I thought I'd—"

"I like him," says Chad.

I stand up straight, somewhat unsure what we're discussing.

"He's adorable, he's polite, and he's upgrading your bathroom. You couldn't possibly ask for more."

I point above us like we can see Mannix through the ceiling. "Him?"

Chad rolls his eyes. "Like it's even a question."

"Please," I say. "I don't have time for hookups, Chad."

"So you've already envisioned hooking up with him. Very telling." He crosses his arms across his chest and nods like he's considering the implications of this.

"I have not!"

"Don't believe you."

"Chad, I hardly even know him."

He takes a self-satisfied sip from his mug.

It doesn't take long before the coffee is finished brewing.

Grabbing my mug with one hand and Mannix's in the other, I carefully make my way up the stairs. The groan of wood being ripped from the floor bounces along the hallway.

"Got your coffee," I call before I reach the bathroom door.

Mannix pokes his head out. "Hey, thanks." He reaches for his cup and grips it with both hands, taking a careful sip.

"Welcome." I lean against the doorframe, observing him over the rim of my mug. "So how's it going?"

Mannix peers over his shoulder and then rubs the back of

his neck. "Not bad. Figured I'd take the floor up first before I start on the tub. Have a clean slate."

"I meant in general," I say a little more quietly. "Like, how are things?"

"Oh." He has to think about this. "Pretty good."

"The Sea Ghost is good?"

"Yeah, great."

"And the ocean?" Internally, I cringe. *And the ocean*. What the hell.

Mannix grins. "The ocean is always good. Always. Better than anything else."

I swallow the lump forming in my throat. I don't know why his words usher in the image of Ella at the railing of her father's boat. She watches three humpbacks as they surface and roll among the waves.

"You're right," I say, and then I clear my throat, hoping he doesn't notice how my voice catches. "The ocean is always better than anything else."

His face softens a little, because, I think, he noticed. "You like your internship so far? I saw that picture you posted of you and two other people at the Nature Center."

"Insta-stalking?"

"You liked my picture of White Crest the other day. It felt like I should return the gesture." Mannix turns back to the bathroom, placing his mug of coffee on the ledge of the bathtub, and then kneels down in front of the linen closet door. He begins to dismantle it by the hinges. "I got the vibe that you were a salt girl." He tosses the old hardware into a waiting bucket. "I figured you must be if you volunteer at MRCA."

"Yeah, I am." I edge around the doorframe so that I'm half

in, half out of the bathroom. "I used be a lot more than I am now. I think I'm trying to reconnect with that Coriander."

"And which Coriander is that?" he asks, lifting from his kneeling position and crouching at the middle hinge.

The Coriander who didn't mind spending recesses in the library reading books about whales, the Coriander who had a best friend she loved, the Coriander who wouldn't have abandoned her, the Coriander who liked herself, the Coriander who was content with herself. The Coriander who didn't feel so lost, so anchorless.

Mannix stands up straight, watching me, waiting for my reply.

"Still me, I guess," I say quietly. "This is the first time I've been to Cape Cod without my best friend."

"She couldn't make it this year?" He tosses the middle hinge into the bucket, and it clangs against its contents. Now the door hangs haphazardly, like a loose tooth.

"No," I say quickly. "She couldn't...."

There's a part of me that wants to tell Mannix what happened. He seems like the kind of person I can confide in. But there's another part of me that doesn't want him to think I'm telling him too much too quickly. Burdening him with all my shit. So I didn't lie, exactly. I told him a less intense version of the truth.

"Okay, well, I have some whales to identify."

"From the house?" He looks out the window, like he's searching for the sea.

"I have fluke pictures I need to match with names." I pull my phone from my pocket and show him a picture of Salt, maybe the most famous whale in Stellwagen Bank. "See? Each humpback's flukes are unique. Like a fingerprint. I need to match some recent photos to the records MRCA keeps."

Mannix squints, like he's suddenly going to recognize this whale. "I feel like that's a fact I learned in school and then forgot."

"Well, I'm glad I was here to remind you."

He takes a step back, gazing down at me. "I'm glad you were, too."

I blink, my mouth parting.

But he smiles, and it makes me feel like that was the reaction he was hoping for.

"So I um, yeah." Taking a step back, I thumb toward the hall and nod my head. "Yeah, I'll get going, and if you need anything, just call."

"I will." He stands in front of the linen closet door, looking up at the last hinge and putting the screwdriver to work.

In the kitchen, Chad continues to pull apart cabinets, tossing endless amounts of lidless plastic containers into the recycling bin and then stacking those that remain neatly. "I know I'm probably in your way," he says over his shoulder, glancing down at the cluttered island. "There's that nice little reading nook in the front sitting room. You could cozy up over there, and as soon as I'm done here, I'll let you know."

"Thanks," I say, gathering my laptop and the binder of whale flukes.

There's a window seat with a navy-and-white-striped cushion and several pillows with a variety of seashells adorning their faces, and I decide this is the best place to get any work done. I pull one of the side tables with a lamp over to the bench and situate my laptop beside me. Fluffing my pillows, I pull my knees up, lean my binder against my thighs, and turn to the first page of whales.

I don't glance up at the clock very often because that seems like torture. I try to set goals for myself. Once I identify two whales, I can get up and get a little wrapped chocolate from the candy bowl in the main hall. If I identify five whales, I can meander over to the window and sneak a peek of Mannix hauling wood from the back of his pickup truck. It's a sorry-looking burnt-orangish-red Chevy that's clearly seen a lot of miles.

I need to focus. And I didn't identify five whales yet, so that means I need to extricate myself from the view of the front yard and zero in on Stellwagen Bank. This is fine. This is easy.

At first, it works. Two whales seem to fly by. No sweat. I grab a chocolate from the green glass bowl on the hall table and linger there for a little while, letting it melt in my mouth. Mannix comes in through the back door, he and Chad exchange some small talk, and I peek in to see if there's anything cute I can witness. Mannix notices and offers me a little wave, which I imitate awkwardly before retreating to my window seat.

When I've managed to ID four whales, I come to a dead stop. There is no way I can move past four. I'm screwed, and it's probably because I cheated after two whales. Two whales didn't warrant a quick spy on Mannix. Two whales meant chocolate, and that was it. You can't con the system.

I flip the page of the binder, my eyes skimming the eight flukes in front of me, and they all start to look identical. Until I get to the bottom right corner, where the image of a whale with a fluke and a half resides. My whale.

Her name is Fraction. She was first documented in Stellwagen Bank off Race Point, in June of 2004. Fraction. Part of a whole. Her name tugs at my attention in a way I didn't expect. It's nice being a part of a whole. It's nice *feeling* whole.

"Hey."

His voice pulls me from Fraction over to the door of the sitting room. Mannix leans in, most of his body still in the foyer. "Hey," I reply.

"I'm gonna pick something up for lunch. You want a sandwich?"

I glance down at my watch and see that it's past noon. "I was going to make some chicken salad. You interested?"

He considers this for a minute. "Sure. I'll help."

I shift my laptop off my lap and leave my whales until later. Mannix follows me into the kitchen, where Chad has expertly rearranged all the plastic containers and their corresponding lids in the cabinets and left a Post-it note plastered to the fridge as our only guide. Opening the door, I find the leftover grilled chicken breasts and hand them to Mannix, and then show him where the knives are kept. Meanwhile, I locate the celery and onion and the jar of mayo.

"Do you have any sour cream?" Mannix asks as he slides a cutting board out from behind the toaster.

"I think so." I stand on my tiptoes to see a little better, and pull the container of sour cream out.

"And some of this," says Mannix, suddenly behind me. He's close enough that I can smell the soap he used to shower this morning, that I can feel the heat from his body. And my body. I clear my throat as he reaches over me and grabs a bottle of Dijon mustard, and then swerves to swipe an apple from the fruit basket on the counter.

"What's the mustard for?" I ask, ducking under his arm and

pretending to be rather preoccupied with pulling apart stalks of celery.

"The chicken salad," he says.

"And the sour cream?"

"It'll taste better than if you used mayo." He begins dicing the chicken. "Where's the pantry?"

I point across the room to the wooden door with the sign that reads BUTLER, and he goes in, obviously on the search for more ingredients that escape my limited sphere of cooking knowledge.

"Dried cranberries," he says, emerging with the plastic bag.

I snort in amusement. "You clearly know more about cooking than I ever will."

"Is that an herb garden your uncle has on the side of the house?"

I don't even know how to reply anymore, so I nod.

"Can I go check it out?"

"I mean, I guess so."

"I'll need some kitchen shears."

I point to the drawer next to him, and he finds what he's looking for. Before I can even ask what he's going to attempt outside, he's through the back door and hovering in Uncle Jack's kitchen garden, among the burgeoning cherry peppers and zucchini blossoms. When he comes back inside, he swipes his hair out of his eyes and presents me with two green stalks of something very fragrant.

"Dill," he says.

"Clearly." I chop the celery and stare at him incredulously. "You're kind of a wonder. Between lifeguarding, and working at the restaurant, and you can apparently cook. And remodel bathrooms."

"Never rescued a whale, though," he says with a half grin as he begins to peel the onion.

"Well, that makes two of us." I don't want to talk about whales right now, or anything that remotely makes me think of Ella. It's easier to avoid that; it's easier to focus on Mannix. "So how'd you get so good at so many things?"

He shrugs and wipes his face with his forearm, carefully avoiding touching his fingers to his eyes. "You get good at the things you have to be good at. I mean, being a lifeguard felt like an obvious choice when it was presented to me. I like being in the ocean, and I like helping people. And cooking has always come naturally, you know? I like to eat, so I got good at making food that I wanted to eat." Smiling, he looks back down at his hands. "Besides, it makes people happy when you feed them."

"Well, that's true," I admit.

He tosses me the apple. "Get chopping and tell me what got you so interested in whales."

I scratch my forehead and take a deep breath. "A whale is the kind of animal that doesn't feel real, you know?"

He scrunches his nose in a way that articulates he does not know.

"Like, they're so huge, and their lives are so different from ours, it makes you wonder how it's even possible that we get to share a planet with them. And when you think about how awful we used to be to them, how awful we still are to them, and yet they never, ever do anything to us. Sometimes they even go out of their way to help us. I just. I dunno. I don't know how anyone can look at one and not think they're in the presence of something greater than themselves."

Mannix nods, placing his hand on my wrist. "I think that's

a good enough chop," he says, nodding at my nearly minced apple. "You can add it to the bowl." He watches me as I follow his directions.

I scrape the chunks from the cutting board into the bowl with the chicken, dried cranberries, celery, and onion. Mannix adds in the condiments, the chopped dill, and a few spices from Uncle Jack's cabinet, then mixes it all together.

"I like what you said about the whales. I mean, even the fact that they breathe air but live most of their lives underwater. That's amazing," he says.

Ella's on the opposite side of the island, watching Mannix and me make chicken salad. *It must be frightening to live in one world, underwater, and rely so desperately on the oxygen of a totally different world*, she says. *Must be terrifying when what you want, what you need is so close, but you're being kept from it.*

I stare at Mannix as he dips a clean spoon in the chicken salad to sample it, then shakes his head, and adds more freshly ground pepper.

I steady my hands on the counter before I say it. "My friend, the one I mentioned before who was supposed to do the internship with me this summer?"

"Mm-hmm."

I swallow hard. "She died last year. She drowned. We were up in Truro."

Mannix lifts his head, his mouth parting. "Cor, I'm sorry."

"It's okay."

"I remember reading about that. That's a really awful thing. For her, and for you, too."

I meet his eyes. "How?"

He's surprised by the question. "How what?"

56

"How did she drown? How does that happen? When one minute I'm looking right at her, and she's in the ocean we've always swum in since we were little girls, and the next, she's gone. Like she was never there in the first place. You're a lifeguard. How does that happen?"

He presses his lips together and plops a spoonful of chicken salad onto his slices of bread. "There are a lot of ways it could have happened. Rip current, or maybe she got stuck on something, or hit her head, or had a seizure. It's hard to know for sure."

I assemble my sandwich, thinking about what he's said. "I guess you're right. I mean, they say you can drown in an inch of water, right?"

"Theoretically, you can." He puts his plate on the island behind us and takes a seat on one of the stools as I retrieve the pitcher of iced tea from the fridge and pour us two glasses. "And this isn't a bathtub you're talking about, or even a pool. It's the North Atlantic. There are a lot of factors at play."

"I miss her," I say quietly. "I miss knowing I could turn to her at any moment and know she's already thinking what I am. Anyway, never mind." I wave away my thoughts.

"I understand," says Mannix, placing my sandwich on a plate and sliding it toward me.

I seat myself beside him, and he lifts half of his sandwich. My bewildered stare alternates between his sandwich and his eyes.

"Cheers," he says.

Smiling, I take half of my sandwich and touch it to his. "Cheers." I bite in. "Wow, whoa." I took too big a bite, and I'm trying to form words around my food.

"Good?" he asks, covering his mouth because it's full and he's polite.

"This *is* good." The combination of the smoky grilled chicken, the pungent dill, the sweet burst of apple, and the tart, chewy cranberry. He's a veritable chicken salad genius, and I'm sitting right next to him.

"Glad you like it."

I take another bite and nod because words don't do this justice. "Can you text me the recipe?" I ask.

He arches an eyebrow playfully. "What, to your phone? Like exchange numbers?" He leans forward, reaching into his back pocket and retrieving his. "Yeah, I can do that. Type it in."

He hands me his open phone, and I add myself to his contacts.

"So," he says a little more quietly. "Can I send you texts even if they're not recipes?"

I blush at this, at the way he can't meet my gaze. "I'd like that."

He nods, letting it sink in. "Me, too."

After we're done eating, Mannix helps me load the dishwasher, then leans against the island and stretches his hands above his head. "Guess that means break is over."

"For both of us," I add, staring wistfully down the hall where I can see the corner of my laptop in the front room. "If you need anything, let me know. I look forward to interruptions."

He pushes himself away from the island and meanders over to the stairs. "I look forward to providing them."

I watch as he disappears at the top of the steps, and then reluctantly return to my seat in the front room. My binder waits patiently for me, and I open back to the page I left off on. And there she is, at the bottom right. Fraction. A whale who will spend the rest of her life living with the consequence of some-one's thoughtless action.

I press my hand over her flukes and then pull out my cell phone. Ella's name waits for me at the top of my contact list.

Cor (1:08 PM): I miss you. I'm sorry.

Chapter Five

At seven thirty on a Monday morning, Provincetown is basically a ghost town. No one is advertising menus outside restaurants, no couples are holding hands and pointing in windows. Even my favorite cop isn't directing traffic at MacMillan Pier.

I cruise up Commercial Street, thankful that I don't need to maneuver the Jeep through throngs of people. When I get to the west end of town, before the Sea Ghost, I pull into the tiny driveway afforded to the Marine Research and Conservation Alliance. I block a Subaru and a beat-up Ford Bronco with the MRCA logo emblazoned on both doors. I'll move if they need me to.

The building is a typical Cape Cod cottage, shingled in cedar shakes with black shutters. I stand in front of the cranberry-red front door, admiring how the Center looks like someone's house.

Before I go in, I check my supplies. In my tote, I have a college-ruled notebook, two black pens (medium point), and a red one, just in case. I have my cell phone and my wallet, and two cans of Diet Coke. I could conquer the world. I start by opening the door.

Though this might have been someone's house before, it's now an open-plan office. Desks line the main room, and behind them is a little makeshift kitchen with a fridge, a microwave, a sink, and a dishwasher. The walls are plastered with posters of whales, sea turtles, sharks, and seals. There's a map of the seafloor of the Atlantic, and beside it, Kyle leans toward Mia, applying eyeliner.

"Hey, Cor," says Mia.

"Oops, don't move," says Kyle, hardly moving their mouth. "This takes concentration."

Mia whispers, "Kyle's showing me how to perfect winged eyeliner."

"Fancy," I reply.

"That's your desk, right across from mine," Mia continues. "Lottie got a phone call and said she'd only be a minute, but she's been gone for, like, ten."

"You don't really want to learn my makeup secrets, do you?" Kyle asks.

"I do!" Mia assures them. "I'll be quiet."

"I can do you next, Coriander," Kyle calls without shifting their concentration from Mia. "Though I think you'd do better with something less dramatic. Something more carefree and sun-kissed."

I pace over to the fridge and line the door with my Diet Coke.

"And there we go!" says Kyle, rolling their chair away from Mia to get a better look. "Yes. Yes, definitely."

"How do I look?" Mia asks me.

"Wow, that's impressive." I return to her side, tilting her chin up to better admire Kyle's handiwork. "Next time I have someplace important to go, you can do my makeup."

"Or a date or something," Kyle adds.

A twinge of something—guilt? Lust? I don't know—pangs inside me, and a vision of Mannix in my uncle's kitchen takes center stage. The Marine Research and Conservation Alliance is supposed to be the place where I don't need any distractions. The place where I can fully concentrate on more important things.

"All right, crew." Lottie breezes in through the back door, tossing her phone on her desk and standing in front of us, both hands on her hips. "A great white beached itself down at Stage Harbor. Who's coming with me?"

"Me!" Kyle leaps up, their hand flapping in the air. "Oh, me. Definitely me."

"Winner," says Lottie, thumbing down the hall. "Use the bathroom before we leave and meet me out by the truck."

I would have gone, I think. To be that close to a great white (and not in fear for my life) is the kind of once-in-a-lifetime experience I signed up for. To be able to save its life, even more so. The realization that I was excited about rescuing a shark surges through my consciousness as I plop down at my desk and organize my whale fluke binder.

"And you two," says Lottie. "Show me your feet."

I blink and then glance down at my shoes. I threw on soft gym shorts and my MRCA T-shirt, so naturally I paired it with sneakers. I hope this was the right choice. I stretch my feet out in front of me, and Lottie gives me the thumbs-up, then moves on to Mia.

"No flip-flops," she tells her.

"I have sneakers in my car!" Mia says.

"Grab them. You two are joining Justin on the boat today for some tagging. Great whites for everyone!"

I lurch from my chair. Being out on the boat is even better than being on any beach in Chatham.

"Justin is down at MacMillan now. Pack yourselves some sunblock, sunglasses, a hoodie, and a lunch, and go join him. He's waiting for you."

Mia practically squeals and then grabs my hand. "I need to run to my car. Will you wait for me?"

"Sure."

We head outside, the morning sun already bright and intense, and I wait for Mia to nab her sneakers from her backseat. "Do you think Converse are okay?" she asks.

"I think they are the perfect sneaker for multiple occasions," I assure her.

We have just enough time for me to pick up some snacks for the trip. I race down to the local shop and grab some elaborate sandwiches and several bottles of water.

When we get to the pier, Justin is standing beside a guy taking tickets from the long line of whale watch–goers.

"Got lunch?" he asks.

I hold up my bag triumphantly. "Vegan sandwiches."

"Rad," says Justin. He's wearing reflective Ray-Bans, and I can't see his eyes.

"Big boat," I comment, admiring the whale watch vessel lobbing up and down on the gentle waves of the harbor beside us.

A blue flag with MRCA's emblematic sea life cracks and flaps in the wind above our heads. "Big enough to accommodate all these landlubbers." Justin bends down and lifts a cooler, then begins walking down the plank. "Okay, let's go."

I glance at the research vessel beside the whale watch boat. It's significantly smaller and a little rusty. There's green gunk growing on the bottom.

"That thing's seen better days," says Mia.

Justin agrees. "We're raising money for a new one as we speak."

"So how do you raise money for things like this?" I ask, following him onto the research boat.

"These whale watches, of course," he says, pointing at the whale watch boat. "And fundraisers. The government allots us some money. We have sponsors."

"Like who?"

"You know, local places. Restaurants. Small businesses. Ecotourism is huge these days, and they want to support those of us who take care of natural Cape Cod."

I ponder for a moment. "What about John Michael Sutton Realty?"

Justin cracks up. Literally has to stop what he's doing to get out his laugh. "That would be rad. So rad. But I'm pretty sure John Michael Sutton thinks Stellwagen Bank is someplace to deposit his money."

I smirk.

"What?"

"He *knows* what Stellwagen Bank is."

Now I've piqued his interest. "How would you know?"

"Because he's my uncle. I'm spending the whole summer with him."

"Dude, get out!" Justin nudges my shoulder in disbelief.

"Let me talk to him," I say. "Let me put something together. He loves fundraisers." Uncle Jack revels in any excuse to get dressed up, drink cocktails, and mingle.

"Wait until I tell Lottie," says Justin. "She's gonna be psyched."

Well, now it's official. But this is totally something I can handle. I mean, how difficult is a fundraiser? I allow my bloated sense of pride to keep me perky as I climb to the front of the boat. At first, the constant swaying back and forth is a bit disorienting, but I force myself to get used to it, because that's what marine biologists do. They go on boats. Mia, on the other hand, is taking to the boat without so much as a queasy burp.

The familiar butterflies inundate my stomach as we back out of our spot. Our captain, Mike, waves to a few of our fellow sailors in the harbor. We cruise along, slowly passing the wharf and the giant portraits of the Portuguese fishermen's wives. I like to think they're watching our journey, wishing us fair winds and following seas when we leave and welcoming us home with malassadas upon our return. As we pass the breakwater, the boat begins to speed up, and my heartbeat follows suit. Cormorants dive and land as we speed by Wood End Light. Captain Mike calls out, "This is the place. Two great whites spotted this morning by fishermen."

The boat cruises along the coastline, heading out and around the tip of Cape Cod, and south toward Highland Light. I lean my elbows over the edge of the railing, resting my chin on the top. I want to see the great whites, obviously. But I could spend the whole afternoon like this, the gentle rocking on the water, watching the Cape go by.

After a while, Justin comments, "The buoys along the beaches have been instrumental."

"How do they work?" Mia asks.

I turn from my place at the railing to hear him more clearly.

"Basically, the tagged sharks send a ping to the buoy if they're nearby, and the lifeguards can signal for swimmers to get out of the water."

"Feels like when we're hoping that sharks stay away, they show up, and when we're actively out looking for them, they disappear," says Mia despondently.

"We'll find something out here worthwhile," Justin assures us as he peers through his binoculars at the horizon.

The sea is flat and listless, and the gentle slap of the waves against the hull of the boat puts me in a trance. It's only the shuffle of Captain Mike's feet and the grumble of the engine as it churns to life again that pull me back.

"Looks like humpies at two o'clock," he says.

We ease toward them and two spouts erupt from the water. Captain Mike cuts the engine, and we float as they come closer. "Get the camera ready," he instructs me as he pulls binoculars out of a bag.

I press myself against the railing of the boat, grabbing the camera that's been hanging uselessly around my neck. My hands are nervous and sweaty.

"Not a mother and calf," says Justin as I take a few shots. He pauses as they pass our boat, skimming beneath the surface of the water. The light collects and reflects over their long white pectoral fins, making the water dance along their skin. Beside me, Mia jots down the relevant information: our coordinates, the weather, the time of day, ocean conditions, and the surface behaviors we're witnessing.

Each whale exhales and then sucks in a huge gulp of air. Their breath smells of salt and fish, and the moisture settles on the exposed portions of the boat. With their final spout, they begin their descent beneath the waves, one of them offering a spectacular salute of the flukes, but the other slips below the waves without a sighting of its tail. I click incessantly, and once they've submerged, check the quality of the shots.

"I think it's Bolt. Not sure about the other one," Justin reports. "Let's follow them, Mike!"

Mike gives him a thumbs-up, and the engine rumbles to life.

"God, they were so close," I murmur, plopping down on one of the white benches below the overhang. Mia does the same.

They're not close enough, Ella complains in my head.

I'm not ready for the memory to come surging back the way it does, but Ella never asks. Lately, she just appears.

Ella hung over the side of the whale watch boat, a little too far, which prompted her dad to pull on her hoodie and bring her back. Her parents were originally from Boston, so they always spent their summers on the Cape. Eventually, our families became friends, and we would rent a house in Truro for a week, then switch over to Uncle Jack's house for however long we wanted to stay after that.

But I lived for my weeks with Ella. I waited all year for our summer traditions. Standing in line forever at Moby Dick's because the fried food was so worth it, mini-golfing, searching the surf for pebbles and treasures, hiding them in the recesses of the bridge that was only accessible at low tide and seeing if they'd last the year there. I couldn't imagine not spending my summers with Ella.

Until I could. Until all of those things we used to do felt silly and pointless.

"Lots of humpies being reported out here today, guys," Mike calls over the roar, pulling me back to the present. "A couple of minkes, too."

"I'd like to spot that finback we heard about last week," says Justin, still studying his binoculars.

The engine lulls and Mike points again. "Two humpies. And three more at eleven o'clock!"

Jumping from my seat, I launch to the side of the boat, Justin close behind. The two humpbacks that we followed are feeding.

"I'm seeing some bubble nets," Justin notes. He points. "See the bubbles breaking at the surface?"

I nod. "They trap the fish and force them together in a clump."

"We can get some fluke IDs over here," says Mike.

I whip around and begin taking the pictures as one of the whales begins to dive. The other two stay at the surface, evidently bemused by the presence of our boat. Almost as though I'm approaching a timid bird I found in the yard, I edge over to the side of the boat, careful not to agitate my companions in the water.

I'm rewarded with the closest I've ever been to a whale. One glides up to the boat and spy-hops beside us. The other stretches itself along our length and flaps its pectoral fin against the water.

"Oh my god," I say. "Look."

Justin follows my gesture to the end of the whale. Half a fluke. "Fraction," he says.

Her eye is right next to the boat, and part of me knows I'm leaning too far over. Part of me knows that if I fall in, it's going to get ugly and fast. But I need to be near her. It's like she's sensed my presence here from the start. First at White Crest, and now here out on the water. Her nearness creates an electricity between our bodies, mine trapped by the land, and hers by the sea, but that doesn't matter to either one of us right now.

They're not close enough, Ella says in my head. She clings to the railing of the whale watch boat, swiping at the blond hair that gets in her face. *Don't you wish they were closer?*

I did wish that. I wish it now, suddenly. I push my body a little farther over the edge, hoping for some sort of proximity, some sort of contact. The kind of contact I've been longing for since Ella died last summer. My hand slips, and I'm not fast enough to grip with the other. The rail digs into my torso, and it's the only thing keeping me on the boat. I'm in too much shock to respond in any other way.

But a firm grip on my arms prevents any kind of catastrophe. Justin yanks me back, grabs me by the shoulders, and stares at me, almost trying to visually assure himself that there's nothing wrong with me and I didn't just purposefully try to fall into the North Atlantic.

Only maybe I did. It's the closest I've been to Ella in a really long time. When I saw Fraction, floating there amid the waves, weightlessly, I could have sworn I saw Ella. I swear, I saw her in the sea.

"Christ, Cor!" he says between breaths. "That could have been dire."

"You need to be careful, Coriander," Captain Mike calls from over his shoulder. "Is she okay?" he asks Justin like I'm not here. My body is still here, I realize. My mind is somewhere else.

"I'm fine," I say, pushing Justin away. "That was amazing."

But Justin has disappeared, my almost-calamity no longer important. "Mike, are you seeing this?"

"Looks like some gear wrapped around the peduncle."

Justin grabs his cell phone and scrolls for the number he's looking for.

"Around which one?" I ask, my eyes trying to focus on all of the multiple feeding whales at once.

"Fraction," says Mia, appearing beside me. She points. "Look. You can see where it's cutting into her flesh. All the pink."

"Can we do something about it?" I ask, turning to Justin.

"This isn't the response boat," he tells me, waiting for someone to pick up. "I'm calling them now. Not sure if there are enough daylight hours to attempt a disentanglement."

From the side of the boat, Fraction blinks at me, rolls over, and submerges herself. All five whales converge, slipping through the waves, spouting, and then diving one last time.

"Let's follow her!" Justin calls to Captain Mike while he's trying to relay our message to the crew on land. "I want to get a buoy on her."

But the thing about whales is that ninety percent of their lives is lived below the surface. So once Fraction and her companions dive, who knows when and where they'll pop up again. Even though we follow, she easily disappears.

And we wait on the water, hoping for the best.

"Damn," Justin mutters, running his hand down his face.

"Is she gonna be okay?" I ask.

He nods. "Doesn't look like anything was impeding her swimming or her feeding. It might be uncomfortable, and it might slow her down a bit. But we'll get her. Don't worry."

I nod, tucking a lock of hair behind my ear even though I know how pointless the action is, how the wind is going to scatter it any which way it likes. But it feels good pretending to be in control of something right now, no matter how much convincing it takes.

Chapter Six

I light a candle that claims to smell like driftwood, but I think they're banking on the fact that you've never lifted a piece of driftwood and taken a good, long whiff. Because the candle smells sweet and aromatic, and driftwood probably smells like rotting dead crab and seaweed.

Outside my window, the voices of Uncle Jack's company float from the fire pit. They're circled around the flames, clutching their cocktails and exchanging laughs and stories.

No one actually likes bonfires, Ella says. She stands beside me at the window, staring down at Uncle Jack's guests. *You end up inhaling and reeking of smoke. The mosquitos are intolerable, and you can never find the appropriate thing to wear. A T-shirt is too cold, and a hoodie makes you sweat.*

I smile down at the flickering light, remembering how

insistent Ella used to get about the things she very firmly believed.

Uncle Jack says something funny. I can tell because he leans in, as if anticipating the laughter, and Chad laughs a little bit too hard. Meandering back over to my armchair, I lift my copy of Dr. Roger Payne's book, *Among Whales*. I'm trying to read as much as I can about humpbacks. Anything that's going to reassure me that we didn't leave Fraction out there to die. Obviously, I know we didn't, Justin promised. But she lingers just outside my imagination, and the thought of her suffering and not understanding why is triggering.

I reach across my writing desk, opening the cover, then pulling my folded list from the pages. I read through my ideas again.

1. ~~Internship at Marine Research and Conservation Alliance on Cape Cod.~~
2. ~~Whale tattoos.~~
3. See Harry Styles in concert.
4. Wear elaborate ball gowns to prom.
5. Real boyfriends. Not crushes.
6. Complete the pebble collection.

Retrieving a blue pen from the MRCA mug in the corner, I add one final entry:

7. Save Fraction.

Ella and I spent our lunches together, quietly, in the library, floating among the whales. This went on for several years. Mrs. Hanson even found us recordings of humpback songs. There were times when we would sit there, leaning against the shelves, headphones too large for our heads hung about our necks, listening to the whales' songs.

"Hey, Cor?" said Ella one afternoon.

I was busy coloring in a lovely illustration of breaching orcas. "Yeah?"

"My dad is taking me to the Museum of Natural History on Saturday."

I dropped my colored pencil. "The one with the whale exhibit?"

Ella nodded enthusiastically, her blond hair falling from her ponytail's loose hold. "And he said I could bring a friend!"

That was me.

"You have to ask your parents' permission," said Ella. "It's imperative."

Probably a word she read in one of her books. Ella was always reading.

"Imperative," I repeated.

When the bus dropped me off at my usual spot that afternoon, I didn't bother milling around with the other kids. I dashed past them, through the snow, and across my lawn. Throwing open the kitchen door, I caught a glimpse of my dad, strumming his guitar on the living room floor, staring up at the ceiling, searching for divine inspiration. Mom was on the phone with Uncle Jack.

"Jack, you know what? Let me call you back. Cor just got home, and she's tracking snow all over the house." She clicked off the phone. "Coriander, I don't want you trudging through this house with your snow boots on."

"Sorry," I said, yanking them off and throwing them at the back door. "But Mom, I have the best news."

"And that would be?" she asked, turning her attention back to the soup on the stove.

"My friend Ella..."

"Yes, Ella. The one with the big words. Go on."

"Well, Ella and her dad are going to the whale exhibit at the museum in the city, and they want me to come!" I was about to explode with whale giddiness. "Can I go?"

Mom looked perplexed. "Isn't that Danielle's birthday party? The one at the roller rink?"

I tried not to let her see my shoulders slump. Even thinking about it made my eyes a little watery. Danielle never invited me to her roller-skating party. She invited every girl in the class except me and Ella. But I was the only one who cared about the obvious snub. I would have done anything to go to Danielle's party. But I didn't want Mom to know.

"I don't want to go to Danielle's birthday," I said. "I want to go see the whales with Ella."

It's not like this was a lie. I always wanted to hang out with Ella and the whales. Only, if I had been invited to Danielle's, I would have bent over backward to make both events work.

"You can go," said Mom, and she turned back to the sink and began loading the dishwasher.

"Whaddya say I tag along, too, kiddo?"

I turned to face my dad, who sauntered in from the living room, pulling his guitar up and over his head.

"Think your friend would mind if I joined you?"

"I don't think she'd mind," I said, though I was always aware that my dad wasn't like other dads. He didn't have a nine-to-five job. He didn't drive a dad car. He didn't watch football on Sundays, and he didn't eat meat.

I chose to push those anxieties aside, only to find them confirmed once we arrived at the museum with Ella and her dad. I suppose, considering the kind of person Ella was, that I hoped her father was a little peculiar as well. Only he wasn't. He wore khakis and a sweater, drove a Lexus, and started talking to my dad about baseball the second we crossed the threshold.

"So, how about those Yankees?"

Dad shrugged and considered. "Well, they were certainly on the right side of the war," he replied. "Though the Confederates gave them a run for their money."

Ella's dad arched an eyebrow. Mine shoved his hands in his pockets and perused the tiny fish behind the thick walls of glass.

It was then that I began to wonder whether I actually drew attention to myself that made the other kids mock me. Like Dad did. Here I was, the year before middle school, reveling in a Saturday at a museum surrounded by whales, decked out in my whale T-shirt, my whale earrings dangling from my lobes, and a whale pendant around my neck. I wasn't at cheerleading practice like half the girls in my grade. Or attending Danielle's birthday party like the other half.

I glanced over at Ella as she scanned the directory to guide us. "This way!" she said, and she grabbed my hand, pulling me down the long corridor to a set of huge open doors.

When we entered, any anxiety I might have had melted away. The exhibit was three stories tall and doused in a pleasant green-blue light to give the appearance of being underwater. There were displays of different species scattered across the room, a history-of-whaling exhibit, and perhaps best of all, a life-size structure of a blue whale hanging above our heads.

I stared upward, heavenward, and the world shrank around me. Suddenly, my fears and my life felt so small.

"I wonder what whales worry about," said Ella, craning her neck to see the whale more fully. "I mean, what would you have to worry about when you're so big?" She sighed.

"Humans, I guess."

She turned to observe me. "It seems kind of stupid to be worried about something that small and out of your control."

"Yeah, I guess you're right," I say.

And then Ella did something she had never done before. She reached her arm out, and she wrapped it around my shoulders. She pulled me close, and we stared up at the massive whale above us.

On the way out, Ella insisted we stop at the gift shop. I found a whale keychain, and the cashier wrapped it up and placed it in a little box. I was pretty pleased with my gift until Ella came dashing past me, a cardboard kit in her hands.

"Look!" she cried. "I'm going to adopt a whale."

"Where did you get that?" I asked, scanning the store.

"In the back. Go and get one, and we can adopt our whales together."

"I don't think so, Cor," said my dad, appearing behind me. He crossed his arms over his chest and then rubbed the back of his head.

"Why not?"

"I think that's our limit today."

"But I only got a keychain." I held up my tiny box to remind him.

"I know...."

Ella blinked and grasped her stuffed whale, the adoption kit, and a thousand-piece puzzle of a blue whale in the Antarctic.

"Come on, we gotta get home for dinner."

After dinner, and a few hours of TV, I didn't say good night to my dad. I thought that would show him. It wasn't until a few years later, after having watched him struggle to maintain a steady income, that I felt ashamed. My cheeks still burn when I think about it.

Besides, Ella left an adoption kit on my doorstep the next morning. We both adopted Fraction. Our whale with the half fluke.

Standing in my room in Uncle Jack's house, I stare at the words on my list for some time, wondering if they're realistic or if I'm kidding myself, but it doesn't matter either way. I'm not letting the sea claim another thing. I watched Ella disappear in the sea, but Fraction won't follow her on the tide. I fold the note up and secure it in the book, then lean back and sigh.

Laughter swells upward again from the backyard, but this time a new voice is among them. I traipse to the window, and standing just outside the fire pit circle is Mannix, in dark tan khaki shorts, a gray Henley T-shirt, and brown leather flip-flops.

I honestly don't think Uncle Jack invited Mannix to his get-together, so his presence must be because of something else. Part of me wants to stay here, in the comfort of my own dwelling. But Mannix is a welcome distraction, and I find myself floating down the steps at the thought of him.

When I get to the kitchen, he's coming through the back door, closing it behind him, and he turns and finds me waiting.

"Hey," he says, then takes a deep breath. "I was wondering where you were. Why aren't you outside with everyone else?"

I shrug. "Not my scene, I guess."

"I get that." He points past me. "I think I left my phone here today. I hope I did, otherwise I have no idea where it is. I'm gonna go check the bathroom." He starts to climb the stairs.

"Need me to call it?" I ask as he goes.

"Sure, go for it," he replies, disappearing around the corner at the top of the steps.

It's silly, but the fact that I have his number and I get to do something so mundane as call his phone when he might have lost it makes me feel like we have this connection that's more than what it is.

"Got it!" he shouts, then trots down the steps, phone in hand. "Thanks for the help."

"Sure thing."

He lingers by the back door, like he has something left to say but isn't sure how it's supposed to come out.

So I give him a nudge. "Where are you headed?"

He thumbs over his shoulder to his red-orange pickup, which is parked in the driveway. "Gonna grab a bite to eat before my shift at the Sea Ghost. I told my coworker I'd cover for him so he could leave early. He had a date he was excited about, so I couldn't say no." He chuckles softly and scratches the back of his head.

Quietly, bravely, I ask, "Do you want some company?"

He seems surprised by this, his gaze darting from his feet to meet my eyes. "You hungry?"

"I'm pretty hungry."

"Come with me, then."

He opens the back door and motions for me to go out first. So I grab my wristlet and keys hanging on the hook by the fridge and head out into the night.

"Uncle Jack," I call as we pass the fire pit. "I'm gonna grab something to eat with Mannix, be back later."

"Have fun," Uncle Jack calls with a wave. "But not too much fun."

"Have all the fun you want," Chad adds.

"What kind of parenting advice is that?" Uncle Jack asks him.

Chad shrugs. "I'm not her parent."

"I'll have the proper amount of fun, thank you for your concern." I duck into the Jeep and follow Mannix down the driveway and out to Route 6.

The sun is close to disappearing and casts the sky in a warm pinkish violet. As we head north toward Truro, Mannix slows, his arm out the driver's-side window, and points to a narrow road heading to the bay. We turn and follow it for a mile or so until we get to a little shack overlooking a small harbor. Boats cruise slowly in for the night, navigating between flashing buoys, and a few tables are set up on the porch with a nice view of the inlet and farther out, the bay. I park next to Mannix's truck and hop out of the Jeep.

"So what do you think?" he asks, shutting his door and then reopening it. He slams it harder this time, then checks the handle to make sure it's really closed. "Wanna eat inside or out?"

"Your choice."

We wait in a long though swiftly moving line to place our orders at the front counter. A girl jots down our selections, something called a Cape Codder salad with grilled scallops for me, and a fried fish sandwich with extra fries for Mannix, and hands us two large empty cups to get our drinks at the fountain.

We don't have a choice where we sit because it's jammed in here. We find a table near a window, adorned with a set of salt and pepper shakers, a lit tea light in a mason jar, and some ketchup and an assortment of hot sauce. Above us, old nets hang from the ceiling, strewn with metal fish with colorful glass eyes that glint in the low light of the dining room.

Mannix places both hands on the table, tapping the wooden top with his fingers as he takes a look around the room.

I press my lips together because it's only just dawned on me that maybe Mannix only took us here because I suggested eating together. Maybe he wanted to grab a sandwich or something fast before work. I don't even know when his shift starts, and now I feel like I'm intruding.

"So my head lifeguard told us the other day that some volunteers from the Marine Research and Conservation Alliance are gonna work with us a few weekends this summer for shark awareness," he says. "Is that you?"

"Yup." I realize my hands are also tapping on the table, and I need to stop before he thinks I'm teasing him. "Our job is to talk about sharks in general—the biology, I guess, and your job is to talk about shark safety in the water."

"Cool," he says. "I can do that."

"Ever see a great white before?" I ask, taking a sip of my Diet Coke.

He leans in, his mouth curved up in half a smile. "Last August I saw one decimate a seal."

"Gross."

"It's natural."

"Still," I say, and take another sip, like soda is going to save me from the vision of that poor seal with those big puppy eyes.

"I don't have to witness it. I wish the sharks all the best. Far away from me."

"I almost saved a guy from a shark attack once," Mannix says, resting against the back of his chair and crossing his hands behind his head in a rather self-satisfactory kind of gesture.

"Liar."

"It's true."

"You saved someone from a shark." I arch a disbelieving eyebrow.

I don't miss how his shoulders slouch just a tad. "I said almost. I helped the guy out of the water."

"That's intense." I lean forward. "You didn't try to swim back to shore? Didn't think to save your own life?"

"Didn't think at all. Just acted, to be honest."

I stare at him for a moment, and distantly, Ella dives beneath a wave. I turn back to the house.

"Cor?"

"Yes." I smile, pretending to be present. But the thing is, I didn't think, either. Just acted. "That's really courageous of you."

Mannix shrugs as our dinners arrive. The french fries on his plate are piled high and steaming, with the perfect amount of flaky sea salt, and I'm starting to regret my choice of a salad. He lifts one and dangles it before me. "You want some?"

"I do." I take it gratefully and bite down while I drizzle the bright green dressing over my salad and seared scallops. "This smells amazing."

Mannix glances up at me, spreading his tartar sauce on the bun of his sandwich. "Try it." He gestures at my salad.

I mix it around, making sure everything is evenly coated in

dressing, and Mannix watches me the whole time. "What?" I finally ask.

"I want you to take a bite of the salad."

I study him. "I feel weirdly pressured."

He props his elbows on the table. "Take a bite."

I jab my fork in, grabbing a few spinach leaves, some crumbled goat cheese, an olive, and half of a scallop, and bring it to my mouth. It's delightfully refreshing, filled with herbs and garlic, and just the right ratio of vinegar and oil.

Mannix waits expectantly.

"This is really good."

Grinning, he sits back and finally takes a bite of his sandwich.

"You're not even going to tell me why you were so determined to have me try the salad, are you?" When he doesn't answer, I start to get a little panicky. "There's something gross in it, isn't there? Something I would have said no to, but now it's in my mouth, and you think it's funny."

He shakes his head. "No, no." Dunking a fry in some ketchup, he pushes his plate toward the middle of the table and motions for me to take more. "It's my dressing. That's all."

He says it so casually, so nonchalantly, that I don't understand what he means. "It's your dressing?"

"I make it and bottle it for a couple of local restaurants."

"Dude." I slap his forearm. "You should go to culinary school! You'd be amazing."

"Nah, I'm good."

He's so modest and bashful. I'm mildly turned on. "But think of everything you'd learn. You're already a good cook; they could teach you how to be an amazing cook."

"I have too much going on here. I couldn't just up and leave."

I pause and consider this. "You're a lifeguard, so that's only for the summer, and a bartender, also more of a summer job, especially in a place like P-town."

"I have winter jobs, too."

"But like, nothing permanent. You're a kid! I mean, how old are you?"

"Eighteen," he replies.

"See? You should at least get some brochures." I pull my phone from my wristlet and start searching culinary schools in New England.

"I can't do that right now," he says, touching my hand and lowering my phone so he can see my face. "My dad, he, um—he was in a boating accident, and he had to have major surgery. He's starting physical therapy in a few weeks, and my family needs me here."

"Oh," I say quietly, suddenly embarrassed by my misdirected fervor. "I'm sorry, I didn't know."

"It's okay." He takes another bite of his sandwich, and we eat quietly for a little while.

"So," I finally say, pushing a cherry tomato around on my dish with the prong of my fork. "Your dad is out of work?"

Mannix nods. "For a while. His job is really physical."

"Yeah?"

"Mm-hmm, he's a lobsterman."

"Wow," I say. Because it's the only thing that comes to mind. The image of Fraction, tangled in rope, rope that could belong to a lobsterman, pushes to the forefront of my thoughts.

"So it's hard for him right now. He can't physically do the job, but he's used to being out on the water every day. He's anxious as hell."

"I bet that's tough."

Mannix nods, staring at his french fries and then pushing his almost-empty plate away. "My mom and I are trying to make ends meet. She takes him to his doctor appointments and physical therapy, and she also works. I try to help her around the house as much as I can."

"And your dad wants to be back on the boat."

Mannix laughs at this. "Sometimes, I'm afraid that if we don't watch him closely enough, he's going to sneak out. Like I have to put childproof locks on the boat."

"Well, maybe he can do something lobster-related that's not on the water," I suggest.

"Like what?"

Shrugging, I try to make this next part sound as nonchalant as possible. "Like the lobster lecture on Friday. Dr. Blair from MRCA is giving a lecture about preventative measures to keep whales from becoming entangled in gear."

"That doesn't sound like something my dad would be interested in," says Mannix, leaning back and crossing his arms over his chest.

"I think it's totally something he'd be interested in!"

Grinning, Mannix replies, "I mean, I know how well you know my dad's likes and dislikes."

"Seriously, though. If we're talking about preventative measures to protect whales that are going to have an effect on the lobster industry, then don't you think lobstermen deserve a seat at the table? My boss, Lottie, said there are a few coming already."

"You're pretty convincing," he says, leaning forward.

"That's my job. Convince people that whales matter."

He stares at me for a moment, his brows coming together seriously. He reaches his hand out, and his pointer finger comes to rest just under my chin, his thumb at my lower lip, and he brushes it gently. I could float away.

"You had a little dressing," he says. "And I can't take whales seriously if I'm too distracted by your mouth." He takes a quick breath, like he's caught himself. "Anyway, I um. I have to get to work."

"I almost forgot."

He pushes away from the table, leaning forward and reaching into his back pocket to fish out his wallet. Before I can grab my wristlet, he shakes his head and frowns. "No, I got this."

"You don't have to," I say.

"My treat. To thank you for keeping me company instead of me eating alone in my truck before my shift."

The waitress brings us our bill, and Mannix leaves her a nice tip and stands, waiting for me to go first, and I start contemplating the dynamics of our evening. There was light flirting, I think, as we pass the front counter and the hostess wishes us a pleasant night. There was that whole touching of my lip, and then he paid for my dinner, which is pretty standard date material. At least, I think we were on a date.

In the parking lot, we stand between our two cars, and I lean against the passenger door of the Jeep. "I like this place," I say.

Mannix looks up at the buoys hung in the net that drapes across the roof of the building. "It's pretty good. Kinda touristy during the summer, but I was trying to think of someplace fast that you'd like, and this was the first thing that popped into my head."

"Well, that's very considerate of you," I say, and he smiles at me. "Whenever I went out with my ex-boyfriend, it usually consisted of one of his basketball games followed by pizza and possibly making out in his car in my driveway just out of the reach of the motion-detecting lights."

Mannix laughs, his head lowering, and he scuffs his sneaker into the seashell parking lot. "He sounds charming."

"Like a prince."

"But I don't want to give you the wrong impression." He looks up and meets my eyes. "This wasn't a date or anything."

"Oh," I say quietly, my face flushing. He's knocked the wind right out of me. "Kinda felt like one to me."

Regardless of this evidently not being a first date, Mannix reaches out and gently clasps my hand. "Sometimes it's better to play pretend. Pretend like it's a date, even if it's not."

"Why would we do that?" I ask. "When actual dates are more fun."

His expression grows serious. "Because when you pretend, you can also pretend all the awkward, inconvenient parts of your life don't exist. The things that wouldn't work in a relationship."

"Like what?"

He stares up at the sky, like explaining this to me is going to take all he has. "Like all of my jobs. Like the whole situation with my dad. Like not going to college. Like you leaving in August. If this were a real date, those things would be there, and we'd have to deal with them. So it's better to pretend. Let this be a distraction instead of something to focus on." He waits for me to say something, but I don't know what it is he expects. "You wouldn't want me any other way."

There are things I want to say, but I'm not brave enough.

Maybe I'm being ridiculous. Probably a little bit immature. But he turns away before any of that can become a reality, anyway.

"Mannix," I say quietly, but I'm not sure he can hear me.

"I've gotta get going," he says, gripping the door handle behind him. "But I'll be back at your place tomorrow morning."

He turns the ignition and backs out of his parking space. I wait and listen as the grumble of his engine fades slowly down the road, till I can't hear the engine anymore. Maybe I can pretend none of this ever happened, and tomorrow will still be totally casual.

But somehow, no matter how hard I try, I can't seem to pretend like I don't know how it feels for his thumb to brush my lip.

Chapter Seven

"No. No," says Kyle. Arms crossed over their chest in complete dismay and disbelief, they stand beside me as I load single-serving appetizers on a tray as quickly as physically possible because I'm falling behind in my duties.

The lobster lecture is more of a success than anyone bargained for. MRCA set up a tent outside one of the local restaurants in P-town, and we are at capacity. The waiters and waitresses who usually work the restaurant are busy doing their own jobs for customers inside, so Mia, Kyle, and I were recruited as waitstaff for Dr. Blair's audience. I can't speak for my two colleagues, but I've never been a waitress before, and I am tragic.

Kyle persists. "You're trying to tell me that this guy leans over the table to wipe dressing *that he makes and bottles himself* off your lip, and then has the audacity to tell you it wasn't a date? You *know* he took you there so he could show off."

I shrug. "Well, maybe that's just it. Maybe he likes the attention."

Which is embarrassing. That's exactly how I felt about Brent. I liked his attention. I liked how people saw me when I was with him, but I'm not sure I ever liked him. And somehow, even though I've only known him for a few weeks, I don't want to be that to Mannix. I want Mannix to be different. I want to be different.

It's hot in here, and I pause for a moment to fan myself. At the front of the tent, Dr. Raymond Blair, the founder of MRCA back in the seventies, stands before a white screen, and every so often, the image of an entangled whale crosses its surface. Tonight's overarching goal is to bring awareness about whale entanglements, to forge a partnership with local fishermen to help avoid these kinds of disasters, and to inform them as to what to do if they ever encounter a whale in distress when they're out on the water.

Mia appears beside me. "Have something to drink," she says. Her thick black hair is tossed up in a high bun, and I wish I'd had the presence of mind to bring my own hair band. "Here," Mia says, pulling a black tie from her wrist and offering it to me like she's some kind of mind reader.

"Oh my god, thank you." I snatch it from the palm of her hand and lift my heavy hair from my sweaty neck, and then gulp down my water.

Mia leans against the table, where I've fully loaded the last tray of stuffed mushroom caps. Now we wait for the garden salads. "I hate these pictures," Mia says quietly, staring at an emaciated right whale. There's gear wrapped around her mouth, keeping her from feeding, and orange sea lice infest her body. "It encapsulates everything that's wrong with people."

I sway so that my shoulder nudges hers. "What do you mean?"

She gives a little shrug. "I mean, this could all be avoided. Every single whale that's ever died from an entanglement. That's our fault, it's on us. It's not natural. It's not sustainable. And it could all be avoided if we considered the impact of our actions."

I swipe at the sweat that's running down my face.

"Here," says Mia, reaching out and smudging just under my eye. "Your mascara's running. Should have worn waterproof."

"I never think to buy waterproof," I say.

In the aisle of the drugstore back in Dusk Hollow lined with sinus medicine on one side and makeup on the other, Ella said, "You can never get waterproof mascara off, even with makeup remover."

"That's true," I agreed, leaning against the handlebar of the mini-cart that I stole from the grocery store parking lot next door, and in front of me, Ella considered two different palettes of eye shadow. It was a Friday afternoon, and when the last bell rang, we'd crossed the busy street to gather supplies for our weekly sleepover.

"Don't buy that one," I said, motioning to the palette in her right hand. "The grays are nice, but there's blue in there, and it's a waste of money. Very few people can pull off blue eye shadow."

"Are you saying I'm not one of those people?" Ella asked, daring me to repeat myself.

"I am. That's exactly what I'm saying."

She snorted out a laugh and hung the palette back on its hook. Examining her other options, Ella then ambled farther down the aisle, and without even looking up, she said, "I think my dad's cheating on my mom."

It was so casually stated that I had a hard time figuring out what she meant. "You what?"

"He was outside doing yard work the other day, and his cell phone kept ringing. You know, like call after call from the same number. So I picked up, and it was this woman. She seemed really flustered that it was me who picked up and not him."

I stood up straight, pretending to be interested in some lip gloss because it felt like that was what Ella needed. Not to make this a big deal. She was eerily calm. "What did she say?"

"That she was Nikki from work, and she had a question about some project they're doing together."

"Maybe that's true," I suggested.

She turned to me and rolled her eyes. "It was a Sunday morning. Who's working on a project with an urgent question on a Sunday morning?"

"I don't know, people do, I think."

She returned her attention to a palette of plum and pink eye shadow. "I think we need some kind of like, I dunno. Mask or something. Something to do before makeup."

I took a hesitant step toward her. "You okay?"

She nodded. "I'm okay." But her shoulders dropped and her face pinched. "I wish he'd realize that his decisions impact more than just him and Nikki from work with the question on the project. Like, not to be selfish, but what about me? What about Mom?"

"I don't think it's selfish to feel that way," I said.

The bell over the glass door in the front of the store jangled, and Ella glanced up. Three basketball players dressed in khakis, button-down oxfords, and skinny ties came in. There was an away game that night, and they were probably stopping for snacks before they had to board their bus.

Brent Tompkins glanced down the makeup aisle, paused when he saw us, and then followed his friends in the opposite direction.

"Oh my god, he saw us," Ella whispered.

"So what?" I picked a lip gloss and tossed it into my cart. "We're buying makeup in a drugstore. It's a thing."

Ella had had a crush on Brent Tompkins since the third grade when she had to stand next to him in chorus and we sang "The Fifty Nifty United States" because she was the tallest girl in our class. I'm not entirely sure Ella and Brent ever exchanged any words after Wisconsin and Wyoming, but that didn't dampen her feelings for him.

"I'm gonna go find a pore-cleaning mask for us and hope he didn't notice me."

"He looked right at you."

"And I'm wearing sweat pants! I look like I just ran the mile."

I considered this. "It's Friday. You did just run the mile. It's what we do every Friday in phys ed."

She motioned at me. "You just ran the mile, and you look put together."

I wore jeans, a tank, and a light cardigan. Together, yes, but not stellar. "That's because I changed after."

"I should have changed," she mumbled as she began her search for the face mask.

I entertained myself while my best friend obsessed over

sweat pants by browsing the snack aisle, seeking out the most appropriate chip-and-dip combo for while we waited for our masks to dry and watched bad rom-coms from the early 2000s. There was the classic salted potato chip with onion dip. But maybe tortillas with jarred queso was the better option. I stared at the jar in my hand, considering.

"That queso's not as good as the homemade kind."

Brent Tompkins stood beside me. He had short brown hair and dark eyes. Some patchy stubble. His red tie populated with oversize Christmas bulbs was askew, but he was kind of cute.

"Is there a lot of chopping involved with the homemade kind? Because I don't have the patience to chop."

He laughed in the direction of his feet. "Cut up some Velveeta and pour the salsa over it, then microwave."

"Huh," I said. "That sounds like the right amount of easy."

"How'd you do on that algebra test today?" he asked while I searched for a box of Velveeta. The grocery section of our drugstore was small but well stocked, and I found a little block of it quickly.

"I feel pretty good about it. What about you?"

I knew the answer to this already. Brent didn't always have his homework complete, and the day before, while we waited for class to start, he'd asked if he could copy mine. He sat down next to me and copied the problems from my notebook to his. When he was done, he glanced at me, and quietly, he told me, "You smell nice."

I did *not* share this information with Ella, and a pang of guilt echoed in my conscience.

Brent shrugged. "Probably not my best performance."

"If you want, I can help you study next time."

I didn't know where those words came from, but I realized once they were out there that I meant it. I wouldn't mind studying with Brent.

"Thanks," he said, reaching for a bag of sour cream and onion chips.

"Getting snacks?"

"Yeah, we have a big game up in Morris County tonight. Long bus ride."

"Totally."

"What are you here for?"

"Oh," I said, glancing back at my cart filled with soaps and makeup. "Ella's sleeping over, and we're having, like, a spa night. I guess." It suddenly sounded so stupid. Getting made up for no one to go nowhere.

But Brent smiled, lifting a tube of concealer. "Fancy. You think this color goes with my eyes?" He held it up to his face.

"You don't match concealer to your eye color," I said, shoving him playfully in the arm.

"What about this?" He picked out my palette of eye shadow, a collection of rosy pinks and soft lavenders.

"No, you should go with shades of plum," I said. "It'll make your eyes seem warmer."

He glanced up at me.

"Not that you don't have warm eyes, it's just—the color would..." I scratched my forehead and cleared my throat. "Really make them pop. Okay, I should, um..."

"Yeah, I gotta get going," said Brent, looking over his shoulder as though his teammates were going to appear at the end of the aisle. "But hey, if you're free some Friday night, you should come to one of my games."

I stared up at him. "Sure," I finally said.

He smiled and then focused on something behind me, and gave a small wave. "Hey, Ella. Still meeting me at the mall next weekend?"

She lifted her hand to wave back and nodded at the same time, but dropped the tube of facial mask clay in the process. As she bent over to pick it up, her cheeks were bright red.

"See you around, Coriander." He sauntered back down the aisle, disappearing behind a display of holiday wrapping paper.

Ella dashed over to me. "What did he say to you?"

I shrugged. "Told me all about queso. Are you going out with him next weekend?" The idea itself was surprising. I was astonished that Brent had even acknowledged Ella.

"I think I tricked him into going out with me."

"What do you mean?"

"In history the other day, I mentioned that I still haven't gotten anything for my dad for Christmas. And he said he hadn't, either. Then he suggested we go to the mall together, and I said sure. But other than that, I don't know what the plan is."

"You little sneak!" I cried, shoving her in the arm. "Going on a date with Brent Tompkins after all these years."

She blushed again and shrugged.

As we stood in line, waiting to check out, I kept thinking about how I should tell her that he'd invited me to one of his games. Maybe I should have made it sound casual, like he invited her, too. Then her feelings wouldn't be hurt. But there was a selfish part of me that didn't want to include Ella. She would have come with me if I asked, but Brent asked *me*. Me. Besides, she had her mall date with him, whatever that was.

When we had all our bags, we trudged back to the high

school parking lot, bracing ourselves against the cold December air and waiting for my mom to come and pick us up. She had said she'd be there by three, but sometimes that meant three thirty.

Beside me, Ella shivered on the curb. "So I got a solo for the holiday chorus concert."

I stared at her incredulously. "Are you serious?" Ella was not a soloist. She tried to remain as unseen and unheard as possible. Which was ridiculous, because she had a beautiful singing voice.

She nodded. "Ms. Ronaldo heard me practicing out in the hall, and she told me I should try out. I don't know if I want to go through with it, though."

"You have to! You sing better than anyone."

She looked up into the clear blue sky and shrugged. "I guess so. But you have to come. I don't want to be up there singing with only my parents in the audience who don't even want to sit next to each other and are only there out of obligation."

"Oh my god, Ella, you know they want to hear you sing, too."

She waved as my mom's car pulled into the lot. "It's a secondary want. I'm a cursory thought." She looked over at me and smiled. "So I have to matter to someone. You're my someone." Opening the back door, she threw the bags in first and greeted my mom, then ducked in.

"That's him, isn't it?"

Kyle's sudden voice beside me jolts me from my memory of Ella, and I follow their pointing hand to the entrance of the tent.

Hesitantly, Mannix Reilly steps inside and waits for an older man to join him, one who uses a cane to get by. This must be his dad. He's tall, like Mannix, with short graying hair that I can see peeking out from under his Red Sox hat.

"How did you know that's Mannix?" I ask.

"I listen very closely when you describe him. Plus you said his dad was in an accident and in physical therapy."

They quietly make their way to a half-empty table where two men are waving them over. Mannix greets them, shaking each of their hands, followed by his dad. They both take a seat, but Mannix scans the audience, casually looking around.

"He's looking for you," says Kyle.

"Stop, he is not."

They shove the last tray of stuffed mushroom caps into my hands and push me forward. "Go serve them. Don't forget to stand close to him—your hair smells pleasantly of coconuts this evening."

"I don't want to, you go."

"He didn't come here for me."

Even Mia is urging me forward, and when I take a timid step and glance back for reassurance, they're clutching each other's arms and grinning inanely.

"Can I interest you in a mushroom cap?" I ask as I approach the table from behind, but I must be too quiet because no one turns to look at me. I clear my throat and take a deep breath. "Mushroom caps? Another drink?"

This time, Mannix hears me. "Cor, hey." He stands up quickly, almost tripping on his chair, which makes his dad chuckle into his hand. "Let me help."

"Oh, no, no. Thank you, though. It's my job tonight. Your waitress. Well, everyone's waitress. I'm good." We stand there staring at each other for a moment, and I don't know what this means. "Mushroom cap?" I offer him the tray.

"Thanks." He takes one.

"Hey, Red," says one of the men at the table.

I glance down at him. "You can't mean me."

The man grins. "Who else would I mean? Look at your hair."

Squinting, I reply, "You can't mean me because I literally have a name tag right here, with my name written clearly in black Sharpie, and I'm making the optimistic assumption you can read, so if you needed me, you'd call me by my name."

This makes Mannix's dad laugh even harder, and he doesn't try to hide it this time. "I like you," he says to me, glancing over his shoulder. "You're a straight talker. Put him in his place."

The guy who called me Red shifts in his seat but is clearly less than entertained. "Another beer, if you would."

I smile tightly. "I'll be sure to send someone over who can get that for you."

Pacing back toward Kyle and Mia, I notice them watching me with wide eyes. "God, what an absolute *dick*," I say when I reach them.

They don't reply but continue staring past me.

When I decide that something is awry, I glance over my shoulder, hoping the idiot from the table hasn't overhead me calling him a dick. But it's Mannix who's behind me, hands shoved in his pockets.

"Hey, I'm sorry about him. He knows my dad, and he isn't always pleasant when he drinks."

"Can't wait to see how saccharine he'll be when he downs another beer." I inform the bartender of his order and then turn back to Mannix. "Hey, these are my friends Kyle and Mia. They're working with me over the summer."

"Mannix," he says, shaking each of their hands. "Nice to meet you."

"Nice to finally meet *you*," says Kyle.

Mannix has the decency to blush at this, but my face flushes so badly that my skin soon matches my hair. Thankfully, the bartender appears at my side and asks where the drink is going. I point to the table, and he heads over.

"I didn't think you were going to come," I say, floundering for something to fill the silence that's engulfed us.

"Yeah, when I mentioned it to my dad, he sounded interested. So I offered to bring him."

Kyle nods knowingly, their eyes wide and a grin splitting their face. "Because you love whales so much, too. I get it. I get it."

"Of course."

"Cor," says Mia, pointing out into the audience. "They're signaling you."

The table beside Mannix's is waving me over.

"I'll manage the next round of apps," Mia assures me.

"Thanks!" I weave through the tables, unable to bypass the guy who called me Red, and as I squeeze by, I catch a glimmer of his conversation.

"I'm tellin' you," he says. "Shoot them." He imitates the sound of a firing gun.

"I don't think that's a logical option," says Mr. Reilly.

"It'd cost less, and we wouldn't have to sit here listening to this shit."

I grab the other table's empty glasses and then stand there, stupefied.

Mr. Reilly catches my eye and shakes his head. "Come on," he says quietly to his table companion. "Give it a break. Let's listen to the speaker." He points to Dr. Blair.

I'm too stunned to move, too baffled to even speak right away. I'm lost in the middle of the aisle, between tables, and in my ear, secretly, Ella whispers, *What makes you think you're so singular?*

Before I can even consider the words, I ask him, "What are you even doing here?"

He stares at me blankly.

Which pisses me off even further. "If you don't care about whales, if you don't care about working together to find a solution, then what's your issue? No one made you come, so why are you here?"

He grins, lifting his beer glass like he's toasting me, and replies, "The open bar."

I can't be near him, so I stalk back to where Kyle and Mia are arranging garden salads for the first course, and I slam my tray down on the table. Mannix jumps. "Are you okay here on your own for a minute? I need some cool air."

"Sure, go," says Kyle, waving me away.

Heading for the flap of the tent that leads out into the dimming twilight, I pull my ponytail down and rub at my scalp, like that's going to calm me down.

"Hey," comes Mannix's voice behind me.

We stand on the narrow brick sidewalk that wraps around the building. About a hundred feet away, people walk up and down Commercial Street, hand in hand, stopping in front of illuminated shop windows and admiring the displays. Beyond them, the bay ripples with the calm of the coming night.

"You okay?" Mannix asks me.

"Honestly, I'm good." I turn to face him and offer him a weak smile. "I was getting a little hot in there and needed to cool off."

"Just ignore Jonesy," says Mannix. "He likes to hear himself talk."

"Nice."

"I'm really sorry."

I shake my head, reaching out and touching his arm. "Don't be sorry. I'm fine. I mean it."

He eyes me warily, like he doesn't believe me. And he's right, he shouldn't. But he hasn't been in my head this whole time. He doesn't know about Fraction, or her entanglement, or her half a fluke, or the way Ella keeps asking me questions, calling me out. "Okay," he says. He runs his hand through his hair and looks back at the tent. "I'm gonna head back in."

"Good idea."

I watch him leave, then let my chin drop to my chest.

Chapter Eight

"Where are we supposed to find tubes in the shape of sea life?" Kyle asks as we drive down Route 6.

I lean back, rolling down the passenger-side window of their Chevy Tahoe and taking a sip from my bottle of Diet Coke. "There's a store in a few miles. On the left." I close my eyes for a moment.

"Hey, hey," says Kyle, snapping their fingers in front of my face. "Stay with me. How will I know when to turn?"

"Trust me," I tell them. "You'll know."

The souvenir shack is littered with inflatable tubes in all shapes and sizes on the lawn, on the front porch, even tied up to the roof. When we get out of the truck, Kyle stares in amazement. "They have everything. I think I'm going to buy that waffle tube for me. I want to float on a waffle."

"Knock yourself out. But first, let's find a whale so Lottie will think we accomplished something this afternoon."

We enter the store, which smells a lot like plastic and sunblock, and wordlessly and almost immediately, we begin browsing the aisles that have nothing to do with inflatable tubes. There are Cape Cod decals for your car (Kyle grabs two), hundreds of sunglasses on rotating displays, and at the far end of the building, there's a glass counter filled with fudge and other candy. We weave through each aisle, admiring all the crap.

"Maybe I want a mug," Kyle muses.

"Oh, look at these," I say, grabbing two coconut cups. "Maybe I want a new bathing suit." I place them on my chest and do a little dance, which makes Kyle bend over with laughter.

"Stop, stop!" they beg, waving me away. "You're gonna make me pee a little!"

This clearly does not make me stop. My dance becomes a little more crazed, and when I do a spin, I come face to face with Mannix, who watches me, head tilted to the side. I drop the cups.

"You break it, you buy it!" calls the lady at the cash register.

"Yup, yes," I tell her, unable to make eye contact with literally anyone. I give her a thumbs-up. "That's fair. Absolutely."

Mannix stands there, still watching me, one hand on his hip and the other holding a pair of sunglasses. He nods and takes a deep breath. "Yeah, that's pretty hot."

"I thought so," I say, placing the coconut cups back on the shelf. "And eco-friendly. A solid use of food waste." Behind me, Kyle has disappeared somewhere, probably in search of a restroom. "So to what do I owe the pleasure of meeting you at this trove of useless shit?"

Mannix is decked out in his red board shorts and a muscle tank. He clearly came from the beach.

"I broke my sunglasses, so I ran out here to grab a pair while I wait for my polarized ones to ship. And lucky me, my timing is impeccable."

"Sunglasses and a show."

Mannix leans an elbow on the shelf beside him stacked with shot glasses. "So what are you up to?"

"Searching for a tube that's shaped like a whale."

"Over there," he says, pointing over my head. "There's a Shamu."

"Orca," I reply.

"But you knew what I meant."

"SeaWorld is a prison, Mannix."

"I believe that. What do you need a whale inflatable for?"

Sighing, I squeeze past him, on the search for my orca. "We convinced our boss to let us make TikToks of what to do when you find stranded sea life. So Kyle and I are on the search for props."

"I can help you out."

"How?"

"Come to White Crest tomorrow. Before lunch. I'll get a few of us together so it doesn't have to be you and Kyle going back and forth filming and starring."

"I don't want to annoy anyone." I stand at the wall, sorting through the deflated packaged tubes and trying to find the orca. There's a doughnut with pink frosting and ample sprinkles, and a giant scallop shell, but I can't seem to find the whale.

"Here you go." Mannix is right behind me, and as he reaches up, his chest touches my back. It is very toned. It is very nice.

I take a deep breath. "I got it." He brings the packaged whale tube down and hands it to me. "And you wouldn't be bothering anyone. They're all my friends."

"But I don't even know them."

He considers this for a minute. "A bunch of us are going mini-golfing tonight. You and your friends could just, I dunno, show up."

This is a big no for me. I am not athletic or competitive, and I would prefer to avoid all situations that would force me to pretend to be either, let alone both. "I don't know if I can tonight."

"Can what tonight?" says Kyle, coming up behind Mannix.

Pointing at me, Mannix turns to Kyle to be the voice of reason. "I invited Cor and you and Mia to come mini-golfing with a few of my friends, and she says she's busy."

"No, she's not," says Kyle.

I scowl at them.

"And I'll pick her up at eight. Yes? Eight, Mannix?"

"Sounds good," he agrees, crossing his arms over his chest and grinning. "Hey, listen." He thumbs toward the cash register. "I need to get back to the beach, but I'll see you tonight. The mini-golf place by the restaurant we went to last week. Remember?"

"Oh, yes." I tap my temple. "I remember."

"Catch you later. Bye, Kyle."

"Bye, Mannix!" Kyle calls after him. Then when he's out of earshot, "What the hell is your deal?"

"What's *your* deal?" I ask, hand on my hip, leaning forward. "I don't want to go mini-golfing."

"He wants to hang out with you! He's the sweetest, and he's so, *so* handsome. I don't get it."

I pretend to browse the collection of foam can coolers until

Mannix is out of the building. "He is all of those things, and he doesn't want to go out with me."

Kyle scoffs. "He literally asked you out thirty-eight seconds ago."

"It's not a date. I had dinner with him last week. That wasn't a date, either. He's not interested. He's just friendly."

"No," they correct me. "He wants to hang out with you, is aware of his previous misstep in hanging out with you, and wants to make it feel like a no-pressure sitch."

I grab a tube shaped like a seal to go with my orca and head for the cash register. "Ready to check out," I say to the woman who chastised me only minutes ago. "Sorry about the cups. They're all in one piece, though."

She grunts as she rings up the tubes but doesn't verbally reply to me.

"Just come mini-golfing." Kyle keeps trying, even as we turn to leave the store with our purchase. "You don't have to stay if you're not having a good time, but I think you're missing out if you don't."

"Fine!" I say once I reach the door of their car. "Fine. You win. I'll go mini-golfing. Pick me up tonight."

"Oh, I will," says Kyle, getting into the driver's seat. "And you're going to have fun, dammit."

I click on the radio as we pull out of the parking lot, and I don't talk for the rest of the drive to headquarters.

I stand in front of my mirror for too long, and the longer I stare at myself, the more messy my hair looks. It's probably fine, but now I'm obsessing. It's only the sound of my phone on the nightstand that forces me to wrench myself away from my own reflection.

The face of my older sister, Peyton, lights up the screen.

"Hey, what's up?" I answer.

"What's up?" she repeats incredulously. "I texted you, like, four times today, and you didn't even acknowledge me."

My shoulders slump, and I stare at the ceiling. "It's been a busy day."

"What are you doing?"

"I had work, and then my friend Kyle and I had to run and get whale floaties, and now I'm about to go mini-golfing with a whole group of people, and I'm feeling anxious."

"Hot lifeguard?" Peyton asks.

"Hot lifeguard." I pause and notice the noise in the background. "Where are you?"

"Out for drinks with my coworkers." Peyton lives in Hoboken and works in New York. She has an adorable apartment that overlooks the Hudson River. She tells me all the time how much she loves the busyness of the city, the constant motion. I glance out the window of my bedroom here in Wellfleet, where two chickadees flutter off into the coming night, and honestly, this is the perfect place. I could spend the rest of my life here.

"What are you wearing?" Peyton asks.

I look down at my outfit. "Cutoff shorts and a pink cami with white polka dots."

"How do your boobs look?"

"Seriously, Peyton?"

"Fine, okay. It sounds nice. Take a pic and send to me. I'll let you know."

"K, bye." I hang up and take a selfie in the full-length mirror, then shoot it to my sister. She replies with a thumbs-up emoji. Good enough.

Outside, Kyle's Tahoe rolls up the shell driveway. I slip on my brown flip-flops and secure my silver stud earrings and then practically skip down the steps. "Going mini-golfing with Kyle and Mia!" I call to Uncle Jack as I race past the kitchen.

"What time will you be home?" he asks, his head inside the fridge.

I pause by the counter where he keeps all his correspondence. "Around eleven?"

"Good," he says, then stands up straight, closing the fridge door. "Hey, did you remember to invite Kyle and Mia out to dinner tomorrow for your birthday?"

Uncle Jack insists on taking me out for my eighteenth birthday, and he also insists that I bring along my coworkers. I think he feels bad that I'm not home with my friends from school, but I knew that going into this summer. And it's not like I've felt like celebrating when I'm around them anyway. Not since Ella.

"Yeah, they're both coming."

"Perfect! And what about Mannix?"

"I'm not inviting Mannix."

"Why not?"

"Uncle Jack. Come on. That's weird. We met a couple of weeks ago."

He pours himself a glass of wine and replies, "You met Kyle and Mia a couple of weeks ago, but you're inviting them."

"Totally different. Listen, I love you, but I gotta go."

"All right, all right." He waves me away. "Have fun."

I grab my key and shove it in my little brown pleather

crossbody bag, then dash out the door. With a yank on the handle, I practically dive into the backseat.

Kyle and Mia both turn and stare at me.

"Well, it took you long enough," says Kyle, watching me in the rearview mirror.

Mia smiles, turning around to look at me from the passenger seat. "But you look really pretty."

"*You* look pretty!" I grin and shove her in the shoulder. "Hey, Kyle, let's get this show on the road. Don't make us late."

"Um, hello? I look pretty, too."

"You always look pretty," I assure them.

They shake their head as they put the Tahoe in reverse. "Liar. Put some lip gloss on."

"Way to call out my dry lips," I mumble, but I reach into my bag and retrieve my gloss from the side pocket.

The ride to the mini-golf place is hardly even five minutes. Just enough time for the cold, nervous shakes and the guilt to set in. Because there are other things I'm supposed to be nervous about, like a whale out in Stellwagen Bank wrapped in rope and struggling. Instead, I'm here anxious about a boy I might never see again after August.

But I hope I do, and I hate this feeling.

I'm the last to get out of the truck after we park, and I adjust my shorts and pull the front of my shirt away from me. Like adjusting what I'm wearing is going to give me the confidence boost required to play well. Kyle and Mia stride on ahead of me, laughing about something I can't hear, but that's honestly okay. I don't want to pretend to find something funny when I'm not even paying attention.

"Do you think I should text Mannix?" I ask them.

"I'm sure we'll find him," Mia says. "This place isn't huge."

We follow a boardwalk path to a wooden booth, where we pay for admission, and then wait by a bench near an unnaturally blue lagoon. A pirate ship sits among spraying fountains and poorly painted stone dolphins that break the surface of the water, and every so often there's the fuzzy sound of a cannon being fired and forced pirate laughter.

"I brought bug spray," says Mia, pulling a spray bottle out of her bag. "Let me spray your legs."

"Good idea," I say, standing.

"Me next," says Kyle.

As Mia crouches down in front of me, Mannix and a few friends approach the wooden booth. "He's here," I murmur.

"Oh, good," says Mia. "We can get started."

Honestly, someone needs to validate my complete and utter dread tonight.

Mannix stands at the register behind a girl who's paying, and he exchanges conversation with another guy who looks familiar. I've probably seen him at White Crest. Both he and Mannix are looking at me. When the girl is done paying, she reaches around to Mannix's back pocket and retrieves his wallet, shoves the change inside, and places it back. Really a familiar move right there. When Mannix catches my eye, he waves, and I awkwardly return the gesture.

"Very smooth," says Kyle.

I straighten my shoulders as Mannix and his group head toward us. "I hate you for all of this."

"Hey," says Mannix, his hands shoved in his pockets as he approaches. He's wearing dark jeans, a green T-shirt, and a pair of Converse. "These are my friends, Maddie, Jacob, Noah, and Kelsey. Guys, this is Cor, Mia, and Kyle."

"Hey," I say.

"Nice to meet you," adds Mia.

"Salutations," says Kyle with a grin.

Everyone starts talking, exchanging stories, places of birth, how their summer's going, high school mascots, and Mia nudges me in the shoulder. "Noah is like...way hotter than Mannix," she whispers, turning so that she's facing me and no one else can hear what she says.

I glance over at Noah, who has fantastic black hair that's whooshed back from his face, a solid tan, and broad shoulders. He is handsome, I'll admit it, but in a totally different way than Mannix. Mannix is handsome because he isn't trying. He's too busy trying to be other things: busy, reliable, thoughtful. He's unassuming.

"I guess so," I reply, and then I tap my lower lip reflectively. "Go offer to be his partner."

"That's weird."

"It's not," I tell her. "It's cute. You're cute. He's cute. Everything will be cute."

Noah and Mannix back away from the group, heading to the collection of golf clubs of all different lengths and organized in barrels against a wall draped in fake fishing nets.

"Hurry up." I nod in their direction. "Before they pair up."

"Okay," says Mia, with a confident nod. "Okay. How's my hair?"

She left it down and slightly wavy tonight, and I run my fingers through the top to poof it a bit. "Perfect. Go get him."

I'm like a mama bird watching her fledgling take her first attempt at flight, but I don't want to be too obvious. Once I see that she has Noah's attention, I turn back to Kyle, but they're already paired up with Kelsey.

I'm left standing with Jacob. He's cute, also tan, with pale blue eyes and shoulder-length wavy blond hair.

"You want to partner up?" he asks me. He thumbs to where everyone else has walked to. "I'll go grab us clubs."

He's gone before I can even tell him I'd like to wait until everyone else gets back, and that's rude. I'm annoyed. But I can still make this work in my favor. Mannix and Maddie, followed by Noah and Mia, amble back over to me, and I straighten my shoulders.

"So," says Mannix, holding out tiny pencils for all of us. His eyes finally rest on me. "You wanna...?"

"Got you a club, Cor," says Jacob. "You ready?"

"Oh, I didn't realize...," says Mannix, taking a step back.

"That's okay," Maddie chimes in. "We can be partners. Give Jacob an actual challenge." She takes her club and a purple golf ball from Mannix and leads the way to the first hole.

Jacob follows her, and Mannix offers me a weak smile, letting me go first. I think Mannix was going to ask to be my partner, but I'm not brave enough to double-check.

I meander over to the aqua lagoon and admire the statue of a mermaid sprawled out on a rock. All around us, families with small children weave their way through the course, and I miss Peyton all of a sudden. I'm not on Mannix's team tonight, and it makes me feel weirdly lonely, and when I'm lonely, I miss home, my safe place with people who really know me.

"Hey," says Mannix, coming up behind me. He holds out a bright green golf ball, dropping it into my open hand. "Try this club. I think I picked the right size for you."

"I got her a club, don't worry," says Jacob.

Mannix rolls his shoulders back.

The club that Jacob snagged for me is significantly too short. "Not gonna work," I say, giving it back to him. I try out Mannix's. It's perfect. "I'll take this one."

Mannix smiles. "I like your braid thing."

I managed to get half a braid crown woven into my hair that runs down into a sloppy bun at the nape of my neck. "Thanks." I take a practice swing. "I like your...hair."

He runs his hand through it, making it messier than it already was. "Me, too."

"Cor," Jacob calls from the green. "We're up first!"

I reluctantly follow him, throwing one last glance at Mannix over my shoulder. He's turned from me and kicks at the sidewalk, head down.

Jacob takes mini-golfing very seriously, and he's soon rather disappointed in my lack of skill and overall eagerness for winning. By the time we get to the ninth hole, I catch him rolling his eyes and then gathering himself, offering me words of encouragement.

"Don't bend from your knees," says Mannix quietly. He leans against the fence that separates the sidewalk from the lagoon below.

"Hm?" I stand up straight.

"You're gonna want to bend at the hips. Not the knees."

I do as he says, take my swing, and my golf ball sails over the green and toward the hole, landing only maybe a foot away. "Look at me go!" I cry, and I hop once.

"Nice one," says Jacob. "That's more like it. Looks like being my partner is starting to rub off on you." He snakes his hand around my waist as I stand beside him, waiting for Mannix to take his shot.

I find an excuse to move farther down the green, away from unwanted gestures of affection. Or is it possession?

Mia goes next, then Noah, and finally Mannix. As he addresses the ball, his eyes meet mine, and Jacob whispers in my ear, "What are you doing after this?"

Mannix's shot is trash.

"Going to bed," I reply. And then, just to be safe, "Alone." Before he even has a chance to reply, I pace over to where Mia admires the lagoon behind us.

"Geez, Reilly, what the hell was that?" Noah asks, scratching his head.

"Not everyone's feeling as confident about their game as you always are," Mannix replies. He follows the ball down the green and then stands casually beside Jacob, like nothing in the world could possibly be the matter.

"Still haven't shaken the nervous jitters?" Noah asks, lining his club up with the ball.

Wordlessly, Mia pinches my elbow.

"Not nervous," says Mannix, concentrating on balancing his golf club vertically on his middle finger.

"Then why were you sweating so bad on the car ride over?"

"Because you're too much of a cheap-ass to buy a car with working AC."

Noah hits the ball and then stares at Mannix in disbelief. "Your truck doesn't even have AC!"

"That's because it's an *antique*."

Jacob straightens his shoulders, focusing his attention on the golf ball at his feet. It's his turn to putt. "Don't know what you'd have to be nervous about, Mannix," he says, taking his swing. "Not like this was a date or anything, right? Just a group outing."

I sneak a glance at Mannix. He doesn't even flinch. "Guess I didn't anticipate this level of competition."

I think they're talking about me, but then again, I'd hate to assume this and then look like an idiot. Neither of them meets the other's eyes.

"Your turn, Cor," says Mannix.

We play like this for the rest of the night, Jacob and I doing only relatively better than Noah and Mia, and no one doing better than Kelsey and Kyle. Mannix and Maddie are pathetically far behind. Jacob goes on and on about himself while we're not playing, telling me all about surfing, and his surfboard, and how I should come to White Crest and he'll teach me how to surf.

When we get to the final hole, I get ready for my turn while Mannix and Noah sit up on a fence behind me, discussing some event at Cahoon Hollow the other day that involved a rather plucky seal escaping from the jaws of a great white.

I take a deep breath, envisioning my golf ball sailing through the downed log tunnel, over the three bumps in the green, and into the hole without much effort on my part whatsoever. When I'm about to take my swing, the bottom end of a golf club nudges me in the back of my left knee.

"Hey," I say, turning to find Mannix looking innocent and still talking great whites with Noah.

"What?"

"You're gonna ruin my shot."

"What?" he repeats, this time shrugging to add validity to his innocence.

I line up again. He nudges me again. This time, I lurch at him, shoving him in the shoulder.

"Whoa, hey. Watch it. If I fall into the lagoon, you know I can't swim."

"Maybe the mermaid will save you," I say.

"You and her have matching bathing suits." He nods in the mermaid's direction.

"She has scallop shells," I correct him. "I clearly wear coconuts."

"I noticed."

"I noticed you noticing."

Noah groans. "Holy shit, could you please either hit the ball or make out with him already?"

"Unfortunately," I say, returning my attention to my golf ball, "I only make out with people I've gone on dates with. And Mannix and I have never been on a date. So that might be awkward."

Noah and Jacob cackle at this, and I'm suddenly sorry I said anything. I was trying to remind Mannix that we had clearly been on something most people would consider a date, but his blush makes me feel like I just sided with Jacob in all of this, and that's not where I want to be.

"Where'd he take you, Cor?" Jacob asks. "The place over by the harbor? Did he make you try his dressing?"

"Jacob," says Mannix, and there's an edge to his tone that makes me second-guess anything I might say next.

But Jacob won't let up. "He's pushy with food. It's like the only thing he's good at, so he has to show off about it."

I think Jacob means this as a joke, the way guys can tease each other sometimes. Only Mannix can't even look me in the eye. His mouth is pressed into a firm, unreadable line. I try to catch his attention, to let him know that Jacob is a piece of shit, but that's not how I'm going to fix this. I whirl to face Jacob.

"It's important to find something to be passionate about that grows with you."

"So is Mannix going to be some ancient chef someday?"

I shrug. "I dunno. Are you going to be one of those aging, wrinkly surfers desperately clinging to their youth someday?"

Jacob's face drops.

I pace back up to Mannix, and when I pass behind him, I say so that only he can hear, "You've got this."

"Hey," he says softly, turning. "Thanks for that."

I nod once, tucking a loose strand of hair behind my ear.

Silently, Mannix squats next to his golf ball, studying the path down to the hole from all angles, then stands, dramatically stretches his arms over his chest, and finally takes a swing. A hole in one. He and Noah hoot and embrace like he hit a grand slam to win the World Series.

I'm pretty sure this means that Jacob and I lost, but I'm fine with this fact, as long as I get ice cream as a consolation prize. There's a place across the parking lot, lit with strands of outdoor lights that softly glow in the darkening night, and I point in its direction. "How about I buy a celebratory frappe for the mini-golf king?"

"I like that," says Mannix, considering. "Ice cream and a title all in one night."

Kyle, Kelsey, Jacob, and Maddie are already in line, and they wave us over to them, and eventually Mia and Noah catch up.

It's nice standing like this. Side by side, considering the twenty-plus flavors of gourmet ice cream they offer, making a joke and laughing at nothing. I lean forward to see the last flavor more clearly, and Mannix's knuckles brush mine. It's small and it's silly, but I wish like hell he'd do it again.

"So what are we thinking?" Noah asks when we all have our ice cream and find an empty picnic table all to ourselves. Behind us, three kids play tag, squealing at the notion of being caught. "Mannix says we're making TikToks tomorrow at White Crest."

I nod, taking a long sip of my chocolate frappe. "Yup, I have the inflatables."

"What are they for?" asks Maddie.

"Our boss wants us to up MRCA's social media presence and reach a younger audience about conservation on Cape Cod, so we suggested TikToks about what to do when you see stranded sea life. Lottie loved it. It's a pretty cool idea," Mia explains. Gently, she turns to me so that only I can hear her and says, "You should invite Mannix to your birthday dinner."

I press my lips together and nod, the idea not quite as ridiculous as it was when Uncle Jack suggested it earlier.

"And then we'll celebrate our TikTok debut at Mannix's party after," says Jacob. "You wanna come with me, Cor?"

I swallow hard and reply as best I can. "Um, maybe."

Suddenly it feels like the entire picnic table must be staring at me, because clearly, I was not invited to this party by Mannix. But I take a breath and steady my nerves. Everyone is still talking about the videos we're making, and no one seems to notice that I'm kicking myself for thinking that Mannix might be more than a decent flirt. Or that I'm worth more than playing pretend.

We hang out for another half hour, and then finally Mia yawns. "Ready to go?" she asks us.

Kyle nods, pulling their keys from their pocket. "Ready."

In the parking lot, we all hug good night, and when Mannix's hug lasts a little longer, I make sure not to make something of it, and move on to Noah.

"See you in the morning," Noah says, and he's adding his number to Mia's phone. At least one of us had a successful night.

I collapse into the backseat and buckle up as Kyle starts the Tahoe.

"Well, that was fun!" they say.

"A barrel of monkeys," I mumble.

"Oh, wow, okay," Kyle says as they back out of the parking spot. "What happened, pouty?"

"Well, there's obviously a party that Mannix didn't invite us to."

"Jacob invited you," says Kyle.

Mia fidgets in the front seat.

"What?" I prompt her.

"I was invited," she says. Then she turns fast enough to give herself whiplash. "But it was by Noah, and he said we should all come, so technically we all were invited."

"See?" says Kyle, monitoring the traffic on Route 6 and then pulling out onto the road slowly. "There we go. We're all invited. Feel better?"

"I don't know how that's supposed to make me feel better. It's Mannix's party, and he clearly didn't invite me. I got a secondhand invite. Oh, I'm sorry. Actually, a thirdhand invite because Jacob is a dipshit."

"You're still gonna go, though, aren't you?" Mia asks.

"Of course not."

"Cor, please? I'll be too nervous, and Kyle's gonna go, right?"

"No can do, my friend," says Kyle. "I have plans with my cousin tomorrow night after we have Cor's birthday dinner."

"Now you have to go," Mia begs me.

I close my eyes and sigh. "We'll see."

Mia sighs and thumps back against her seat. I'm not trying to hurt her, and part of me wishes I had the eloquence and presence of mind to tell her that. That she's bycatch in my net of irritation.

What makes you think you're so singular? Ella nags.

And if she were really in the car with me, I'd tell her it's easy being singular. It has been ever since she died. That way it's not my fault when everything goes wrong. You can't destroy what you never had.

Chapter Nine

I don't have to sit in Mia's driveway for too long before she bolts from the back of the house and plops herself down in the passenger seat of the Jeep.

"Sorry I'm late," she says.

"No worries."

We're both wearing gym shorts and our MRCA T-shirts, with the whale, shark, sea turtle, and seal insignia on the breast pocket, but Mia has a little something extra on her shoulder. As I pull out onto the dirt road that leads to her house, I pluck some gauzy white material from her shirt and assume it's a spiderweb.

"Shit, is there a bug on me?" She practically lurches from her seat, and I place a hand on her arm to keep her within the moving vehicle.

"It's okay, just an old web."

"It's the outdoor shower," she says with a groan, rubbing at her eyes with the heels of her hands. "I have to drape my clothes over the door so that I'm not prancing around the yard in a towel, and there are so many bugs, Cor. Every day. Like, I swoosh them all away, and then they come back with a vengeance."

"That sucks."

She settles and then suddenly remembers what day it is. "Happy birthday!" she cries, and reaches over the console to hug me.

"Aw, thanks," I say.

"I got this for you." Mia hands me a little gift box wrapped in rainbow confetti paper.

At a red light, I open it and inside is a pair of sand dollar earrings. "Mia, I love them. Thank you so much." I lift from my seat, using the rearview mirror to secure them in my ears.

"I'm glad." She's quiet for a minute as we turn off Route 6 toward White Crest Beach. "So," she finally says. "Have you thought about whether you're coming to the party tonight?"

I tap my fingers against the steering wheel to the beat of the song on the radio and reply, "I'll see how awkward it is when we get to White Crest today. I don't know if I want to go if he didn't even think to ask me. It'll be weird."

"It's okay," she says, staring out the window at the passing pine and oak trees. "I get it. I do."

I'm not sure if she understands how this in-between feels like swimming, the way your feet almost touch the bottom, and your toes brush up against the flailing fronds of seaweed, and if you don't act quickly, if you let yourself become entangled, then it'll anchor you to the seafloor. I have to keep moving.

With a slow breath through my lips, my gaze is captured by

the deep blues and greens of the Atlantic out my window. Below the cliffs, the waves, with their frothy crests, crash against the shoreline, and I remind myself why I'm here. It's not about parties, or boys, or getting noticed. It's about doing the work that I was supposed to complete with my friend.

We pull into White Crest's parking lot, which is filling up slowly. Several chairs and umbrellas dot the beach below, and Kyle stands at the whiteboard with Noah, Mannix, and Maddie.

"What are you doing?" Mia asks as we climb out of the Jeep.

"I'm writing all the pertinent info on the board," says Kyle. They're also drawing seashells in the corners. "Because Mannix has the handwriting of a kindergartner in a paint mixer."

"That's vivid," says Mannix. He crosses his arms over his green lifeguard T-shirt and spares me a glance.

"We're gonna head down to the beach and blow up the tubes," I tell them before Mannix feels obligated to say something to me.

"Hey," says Mia behind me, and when I look, she's batting her eyes at Noah.

"Hey," he says. "Can I help you carry something?"

"Sure, thanks." She hands him a bag and some props we collected from the MRCA's junk shed at the back of the property.

I begin my trek down the sandy path toward the water and locate the perfect spot. Away from all the people and close enough to the ocean so that we can include a view of the water. Tugging a blanket from my bag, I whip it open and spread it out before me, then plop down and begin blowing up the tubes.

The whale is huge. Which makes sense, it's a whale. But I don't know if I have the lung capacity to complete what I've started. I give it a go anyway.

As I'm exhaling every last molecule of oxygen I have to offer, a shadow passes over me. I look up, still attached to the tube.

"Hey," says Mannix, shading me from the sun.

"Hey."

"You can't blow that up by yourself."

I take a break for several deep breaths and a few words to spare him. "I'll be fine. We have the whole morning."

"You're gonna make yourself sick," he tries again. "I'm gonna run up to my truck. I have a pump we can use."

I keep blowing, and eventually he returns carrying something that looks a little bit like a drill, but apparently it's going to inflate this whale much quicker than I possibly can.

"Come on," he says, urging me to stand up.

"It's fine," I assure him, but I take his hand and let him lift me to my feet. The sudden change in altitude makes me dizzy, and I sway despite my best efforts.

"Whoa, hey," he says, dropping the pump and gripping both my arms. "You okay?"

I close my eyes, my fingers digging into his wrists.

"Just stand still for a minute," he says. "I got you."

"Thanks," I tell him quietly. "I think I'm okay."

"You sure?" He tilts his head to look me in the face, as though I'm incapable of lying if we make eye contact. This turns out to be kind of true.

"I'm gonna sit back down."

He lowers me slowly by the hands to the blanket again, then plops down beside me and begins inflating the whale. We're quiet for a little while, just us and the lull of the waves. A few surfers paddle out, and I like to watch how graceful they are, how quickly they assess which wave is going to be the one and then find some way to hoist their bodies onto their boards and balance themselves to ride the surge back to the shallows.

Beside me, Mannix shifts and turns in my direction. "So I didn't get a chance to tell you yesterday that I'm having a party tonight. You know, if you wanna come. It's really casual."

Guilty invite. "I can't," I say.

He sighs. "I'm sorry, I should have mentioned it...."

"It's okay, I'm just busy."

"Doing what?"

I scratch my forehead. This sounds so pathetic in my head, and I can only imagine how much saying it out loud will amplify it. "It's my birthday."

His eyebrows jump. "Oh, happy birthday. I didn't know." He stares out at the water for a while. "So are you seventeen? Eighteen?"

"Eighteen," I reply. "I'll be a full-fledged adult senior."

"How are you celebrating?"

"Uncle Jack is taking me and Kyle and Mia out for dinner."

"So come to my party after."

"I don't know what time we'll be finished."

He laughs at this, pulling his knees up to his chest and wrapping his arms around his legs by linking his hands. "I'm pretty sure the party will still be going on. My mom and dad are in Boston this weekend to see his doctor, so the place is mine."

"Wild rager?"

He shakes his head. "Nah. Just some friends getting together, grilling, maybe having a beer or two. It's for people I went to high school with. Honestly, I didn't even think about anyone outside that circle until Jacob brought it up."

"We'll see," I say quietly.

Mannix sighs, stretching his legs out and leaning toward his toes; then he jumps up, like sitting is too much right now. He walks to the water, then turns back to me. "I'm really sorry I didn't ask you. I was honestly so caught up in going mini-golfing with you, and you meeting my friends, that I didn't even remember I was having a party. But I would have—"

"No, honestly." I stop him midramble. "I'm not mad at you. I'm mad at me, and I'm trying to do what I should have done the other night when you told me you weren't interested. I'm taking a step back. It's okay."

He runs his hand up his right arm and squints in the brightening light of the sun. "I didn't say I wasn't interested," he says quietly.

"Let's not do this," I tell him. "Please. Whatever it is you mean, it's fine. I'm not offended. I'll come to the party. I'll even bring some chips."

"Okay," he says in a tone that implies that it doesn't feel one hundred percent okay.

Next to me, my orca is fully inflated and looks ready for its close-up.

"All right," says Noah, clapping his hands as he reaches the bottom of the cliff. "Are we ready to film me in my debut?"

"You've never made a TikTok before?" Mia asks, coming up beside him.

"I don't have time for that," he says, but he's grinning, clearly thrilled with the idea that he's about to be in his first one.

"I think we should put the whale halfway in the surf," I suggest, dragging it toward the water. "That way it looks more realistic."

"It's an orca," says Noah. "We don't get a lot of those."

"There's one they spot off Chatham from time to time," I tell him.

"Old Thom," Mannix adds.

I glance up at him and smile. "That's him."

"How old is Old Thom?" Mia asks.

"Not that old," I say. "He's maybe a teenager. But he's named after a famous orca who lived off Australia. He and his pod used to help the whalers hunt larger baleen whales, like humpbacks. He would alert the whalers when he had one cornered, and in return, they'd let the orcas eat the tongues and the lips of the dead whales. They had a truce, an alliance, until Old Thom died."

"What happened to him?" asks Mannix.

"A whaler fought him for the carcass of one of the whales they killed and damaged his teeth. Old Thom probably died of infection and starvation. The whaler said he regretted what he did to him for the rest of his life. He had to live with that guilt." My mouth twists strangely, and I don't want to break in front of everybody. Not when we're supposed to be having fun, not when they'll never understand how this story devastates me from the tips of my curling toes in the sand to the pit in my roiling stomach.

"That's a pretty gruesome alliance," says Mannix, staring out at the water.

"Yeah, well. Maybe the whalers saw something in the orcas they understood," I suggest; then I pretend to cough, to hide the crack in my voice. "And maybe the orcas trusted them."

Noah stands beside Mannix, nudging him with his elbow. "You ever see our Old Thom when you're out on the water with your dad?"

He shakes his head, scratching the back of his neck. "Nah, not me. Wish I had, though. Next time, I'll tell Dad about the orcas off Australia. He loves stories like that."

"Okay," I say once I get our inflatable situated. I stand up straight, my hands on my hips. "Who's riding Old Thom?"

"I'll give it a go," Mannix volunteers. He approaches the tube and stares at it for a minute, then straddles its back, behind the dorsal fin. "Am I gonna pop it?"

I tilt my head to the side, watching as his weight makes the whale's head rear up unnaturally. "I don't think so. But it looks like it's in pain."

"Well, this is supposed to be about what not to do when you find stranded marine life, right?" Noah asks.

"Right."

"So we shouldn't do this." Noah points to Mannix.

My face still scrunches. "Yeah, but it doesn't look right. Mannix is too big."

Mannix lifts himself from the back of the whale. "I have an idea." Before anyone can ask what that might be, he goes jogging down the beach, stopping at a semicircle of beach chairs and chatting with two parents and a little kid. By the time he's done, he and the kid are walking back toward us.

"Did you steal someone's child?" Noah asks.

Mannix ruffles the boy's hair. "This is Jackson. You ready to star in your first TikTok, big guy?"

Jackson, still decked out in his shark board shorts, nods once. "Ready."

"So here's what I need you to do, buddy," I say, pointing to our whale. "We're going to pretend that this is a real whale that's stuck on the beach, and he wants to get back in the water."

Jackson gives me a firm nod.

"First, you're going to act the wrong way. You're going to poke him and climb on his back."

"That's not nice," says Jackson.

"No, it's terrible. But don't worry, because then we're going to do the right thing."

"Okay," says Jackson, and he hops on the whale's back.

After filming a few takes of Jackson playing with our orca, we move on to him running to find a lifeguard when he notices the stranded whale. Then Mannix getting on his phone and pretending to call the stranded marine life hotline. Then me and Mia jogging up, applying damp towels to the whale to keep him cool, then successfully refloating him. We all wave goodbye as he drifts out into the Atlantic.

Standing there, I shade my eyes with my hand. "We're gonna need to get that whale back."

"I'm on it," says Mannix, and he wades into the water, diving in after him.

"So," says Mia beside me as Noah and Jackson play a game of tag. "Are you coming to the party tonight?"

"Yeah," I reply, still watching Mannix as he emerges from the surf, whale in tow. "I'll come for a little bit."

"Did he ask you?"

"He did."

"I knew you were worrying for nothing. He likes you."

I turn to her, crossing my arms over my chest and shrugging. "Honestly, it doesn't even matter if he doesn't. That's not why I'm here this summer, you know? It was my little wake-up call to get my priorities straight."

"Well," says Mia, "I think you can have priorities and fun all at the same time."

"That was delicious," says Uncle Jack. Outside the Sea Ghost, we trail down the dimly lit cobblestone walkway, waiting for Chad to finish getting the recipe for the cocktail he'd had at the bar.

"Thanks for dinner, Uncle Jack," I say, linking my arm through his and resting my head against his shoulder.

"Of course." He kisses my temple.

"That cake was amazing," Kyle adds from behind us. "But I'm heading back this way." They point up the opposite end of the street. "I told my cousin I'd meet her around nine, so that gives me enough time to hike back."

"Do you need a ride?" Uncle Jack offers.

"No, thanks," says Kyle, resting their hand on their stomach. "I need to walk off that meal."

"Are we gonna head out?" Mia asks me as Chad emerges from the restaurant. "Meet you at Mannix's?"

"Going to see Mannix?" Chad asks, raising his brows at me.

I shove him gently in the arm. "He's having a party and Mia and I are going."

"What time will you be home?" Uncle Jack asks. "You have work in the morning, and then we need to start planning that fundraiser."

When I mentioned hosting a fundraiser for MRCA, Uncle Jack was all too thrilled to get started. Tomorrow afternoon, we have a meeting back at the Sea Ghost to talk about the menu. "Around midnight?" I say.

"Text me when you're on your way home," he says.

"Uncle Jack, I'm eighteen today. Remember?"

He blinks. "Text me when you're on your way home, and I don't care if you're thirty-five."

"All right, all right," I acquiesce. I kiss his cheek.

"Drive safely, and no drinking."

"I know. Love you."

"Love you, too."

I follow Mia to where our cars are parked, and before I hop up into the Jeep, I ask her, "Do you know where you're going?"

"Nope," she replies. "I figured I'd follow you."

Mannix lives in Wellfleet, too, and my navigation points me down a sandy dirt road shrouded on either side with scrub pines and oak trees decimated by some disease that looks like green foam on the branches. I'm nervous. Despite all my efforts to not think about this party all day, I have. I've thought about it way too much. I pull up along the street where several other cars are parked, and turn off the Jeep.

Ella's in the passenger seat, and I turn to her, instinctively.

"I want him to like me," I say out loud. "I don't know why, but it matters. He matters."

You're allowed to like him, Ella says.

"I don't want to use him," I say quietly. "And I don't want to be used."

But that's the thing. If you were using him, like you're so afraid of, you wouldn't acknowledge that. It wouldn't even cross your mind. And believe it or not, if he were using you, you'd know that,

132

too. She pauses, then says the words I need to hear. *Trust yourself. He's not Brent.*

And with that reminder, I hop out of the Jeep and wait for Mia to join me. There are shrieks and laughter coming from the house my navigation insists is Mannix's. He lives in a typical Cape Cod saltbox, with cedar shakes that are dark with age and mold, and fading burgundy shutters and trim.

I pull on the hem of my skirt, suddenly feeling ridiculous for having taken such meticulous consideration in choosing it. I adjust my hair, loosely braided from my forehead down, over my shoulder. The sun is about to set, and Mia and I glance at each other timidly.

"I like your skirt," she says.

"Thanks. I like your dress."

"We've got this."

"Totally."

I knock hesitantly on the glass of the storm door, and try to peek in to see if I can spot anyone. Or maybe we should go around the back. The front room is dark and empty, and no one answers the door.

Gathering my resolve, I open the front door and step inside. There are jackets and purses piled in a corner, and Mia and I hide our bags behind the armchair near the fireplace. The mantel is lined with pictures of Mannix throughout the years and pictures of someone else, too. His brother, probably. Beyond the living room, I make my way to the kitchen and the slider door. There are some people in the backyard, circling around the grill with its platter of hot dogs and hamburgers; others mill about with bottles of beer in their hands, and several people sit around a huge bonfire. We step out.

They stare at us as we get closer, and I tuck a piece of loose hair behind my ear, offering them a small wave and a quiet "Hi."

"Is that her?" one guy says from over at the bonfire.

Mannix, standing at the grill and handing someone a plate of burgers, turns to see who his friends mean. "Hey! Cor, Mia, you made it." He places the tongs down on the side of the grill and heads over to us, wrapping me in a hug. "Happy birthday."

"Thanks," I say.

"Hey, Mia." Their hug is more casual. Maybe because it's not her birthday. "Let me get you guys a beer."

Mia touches my arm and whispers, "We're not twenty-one."

I try not to laugh at her. "Neither is he."

"But I'm driving myself!"

"It's okay," I tell her. "You can tell him no."

"I don't want to be rude."

"So take it and pretend like you're sipping from it, or leave it on a table somewhere. You don't have to drink it."

"That's such a good idea."

I nod over to the fire, where a few people are congregated, sipping from their drinks and laughing. "There's Noah," I say.

"Come on," says Mannix, returning from the cooler and offering us two beers. "Come sit with us."

I follow him, Mia close behind, and after she and Noah awkwardly say hello in the cutest way possible, I seat myself on a wooden chair that Mannix offers me. "Guys, this is Coriander and Mia. They're spending the summer interning at MRCA, and we've been working together on a few things."

Everyone offers us a "Hi."

"So," I say after taking my seat and a sip. "Is this party for anything in particular?"

"Just wanted to have one while people are home from school."
Mannix shrugs. "Give it a month, and everyone will be gone.
And I'll still be here." He chuckles quietly and rubs the back of
his neck.

Mannix remains standing next to me, chomping down on a
hot dog.

"Sit here," I offer him, inching over, but it's obvious there
won't be room for two of us in this seat.

He sits himself down on the arm of the chair so that our
knees and upper arms touch. I'm getting a little gooey inside.
And the beer isn't exactly helping. I like this closeness.

Out of the corner of my eye, I notice Jacob meandering over,
then the empty lawn chair beside me.

"Hey, Cor," he says.

"Hey, Jacob." I stand politely and offer him a brief half hug.
No mixed messages.

He stands next to the chair even after I've sat back down,
focused on Mannix. "Just talked to Kayla," he says.

Mannix regards him, his beer hanging midway to his mouth.

"She might stop by later, but she's not sure yet. I'm surprised
you didn't invite her."

Mannix frowns. "I didn't even know she was home."

Shrugging, Jacob finally takes his seat. "I figured you would,
considering how close you always were."

Mannix doesn't reply this time.

"You hungry?" Jacob asks me. "I was about to get a hot dog."

"No, thanks," I say. "I'm good for now." I turn my attention
back to Mannix, but he's visibly tense as Jacob lifts from his
chair and saunters over to the grill. I don't know who Kayla is,
but she's making things weird without even having shown up,

and my mind spirals to reclaim what it felt like with Mannix before Jacob came over.

Before I can think of something to say, Mannix turns to me. "Hey, have I told you about the secret passage?"

I frown. "No. What are you talking about?"

Mannix grins and turns to his friends across the fire. "Guys, go get the stuff, and we'll show Cor and Mia what it's all about."

His friends pick up a box near the porch, and others the cooler of beer, and they head into the woods. I stick close to Mannix, though, and we stop every so often to talk with different circles of friends.

After a while, Mannix nods to a line of trees and leads me toward the woods.

"Where are we going?" I ask him.

"You'll see," he says with a secretive smile that I'm inclined to trust.

I'm not usually the kind of person who goes traipsing off through the woods. It's dark, and the woods are filled with nighttime animals, and I'm probably delicious if the bugs around here are any judges in the matter.

"Are you having fun?" he asks me.

"Yeah, I am."

"Good." He smiles at his feet. "I was nervous about inviting you."

My heart stumbles a bit in accordance with my feet.

"Watch your step."

"Why were you nervous?"

He shrugs, almost a little embarrassed. "I dunno. I guess I thought I screwed up when Jacob invited you before I got the chance. Honestly, I didn't think you'd want to come if it was a bunch of people you didn't know."

Quietly, I reply, "I know you."

Mannix looks down at me. "I'm really glad you're here."

We've been walking along this path, only the light of the full moon and Mannix's knowledge of his own property to guide us, following the sound of laughter and playful squeals coming from a close distance.

He glances over at me, checking to see if I'm paying attention, as the branches and vines before us break open, revealing the shore of Cape Cod Bay. His friends all laugh and drink on the beach, waving when they see us. With the moon behind us, the water shimmers and swells. A red-and-gold firework explodes from the sand and cracks apart in the sky, illuminating everything around us.

I cover my mouth with my hands. "This is amazing," I say, running my hands up and down my arms. The night has gotten colder, and my cardigan isn't enough.

"Here," says Mannix, pulling his hoodie up and over his head. "I'm too hot anyway."

"Thanks." I slip it carefully over my braided hair and push my arms through the sleeves. It's still warm from his body and smells like fabric softener and boy deodorant.

We stand quietly for a while, my hands shoved into the pockets of the hoodie, watching the sky explode in shimmering color, and I think, This is one of those moments, isn't it? That the girls at home always talk about, with boys who have somehow inhabited their priorities. Why they want to be young forever, and growing up is so tough. Because it is. But shit, at least I have the opportunity to grow up. At least I didn't disappear, wordlessly, under the surface of some deceptively calm sea. If I could inhabit this moment for the rest of my life, me standing this close to someone who's practically a stranger, feeling the tingle of possibility in every nerve ending of my body, I probably would.

I'm so lost in my own thoughts, I hardly even notice the way Mannix slips his hand into the pocket of my hoodie and threads his fingers through mine. He peeks down at me, then smiles shyly and returns his attention to the sky.

Chapter Ten

I'm awake. But my eyes are crusted shut. My head is pounding and swimming all at once, and I think this must be like the plague or something. I'm leaning on some lumpy pillow, and my eyes decide this is a good enough reason to finally open.

I'm in Mannix's living room, surrounded by several sleeping bodies, and I'm lying against his. He's propped up on the couch, head back, mouth open, snoring, and I'm curled into the side of his torso. I'm salty and sticky from last night at the bay. My feet are covered in rough sand, and I have no idea where my shoes are. The stale tang of old beer claws at my throat. I need water.

I detach myself from Mannix, careful not to step on anyone as I tiptoe across the living room to the kitchen. I grab a cloudy glass from the oak cabinet next to the sink and fill it with tap water. Tastes like iron, but it does the trick. I gulp it down, but my head still hurts. I need something to eat, and then Advil. For the love of god, Advil.

I squint to read the time displayed in green on the stove dash, and it's after ten in the morning. Uncle Jack.

Uncle Jack must be losing his mind right now. Lottie must be seething, wondering why I'm not at work when she expected me over two hours ago. I search for my wristlet, hidden behind the armchair in the living room, and then, sneaking out the back door, I quickly look around to see if my sandals are anywhere to be found, but no luck. They're a casualty of the night, and I'll need to let them go.

I cross the street and jump into the Jeep, ripping my phone out. Six missed calls from Uncle Jack. Two missed calls from Lottie. One text from Mia.

> **Mia (8:23 AM):** I tried to wake you up when I left last night, but you told me you were fine. 🗿

Holy hell.

I dial Uncle Jack first. He picks up, and I cry, "I'm here!"

There's silence on the other end. Then, "Get. Home. Now."

I'm shaking. "Okay. I'm sorry. I should have called."

He hangs up. I cover my face with the palms of my hands and then look back down at my phone. Lottie. Time to face the music. I dial, but it keeps taking me to her voice mail. I leave a message anyway. "Hey, Lottie. It's Cor. I know I'm late for work, but I'm on my way. I didn't hear my alarm. I...I'll be there soon."

Dropping my phone on the passenger seat, I turn the key

and head home. I don't bother with the radio. I'm too focused on what's ahead of me—fresh pavement and hell.

Inside the house, Uncle Jack sits at the edge of the sofa, staring out the window. He doesn't greet me with a huge hug, he doesn't even turn when I walk through the door, dropping my keys on the kitchen counter. I don't know what to say.

"Your mother called while you were gone," says Uncle Jack. His voice is quiet, controlled. His hands are steepled, and he props his chin on his fingertips. "It's difficult, lying to your sister. Telling her that her daughter is asleep, safe and sound in her room, when in reality, you have no idea where the hell she is. When all you want to do is cry to your big sister because you don't know what to do."

My lip begins to tremble against my will.

"You will never do that again."

"But I—"

"Don't speak to me right now, Coriander. Don't say one damn word, because I don't care. If you are going to stay over at someone's house, anyone's house, you will call and let me know. That's all. That's common courtesy. Common decency. Instead, I'm up all night, wondering if I'm a lunatic if I call the cops because you told me you'd be home by midnight. I tried calling Mannix's cell, but no one seems capable of answering their phones. Not fair, Coriander."

"Uncle Jack," I begin, tears choking me a bit.

"That was selfish. That was you only thinking of you and your good time. And if that's the way you're going to act, then you can't stay with me."

My mouth tries to form words, but it's pointless.

Uncle Jack stands up, walks into the kitchen, grabs his brief-case, and says, "I'm showing three houses this afternoon. I'll be home around five. I'll call if anything changes." He leaves, but he doesn't kiss me goodbye.

I take a fast shower because my hair is salty and sticky, my skin reeks of sweat, and I feel like the stink of stale beer emanates from my body. Not the way I'd like to greet my coworkers at MRCA. I twist my hair into a damp knot on the top of my head, brush my teeth, hop into the Jeep, and speed up Route 6 to P-town.

When I get to MRCA headquarters, Lottie, Justin, and a few other members of the disentanglement team are heading to their truck. I park on the side of the road, leaping from the Jeep and running up the sidewalk.

"I'm here, I'm sorry I'm late," I say so quickly that the words warp and meld together.

Lottie stares blankly at me. "It's fine. We're heading out with the entanglement response team to see about Fraction."

I hear what she says, I honestly do, but I can't seem to force it all to be coherent. "Should I put my things down and come back out? Are you headed to MacMillan?"

Lottie opens the hatch of the beat-up Ford and begins loading in the equipment. "No, you're good. Kyle and Mia are enough."

From the driver's-side door, Justin glances over at me, his face unreadable, but when he looks at Lottie, I feel like he might be pleading for me. Maybe I'm imagining things, though. That's a possibility, because now I'm desperate.

"Please," I say quietly, stepping up beside her. "I screwed up, and I'm so sorry. But please let me come. I want to be there when they disentangle Fraction."

Lottie rearranges a few boxes, and without looking at me, replies, "You could head over to the Nature Center. You'll see some filing that needs to be done in my office. I'd appreciate it." She brings the hatch back down and circles around to the passenger seat.

Mia and Kyle both offer me wide eyes, but I turn away so that I don't have to give them some kind of emotional reassurance, like filing Lottie's shit is going to be equal to them witnessing the disentanglement of the whale that matters to me. I don't have that. So they climb into the truck and roll out of the driveway, disappearing down Commercial Street.

The Nature Center is set off Route 6 and outside the hustle of Provincetown. Surrounded by the dunes and scrub pines of the National Seashore, it's a world apart, and maybe it's better that I have to spend the next few hours here doing tedious work like sorting forms. I like cleaning, finding order in chaos, and if there's one thing that the Nature Center's office is lacking, it's my organizational skills.

Filing cabinets overflow with papers that spew in multiple directions. I start by browsing the supply closet, and at the top of the highest shelf, a package of manila file folders hides behind several reams of printer paper. I retrieve a packet of colored stickers and a fresh box of black Sharpies and seat myself cross-legged on the office floor, spreading out the mess and making piles. I label my manila folders, I color-code them with my stickers, and I put them in an order that makes sense for everyone. It takes me almost three hours, and by the time

I'm done, I'm a little hungry, but it's not like there's anything to eat here.

I wander out into the main room of the building, where the skeleton of a right whale hangs from the rafters. I stand beneath her, looking up into her rib cage, where her heart once dwelled. Everyone should stand under the shadow of a whale's skeleton, knowing full well that her death was caused by people. Everyone should have to look up and feel the weight of that hovering above them, suspended only by the clear, almost invisible strings attached to the ceiling. Then maybe adapting the fishing industry to help save them wouldn't seem like the end of the world because you'd already know what that looks like.

Across from me, several displays about the marine life of Cape Cod line the wall, and I'm drawn to the humpback songs. I lift the headphones from their hook and secure them over my ears; I press Play and close my eyes. Their spectral cries make me feel like I'm eavesdropping on something that was never meant for me, like I don't deserve to witness anything this astonishing. For a moment, I drift beneath the waves, their songs lulling me into my thoughts.

On the night of Ella's holiday chorus concert, I was at Brent's basketball game. I sat with the girls who were dating basketball players. I was included in their stories and their jokes, and they asked me questions about Brent, like we were already a couple and I was a part of something. Something I thought I had wanted to be a part of for so long.

But I kept looking at my phone, knowing Ella's concert started soon and that I needed to be there. When the game ended, Brent scoring the winning shot right at the buzzer, I tried to sneak away, but he caught me in the parking lot.

"Come on, come with me. A bunch of us are going to the diner. I'll buy you pancakes."

I hesitated, staring at my feet.

"What is it?"

"Didn't you go out with Ella last weekend?" I asked him. Maybe I could remind him of their date, their trip to the mall.

Brent scoffed, his expression confused. "You think I went on a date with Ella? Are you serious?"

"Yeah, I'm serious."

"Why do you think I went out with Ella, Coriander?"

"Because she's smart, she's pretty..."

"No chance. She's your best friend. I spent the night asking her things about you."

I was both flattered and remorseful about his response. Ella had waited a really long time for Brent to even notice her, and for him to admit that he only used her to get to me...it felt like it was my fault.

"Come on," he said quietly, reaching out and tucking a lock of hair behind my ear. I shivered at the touch of his fingertips. "Come to the diner."

I wanted to go to the diner. I really wanted to go to the diner. But I told him, "I have to go to the holiday concert. I promised Ella, she has this solo, and she's so nervous—"

"What time?" he asked, adjusting his gym bag over his shoulder.

"Six minutes ago."

"Let's go." Brent grabbed my hand, and we raced across

the parking lot toward the auditorium, laughing hysterically, the icy air with its sharp fingers branching into my lungs with every gasp.

We burst through the foyer, stopped by our algebra teacher, who asked if we had any donations for the soup kitchen (Brent tossed a five-dollar bill into the can), and then slammed open the doors to the auditorium, suddenly bathed in the darkness and rising voices of the choir.

Ella stepped forward onto the stage, the spotlight shining blindingly on her, and she shivered. Everyone in the audience turned to see who was making a scene in the back of the theater. We tried to tiptoe down the aisle, our hands clasped together, shushing each other, but the laughter wouldn't stop. Finally, we found two end seats in the second row. Parent glares ensued.

But something was up. I didn't even notice it right away. The piano accompaniment kept playing, then would softly fade away and start up again. Because the song was trying to go on, but Ella wasn't. She stared at me. Finally, shaking herself out of her distraction, she must have realized that she should sing. But her voice was so quiet as it quivered out into the shadowy auditorium. No one could hear the words. No one could hear her voice. I had silenced her.

I pull the headphones from my ears and lean forward onto the display, head hanging, fingers turning white supporting the weight of everything. Then I suck in a sudden breath, pinching the bridge of my nose. I can't stay here at the Nature Center anymore. I did the filing. I did it better than Lottie will have expected. Now I have to get out of here.

Outside the building, the air is heavy and hot. I lock the

doors behind me and then climb into the Jeep. I don't know where exactly I'm headed. I don't want to go back to the house—the feeling of guilt still pervades within the walls. And Provincetown will be too busy, too overwhelming. The beach, too.

I start to drive, heading down Route 6 toward Wellfleet, and I'm not even making any conscious decisions. The Jeep takes me where it wants. And where it wants is Mannix's driveway.

All the cars from last night are gone. The neighborhood is quiet except for the drone of lawn mowers and a few cawing crows. I travel the sidewalk up to his front porch, and beyond the storm door, I can hear water running and the muted clink of dishes in the sink. My hand hovers over the doorbell, because I know what this is. This is a distraction. I ring it anyway.

Mannix's shadowed outline appears in the living room, and he pushes the storm door open, forcing me to take a step down to avoid its swing.

"Hey," he says. "I wasn't expecting you."

I shove my hands in the pockets of my shorts and shrug. "Can I come in?"

"Yeah, of course." He steps aside and allows me into the living room. "Everything okay?"

I wander to the kitchen, taking in the complete and utter chaos from the party last night. "Holy shit, this place is a mess."

Wordlessly, Mannix agrees.

"No one stayed to help you clean up?"

He gestures around the room. "Just me."

"I'll help you," I say. This is good. This is perfect. This is like filing at the Nature Center, something mundane and physical that will get my mind off my shit decisions from last night.

I grab a black garbage bag and begin clearing off the kitchen table. "I'm sorry I left so quickly this morning."

"It's okay," Mannix replies.

"I had work, and I shouldn't have stayed over, and I forgot to tell Uncle Jack my change of plans, so things were kind of a mess."

"It's fine."

I grab the tray of what used to be nachos and begin scraping the remains of dried salsa and crusty cheese into the bag. "Are you all right?" The question is quiet, like I'm afraid to ask it out loud for fear of what his response might be.

At the sink, Mannix shrugs. "I get tired of having to handle everything, you know? Like, I host the party, I provide the food, everyone comes and has a good time, then they leave me to pick up after them, and my parents are due home in about..." He glances up at the clock above the sink. "Three hours."

"Mannix, I—"

"I don't mean you," he says quickly. "Not you. Not at all." He turns back to the sink, shutting the water off and drying his hands on a checked dish towel. "Is that ready to go out?"

I look down at my massive garbage bag. I've overstuffed it, and I'm hardly capable of cinching it closed.

"I'll take it down to the trash can." He lifts it, making sure his grip is secure, and exits out the slider door and down the steps of the back porch.

I keep puttering about the kitchen, cleaning things as I go, the sound of Mannix's footsteps crunching on the seashell driveway drifting in through the open windows.

"Son of a bitch."

I crane my neck to see what Mannix is cursing about.

Midway down the driveway, the garbage bag has split open at the bottom, all of its contents sprawled out before him. He stands there, hands on his hips, face turned upward to the sky, chest heaving.

I've been him before, so overwhelmed that the smallest setback feels colossal, and he's the last person in the world who deserves to feel that way. Automatically, I search under the sink and find rubber gloves and the extra garbage bags, and I join him outside.

"Hey, this is fine," I say, touching his shoulder. "I'll help you. You don't have to clean it up alone." I kneel down in the broken shells, wincing when one digs into my bare knee, and begin gathering the refuse and shoving it into a new garbage bag.

Mannix squats down beside me and takes a long, shaking breath.

"Do you wanna go inside? I can do this. Go get a drink of water, you'll feel better."

He shakes his head, tossing a few paper plates and half-eaten hamburger buns into the bag. "We can do it together."

I sway into him playfully, and he wears a strained smile.

"Clearly I came back so that I could smell like garbage with you."

This at least elicits a soft chuckle from him. "You smell like almond."

"I'm impressed with your ability to identify ingredients."

After a while, the driveway is cleaned up, and whatever's left is hopefully biodegradable and will be washed away with the next rainstorm. After he deposits our newly secured bag of trash in the can at the end of the driveway, I follow him back into the house and to the sink.

Warm water flows from the faucet, and I pump lemon-scented liquid soap into my hands. Mannix appears beside me, our hips gently bumping together as we share the stream.

"You want some soap?" I ask, like he's completely incapable of getting it himself.

"Please."

I pump some into his waiting palms, he washes for maybe a second, and I scoff when he reaches across me for the dish towel.

"What?" he asks.

"You're supposed to wash your hands for twenty seconds or until you've sung 'Happy Birthday' twice."

Reluctantly, he returns his hands to the water, and I reapply the soap. Our fingers brush up against one another as he murmurs, *"Happy birthday to you, happy birthday to you..."* He pauses for a moment. "Did you get what you wanted for your birthday?"

My eyes rove from his elbow up to his shoulder and then settle on his mouth. "No."

He presses his lips together, and when he finally speaks, his voice is quiet, his gaze gently meeting mine. "What did you want?"

I laugh quietly, looking back down at the sink, then shut the water off, flicking the excess droplets from my hands. "I think you know."

Mannix cocks his head to the side. "Maybe you could show me." His eyes are half lidded, studying me, and I reach up to brush his hair out of his gaze.

Pushing up on my tiptoes, I steady myself, one hand gripping the edge of the counter and the other touching his wrist.

My thoughts are hazy and haphazard, and I'm working on instinct, not logic. He inclines his head, the bridge of his nose brushing mine, and my hand climbs up his forearm until it's under the sleeve of his T-shirt, leaving a trail of warm water in its wake, my fingers digging gently into his skin. When our mouths meet, he presses his palm against the small of my back so our stomachs touch.

Warmth spreads through my belly as I reach my hands up, grasping his T-shirt like I need something to hold on to in order to keep standing. I snake my arms around his neck, pressing myself against his chest, kissing him harder.

I thought first kisses with new boys were supposed to be shy and nervous, but the more I have of Mannix the more I want. His hands trace down my ribs and rest at my hips, and his tongue darts across my mouth, past my lips. He reaches around my back, his fingers finding the clasp of my bra, and I pull away, breathless.

"Maybe we go a little slower," I say, overwhelmed now with new emotions I wasn't expecting today. I wasn't expecting this.

He nods and kisses me again. When he steps back, he smiles at his feet. "Okay."

"What is it?" I ask, smiling so that he knows I want to share this, too.

Shaking his head, Mannix takes another deep breath, lifting my hand so that we're palm to palm, each following the other's trajectory. "Just that it's weird how one day you're a girl in a parking lot I think is pretty, and another you're saving me from drowning."

My bottom lip trembles. I couldn't possibly be that for him, a boy who's only recently appeared in my life, completely unexpected and uninvited but welcome. I couldn't possibly keep him above water when I couldn't even do that for my best friend, half of my heart. But I'm relieved and terrified all at once.

I shake my head, trying to wrestle the feeling from my thoughts. "So what does this mean?"

Mannix's hand weaves its way through my hair, and I lean into his palm. "It means I like kissing you."

I smile and close my eyes as his lips find mine again. "I mean besides that," I say against his mouth.

His voice is quiet, his forehead pressed against mine. "It means I'm tired of fighting myself over how I feel about you. I'm tired of pretending like I can keep away, or like I don't think of you almost every waking moment."

"Even though I leave at the end of August?" I ask quietly.

"Whatever this is," says Mannix, gesturing between us, "whatever it's going to be, I want it. And when we're standing at the edge of summer, and we're forced to look back and define this or figure out what it's going to be moving forward, we can step over the edge together, when we have to."

"Okay," I say, smiling, and lift my mouth to kiss him again. "Can we go for a walk? Maybe get out of here for a little bit?"

Mannix glances around the kitchen. Everything is cleaned up except the dishes in the sink, but they should be fast. "Yeah, let's go."

We walk hand in hand down his street and toward Wellfleet Bay Wildlife Sanctuary, traveling the boardwalk over the tidal marshes. I stop a few times to take pictures with my phone. I want my Instagram to be overburdened with Cape Cod this summer, with dunes, and whales, and lighthouses, and boats, and harbors, and fried scallops, and maybe Mannix. I want to look back and know that this is what mattered to me for three months out of the year. This and only this.

Mannix watches a crane in the salt marsh. It stands perfectly still, one foot up, like some relic from prehistoric times, and when he turns to point it out to me, I snap his picture before he can protest.

"What was that for?" he asks, his lopsided grin making me giggle.

I shrug. "Dunno yet. Maybe just for me."

"Then you owe me one."

"It's a deal."

I step forward, latching my hand to his, and we keep walking.

"I know this place," I say as we travel a sandy gravel road toward a high hill of sea grass and beach houses that overlook the bay. "I used to walk here with Ella."

"Oh yeah?"

"Uncle Jack's house is only a fifteen-minute walk that way." I point northward. "But Ella and I always liked the idea of that bridge."

Mannix looks ahead of us and then laughs. "Because you can only get over it at low tide?"

Before us, a rattly wooden bridge spans the width of the waterway that cuts through the marsh grass. There's only room for one car at a time to make it across, and when the tide rises, you're stuck on either side. Cedar shake homes overlooking Cape Cod Bay dot the island beyond the bridge.

"Well, yeah," I say. "There's something dramatic about that, right? Knowing you only have so much time? Otherwise you're screwed."

153

"So would you be afraid of being stuck, or afraid of not making it to the other side in time?" Mannix asks, staring at the island.

I consider this. "Afraid I wouldn't make it to the other side in time. You?"

He crosses his arms over his chest. "Afraid of being stuck."

We travel to the middle of the bridge, then lean over the railing, looking down at the brackish water that ripples through the marsh grass. Tiny fish dart from bank to bank. "So every summer, Ella and I used to take a trinket like a pebble or a shell, and we'd wade down the bank into the water, then hide it in one of the supports under the bridge."

Mannix glances over at me and laughs. "Why?"

I shrug. "To see if it would make it until next year. If the tide or a storm would wash it away. I dunno, it's silly, I guess."

"Did you hide one last year? Before...you know..."

I dangle my hands over the railing, thinking about my last summer with Ella. "We weren't really talking last year."

"I'm sorry," says Mannix, pushing away to stand up straight.

"Totally not your fault." I begin my descent back down the bridge. "I need to get back to the house before Uncle Jack gets home. Tell him I'm sorry."

He catches up to me, and we travel the planked path back the way we came. I peek over my shoulder, briefly, like that'll be enough to catch a glimpse of any hidden shell or stone under the belly of the bridge.

But we turn a corner and it disappears behind a wall of rippling sea grass.

Chapter Eleven

My face melts into the palm of my hand, and I sigh as the midafternoon sun shoots death rays into my tiny shack on MacMillan Pier. There's a subpar air conditioner to my left, and it whistles a trickle of cool air that easily slips out the sliding window in front of me. What a waste. I take a picture of it and send it to Uncle Jack, followed by a text.

> **Cor (12:22 PM):** It's hot. Want to bring me ice cream?
> **Uncle Jack (12:23 PM):** Don't push me.
> **Uncle Jack (12:23 PM):** We'll get ice cream after dinner.

With every day that passes, Uncle Jack is less and less mad at me about not calling when I stayed over at Mannix's. The fact that he's taking me out for ice cream later just proves that we're back to normal.

I tap my pencil against my dependable notebook. I've been switching back and forth between writing ideas down for our Barnacles and Brunch fundraiser next week and preparing for running summer camp at the Nature Center. Lottie asked me to cover a shift for one of the naturalists who needs to take an emergency trip to Utah. I don't know what I'm supposed to teach preschoolers and kindergartners about Cape Cod ecosystems, but Lottie trusts me enough to take care of this, so I can't let her down.

It's honestly the first real thing she's asked me to do since missing out on Fraction's disentanglement. They tracked her far out into Stellwagen Bank, now tied even more elaborately in fishing rope, dragging a lobster pot behind her, weighing her down, making her tired. They were able to cut some of it away, but not all of it.

I shake my head to get the image of her hopelessness to disappear.

Clusters of people amble by me and my exhibition of whale keepsakes. I have several hoodies (which are almost laughable at this point) in multiple colors and sizes. Plush toys, keychains, magnets, all displaying the insignia of the Marine Research and Conservation Alliance. In the next shack, a guy named Clive sells tickets to the whale watches throughout the day.

Justin usually acts as the naturalist on board these trips, explaining to our seafaring tourists the wonders of Cape Cod Bay and Stellwagen Bank. But he hasn't shown up yet, and he's an incredibly punctual kind of guy.

The line of passengers grows increasingly long as the hour approaches. I check my wristwatch. Quarter to one, and still Justin hasn't shown up. I watch the crew, a bunch of kids my age or slightly older, pulling their cell phones out of their pockets and looking up toward the parking lot. Finally, I spot Justin's man bun bobbing in between tourists.

"Jesus," says Captain Mike, coming and leaning an elbow against my counter. He's a short man, maybe sixty, with salt-and-pepper hair and a neatly trimmed mustache to match. He wears khaki shorts and an MRCA T-shirt tucked in. "I was getting a little nervous."

"Sorry, group," says Justin, approaching us at a slower pace than usual. He burps and then stops midstep. "My stomach is *raunchy* today."

"You okay?" I ask.

"I'm good. I took some kind of minty, milky liquid before I got here."

"And you think you'll be okay on the boat?" Captain Mike prompts. "The water's a little choppy today."

"Dude, I'll be fine." He waves us away, but I can't help but notice that he's looking a little green around the gills. "Hey, Cor." Turning to me and placing both hands on the counter, Justin sways a little and then steadies himself. "What do you say you close up shop and come on this trip with me and Mia? Do some ID'ing and recording? Kyle will be along soon, so don't worry about the stand."

I dash out of my tiny entrance and gather all my products. No time to organize them neatly like I typically do at the end of the day. I toss them into the shack, stuffed animals with

T-shirts, hoodies with baseball caps, and lock the door behind me. It's chaos, I tell you, but anything to escape the shack for the afternoon.

"Ready."

Captain Mike escorts me down the gangplank, handing me a clipboard and pointing to a chart. "It's all right here for you," he says. "You see a whale, ID it, you jot down the latitude and longitude, and then any surface behaviors you witness."

"Got it." Although, I think to myself, that's a lot of things to consider all at once. I don't think Captain Mike notices, though. I glance behind me, and Justin stands at the top of the gangplank, collecting tickets from passengers and greeting them with a halfhearted smile.

Following Captain Mike and Mia up to the flybridge, I'm amazed at our view. I can see almost all of the harbor, even out over the other boats to the breakwater where the cormorants dry their wings in the obliging light of the sun.

"Okay, I think that's everyone," says Justin as he eventually joins us on the boat. Even in the harbor, where there are no waves, the boat lilts a bit, and Justin winces at each and every undulation.

Captain Mike sounds the horn, we ease out of our space in the harbor, and our journey begins just past the breakwater.

Justin grabs the microphone and begins his speech. "Good afternoon, everyone. My name is Justin Burke, and I'm going to be your naturalist on this trip." He continues with the necessary discussion of life preservers, where they're located, how to wear one. Once that's complete, he describes the water surrounding Cape Cod. It's rich in nutrients, it attracts all kinds of sea life, specifically the humpback whales.

Humpbacks are the draw for whale watchers. I've seen plenty of other whales. Fin whales, minkes, pilot whales, and right whales in the spring. But humpbacks like to put on a show.

Justin discusses the important points of humpback whales. They have baleen and not teeth. They mate and give birth in the winter in the Caribbean, and then they travel up to the colder waters off Cape Cod and Canada to feast on sand lances and herring. I've been on so many whale watches, I could recite this word for word.

He misses a few of the things the naturalists usually say, and steadies himself on a nearby seat because he looks like he's about to lose it. Finally, he tells our passengers we're heading out to a group of feeding humpbacks that have been active for a good part of the morning. He clicks off the mic and collapses on the seat beside me.

"You're not gonna make it, Justin," says Captain Mike, his eyes focused on the horizon as he steers the boat.

"Did you eat some bad tofu?" I ask.

He shakes his head and rubs his eyes. "I think it's the sprouts."

"I thought sprouts were supposed to be good for you."

Justin only nods, and his lack of a verbal response confirms for me that he's hesitant to open his mouth. I pat his knee to make sure he knows I understand.

The boat chugs along through the choppy water. I take a few opportunities to venture out to the top deck and peer over the side. No sign of any sea life.

I lean over the railing of the deck, trying to see if any whales appear. A sleek gray back and a tiny dorsal fin slice through the water. A few kids beside me wonder if they've seen a dolphin.

"Definitely a minke whale," I say, leaning toward them. "Dolphins swim in pods. Minkes usually swim alone."

"Oh," they reply, and nod, as though it's suddenly all clear.

Minke whales don't make a spectacle at the surface, and they rarely stay in one place for too long, so we keep moving.

Little groups of gray seals cling to the shoreline, their heads bobbing up and down as they observe the humans that wander along the sand. These clusters have become more regular over the past few years, drawing ire from fishermen and the appetites of great whites.

Under the shade of the flybridge, Justin sips something fizzy from a plastic cup, making a face every time he swallows.

"Coming up on the humpies," says Captain Mike. He cuts the engines as the tiny black bodies grow larger upon our approach.

There's always this buzz of anticipation when I'm out here. Seeing them swimming and feeding almost makes me forget about Fraction, somewhere suffering.

Almost.

"Ladies and gentlemen," says Justin, picking up the mic and clearing his throat. "We're approaching a large, feeding group of…humpbacks. Humpback whales." He drags a slow breath.

I watch him silently.

"As I said before, humpbacks don't have teeth," he continues, his voice cracking. "They have baleen, which is…"

His face is so pale that I think I can see his green and blue veins. "Justin?" I whisper.

He drops the mic and makes a dash for the side of the boat. He heaves.

Captain Mike's eyes begin darting around. "Now what?"

"What do we do?" I stare out at the giant gaping mouths of

the humpbacks as a huge flock of sea gulls caw and call to one another, sometimes brazenly landing on the faces of the whales in hopes of catching a stray fish.

"Pick up the mic," Captain Mike instructs.

I follow his directions and then stare at him, waiting for more.

His eyes widen in disbelief. "Talk, Cor! Talk about the damn whales!"

"Me?" I almost can't believe what he's suggesting. I'm honestly just a kid. No degree, no schooling in biology other than honors bio my sophomore year. Which I aced, but still. "What am I supposed to say?"

"You've been out here before, you know what they're doing. You know what Justin says. Repeat!"

You've got this, says Ella, appearing at the railing. *Show them what you know.*

I focus on the whales, and I try to find some words. Any words to unscramble and put together into a logical, cohesive sentence. Captain Mike looks at me expectantly, and I don't want to let him down. Or Justin, who is now a permanent fixture attached to the railing. Or Ella. Especially not Ella. One of the crew helps Justin down the steps and to the bathrooms, and I'm on my own.

From the bow of the ship, a beautiful, trumpetlike noise rings out, and I glance at Ella. *Dome*, she says. *You can recognize her by the sound she makes when she comes up to breathe.* I'm still frozen as Ella stares back out over the whales. *Trust someone, Cor.* Mia appears beside me, opening up our giant binder of whale tails, ready to ID and feed me facts. She nudges me, and I feel bolstered enough to go on.

"Ladies and gentlemen, my name is Coriander Cabot, and I'm an intern with the Marine Research and Conservation Alliance. I'll be taking Justin's place this afternoon due to unforeseen circumstances. That noise you're hearing, that's Dome exhaling. She's a regular here at Stellwagen Bank, well into her thirties, and has had ten calves."

Captain Mike breathes a huge sigh of relief, his shoulders visibly relaxing.

"Humpback whales are voluntary breathers. We are not. Every time a humpback breathes, they need to think about it, even while they're sleeping. So a humpback's brain sleeps one side at a time to make sure they're still able to breathe at the surface of the water."

"We have Pepper, next to Dome," Mia whispers to me.

"We've just ID'ed another whale, Pepper. You'll see her diving now, that signature hump that appears when these whales take a dive. Wait for the flukes." She salutes us with her beautiful tail, and the cameras begin to click incessantly. "Awesome," I say, and I say it into the mic, even though I was hardly conscious it came out of my mouth. "You'll notice that slick-looking patch on the water after they dive. Whalers used to think that was residual oil from the whales left on the surface, but it's actually the pressure the whale's flukes produce on the water from below."

A few children sigh despondently, almost as though they think the whales are gone forever.

"What we're going to be looking for are bubbles forming a circle. These whales are bubble-net feeding right now. Basically, the bubbles trap the fish in a tight ball, making it easier for the whales to get a mouthful."

Just as I say this, a bubble net forms at three o'clock. Beautiful teal spirals of bubbles that look as though they reach down to the seafloor in a perfect cone break the surface, followed by the gaping mouths of four whales. Their sleek black bodies are only a few feet from the boat. Cheers erupt, people point. It's one thing to look at pictures of whales online or in books. It's another thing entirely to see them next to your boat, almost the exact same size.

From the opposite side of the boat, a massive tail and almost half the body of a humpback stick out from the water and then come crashing down in an explosion of shimmering spray and foam.

"That's Lightning, over there, doing some kick feeding."

There's a mass movement from one side of the boat to the other. There's so much surface behavior, though, it almost doesn't matter which side of the boat these people choose. We're surrounded by whales.

I keep my eyes peeled for Fraction, but I don't see her. I remind myself that the Atlantic is sort of a big place, so I can't expect that she's going to be where I am every time I venture out on the water. Still, the thought of her tugs at my heart. I hope she's okay. I hope she's not afraid.

We stay with these whales for another half hour, and even more come to join them. The sea, the sun, the gulls and shearwaters, the whales, all make for a near-perfect afternoon.

"Some show, eh?" says Captain Mike.

I nod, leaning on the bench with one knee.

"Something missing?" he asks.

"Oh, you know. Everyone comes on a whale watch and they're looking for the breach. I wish one of them would breach for us."

"Probably too full now," Captain Mike says with a chuckle.

And just as we resign ourselves to our breach-less fate, a little calf, not even half the size of the other feeding whales, propels himself out of the water, long pectoral fins spread wide in joy, and lands with a splatter beside his mom.

The boat erupts in laughter and cheers, and they applaud this baby's show.

"Well, there you go." Captain Mike grabs my shoulder and squeezes.

I switch on the mic. "Folks, you can't ask for a better encore than that. Just as we're about to head back to Provincetown."

We ease away from the feeding whales, and when I glance back, I see the little head of the calf pop out of the water, spy-hopping. Almost like he's wondering where we're going, because he wants to play some more.

I smile. "See you later, buddy."

The afternoon cools down as we approach Provincetown Harbor. It's only when the boat is parked and settled that Justin finally emerges from below.

"Well?" I ask.

"I guess I'm fine," he mutters. "I want to go to bed."

"Your girl here did a bang-up job, Justin," says Captain Mike, jerking his thumb in my direction. "She's a keeper."

"I never doubted her," says Justin, crossing his arms over his chest. "Sorry to leave you hanging like that."

"It was fun." I think for a moment. "Nerve-racking, but fun."

"See, if I hadn't gotten sick, I would have deprived you of this important life experience," says Justin as we walk back up the gangplank. Kyle waits for us outside the souvenir shack, waving frantically like they haven't seen us in days.

"Yeah, it's something like that."

"What's up?" Justin asks, hauling a bag up onto his shoulder and eyeing me suspiciously.

I try to wave it away, but I can tell that won't work with Justin. "It's just that Lottie told me to man the merch shack today, and I've kinda been on thin ice with her. I don't want to get in trouble."

"Hey," says Justin. "Let me deal with Lottie. I made an executive decision, and you were phenomenal. She'll hear about it. Cool?" He offers me his fist for a bump, and with an attempt to gather my courage, I meet it.

"Cool."

"It was so natural for you," Mia says once Justin disappears into the parking lot. We stand beside the merch shack while Kyle does their best to showcase our array of hats. "I get too nervous talking in front of live crowds." She shrugs, still clutching her binder where she recorded location and surface behavior that we witnessed today out on the water.

I try to find the words to explain why something like this afternoon comes so easily to me. "I think if we don't share what we know, then we can't expect to save them, right? They need all the help they can get, and that helps me overcome any shyness. It's about more than me and my feelings."

Mia nods, which makes me feel successful in not feeling like a complete weirdo. I hook my arm through hers and we cross through Provincetown and back to headquarters together.

Mannix and I are back to back, tackling opposite walls in the upstairs bathroom and swathing them in a coat of deep navy blue. I've always liked painting. There's something weirdly soothing about rolling a new color over an old one, about changing a room's whole perspective, starting over.

"If you have other things to do, I've got this," Mannix says over his shoulder. He stands on a three-step ladder, carefully edging the space where the wall meets the ceiling.

"I'm good." I take a step back, admiring my full coverage of the wall. I make extra sure that no white splotches of primer are peeking through. "Besides," I say, squatting down by the tray of paint and coating my roller again, "it's not like I'd be getting a ton of work done with you down the hall anyway."

Maybe that shouldn't be true. Maybe there should be clear boundaries when there's work to do and when I have time for Mannix, but no matter how logical that sounds, I push it aside because I like what I'm doing right now. I like that when I'm with him, I don't think about dead friends and drowning whales.

When I look up, Mannix is crouched down in front of me, studying me.

"What?" I'm suddenly embarrassed. A lock of hair falls loose from my ponytail, and I tuck it away behind my ear.

Wordlessly, he leans over the tray of paint, tilting my chin up with his finger, and kisses me softly.

I open my eyes, wishing he had kissed me for a little longer. "Why'd you do that?"

He shrugs, smiling, then lifts his paintbrush again and dips it into the can. "Nothing. I guess I wanted to make sure that the other day happened."

"That's supposed to be something I would do."

"Well, maybe we can both be mutually insecure and make out all the time."

"I'm not opposed to that."

He glances up at me and smirks, then grabs the handle of the paint can and carries it with him to his mini-ladder.

"So are you off today?" he asks me.

"I'm off for the next two days, but I'll probably be getting ready for the Barnacles and Brunch fundraiser with Uncle Jack. Apparently we have a final tasting this afternoon at the Sea Ghost."

Mannix frowns, pausing. "Why does this sound like a wedding?"

I stand and continue rolling the wall where I left off, careful to avoid the edges of the blue tape that protects the bright white trim of the door. "Probably because it's the same level of pomp and circumstance."

We're quiet for a little while, and when I've finally trimmed around the door, I stand back and admire my work. "I think this is fairly close to professional level, if I do say so myself."

Mannix comes up beside me, admiring my work. "You're hired."

"Does that mean I get to come with you on all your odd jobs?" I ask, grinning and looking up at him.

He leans down and kisses me. "I don't think that would be efficient at all."

When he pulls away, I glance down, and a wet blue splotch streaks across my stomach. "Oh no."

"Oops."

I pull my shirt out away from my body and try to assess the

best way to salvage it. "You're going to send me to this tasting looking like a Smurf." I'm pretty sure it's a lost cause, but I at least have to change.

"Here, let me help." He steps over, still holding the paintbrush. "I can fix it. I know the Sea Ghost like the back of my hand. The most important part about showing up to a place like that is looking like whatever you're doing is purposeful, you know what I mean?"

I frown. "I have no idea what you mean."

"Like this." He runs his paintbrush along the inside of my forearm, from wrist to elbow.

"Mannix!"

"Or maybe this." He swipes my forehead. "Now it's like a look you were going for, you know?"

"You pain in my ass." I grab my paintbrush from the tray and slap it across his stomach.

"You wanna play that game?"

"I'm here for it."

He dips his brush into the bucket of navy blue and flicks it at my face. I scream involuntarily and jab my paintbrush in his general direction. It makes contact almost immediately with his torso, and when I open my eyes, he has me pressed against the door behind me, both his hands on either side of my body, his chest heaving, a grin crossing his face. "Your move," he says quietly.

"You make it sound like a challenge."

"Maybe it is."

I grab his T-shirt and yank him toward me, our bodies colliding, our mouths finding each other immediately. His hips pin mine to the door, and his hands move up my shirt. I can't grab enough of him, pull him close enough.

"Better than paint, right?" I ask a little breathlessly.

"So much better than paint."

Downstairs, the back door to the kitchen opens, keys jangling, and Uncle Jack and Chad return home from wherever they've been all afternoon.

"Cor!" Uncle Jack calls. "Ready for the tasting?"

Mannix rests his forehead on my shoulder, then kisses along my collarbone, up my neck.

"Don't," I whisper halfheartedly.

"You could go to the tasting, or you could just stay here."

I trace my fingernails through his hair. "Where you're supposed to be updating a bathroom."

He groans and inches his body from mine, his finger tucked in the band of my shorts, almost anchoring me where I am.

"I'll be right there!" I shout out the door. Then I turn back to Mannix. "I have to wash up and get changed."

Exiting the bathroom, I swerve into my room, pausing before shutting the door, trying to catch my breath. I leave it halfway open and check over my shoulder to see if Mannix follows me. Rummaging through my dresser, I find a white tank top and peel off my ruined T-shirt. As I pull the tank over my head, my bedroom door creaks open and Mannix stands at the threshold holding a wet washcloth and staring down at the jar of pebbles on my nightstand. He lifts it, trying to get a better view of those that have settled on the bottom.

"It's my collection," I say in explanation, even though he hasn't asked anything.

"Pebbles?"

"It was Ella's and mine," I add, taking the washcloth from his hands and wiping it over my face. "We used to collect stones from every ocean beach on Cape Cod. So I figured I'd finish it for us."

"Which beaches do you have left?"

"Race Point," I tell him as he places the jar back beside the anchor lamp. "I keep trying to get up there, but every time I get in the Jeep, I feel like..." I can't finish, so I scratch my head and put in a pair of earrings.

But Mannix still stares at the jar. "Like once you find the pebble, that last piece you have of her will be gone," he finishes for me.

I lower my head. "Yes."

"Yeah, I get that."

I watch him for a moment, the words gathering in my thoughts. "Do you want to come with me to the Barnacles and Brunch fundraiser?" I ask.

I've surprised him, I can tell, because his mouth moves uselessly before any words come out. "I'm working the event," he finally says.

"So get someone to cover your shift," I suggest, crossing the room to him. I link my hands to his and stand on my tiptoes, kissing him once. "Please?"

"That's a lot of tips you're asking me to miss out on. This event is huge. I was lucky I even got a shift."

"It's just one afternoon!"

"Cor," he says, and sighs.

"Please? I want you to be there with me."

"I will be there. Behind the bar."

"No, *with* me, with me. Dressed up and handsome and meeting people. It's different."

He takes a step back, scratching his forehead. "Okay," he finally says. "I'll find someone to cover my shift."

I jump once and then wrap my arms around his neck. "I owe you one," I tell him.

"You owe me several." But when our mouths meet again, his shoulders relax, and I know he's mine, and he can't be that mad.

Chapter Twelve

Kyle faces me from across the main room of the Nature Center. It's massive, and it has to be because it holds the skeleton of a fully grown right whale. I sit at the information desk, and Kyle is perched on a stool behind the souvenir stand.

"Okay, hold up ten fingers," they say.

"Can't you come over here?" I call across the room, my voice bouncing along the whale's vertebrae.

Her name was Mosaic, and that's the first thing I tell people when they come to the Nature Center to see her. What her name was. Because when you name something, you give it a life and a purpose outside of a headline. When you name something, it means they mattered. She had a name.

"No, obviously," Kyle replies. "If Lottie or Justin comes in unannounced, then we can pretend we were doing actual work. Now hold up ten fingers."

Both hands go up, fingers spread wide.

"If you put down five or more fingers, that means you're a weirdo."

"I already hate this game."

"Coriander Catherine Cabot, play along."

"My middle name is Rose."

"But that doesn't alliterate. Okay, put down a finger if you've ever been obsessed with a character on TV."

A finger goes down. "Why does that make me weird, though?"

Kyle pulls a scrunchie from their wrist and throws their long hair up into a ponytail. "You don't trust the process. Let's keep going. Put a finger down if you've ever talked to yourself when you're completely alone."

Another one goes down.

"Put a finger down if you have three or more customizations for your Starbucks order."

"This doesn't feel fair."

"Finger down."

I do as they say.

"Put a finger down if you put the milk in before the cereal."

I arch an eyebrow, but at least one finger stays up.

"Put a finger down if you still sleep with a stuffed animal."

"Kyle, you're judging me." I sigh. "Besides, none of these things are reasons people have found me weird."

They pause for a moment. "I don't think you're weird, you know," they say gently.

I smile down at my lap. "Yeah, well. You're in an exclusive group."

"Listen," says Kyle, putting both their elbows on their desk and staring determinedly at me. "I've gone through a lot of shit, too. And people are alarmingly mean, but not all of them. Definitely not all of them. You start to realize that the people you should let into your life are the ones who ask to be a part of it. Why would we struggle to include people, hold people close, who aren't on our side, you know? Once you let the asshats go, everything else falls into place."

I'm quiet for a moment, probably waiting for Ella's voice to show up in my head, but she doesn't.

"What?" asks Kyle.

I shrug. "Just what you said makes sense."

"It should. I can't even tell you how long I chased people around for their approval. Lost friends because I wanted to make sure I was seen, I was accepted, by people who never really mattered, you know?"

I nod fervently. "Yeah, I know. I've done that, too."

"I knew we were kindred spirits the moment we met."

Staring down at my lap, I smile at my fingertips, then look back across the room at Kyle. "Surprisingly insightful from a person who just changed my middle name because the old one didn't flow."

"Who's ready for lunch?"

Kyle and I both turn to the entrance to find Mannix and Noah breezing through the door and carrying takeout bags from Marshside Deli.

Noah hoots and shakes the bags triumphantly, then takes in the entire room. "Hey, where's my girl?"

"Mia's running the Under-Twelve Beach Cleanup today at

Head of the Meadow," I say. "But Kyle and I never say no to sandwiches."

"No kiss hello?" Kyle calls from across the room, eyeing me and Mannix in disbelief.

"I'll give you a kiss," says Noah, leaning in with puckered lips to peck Kyle's cheek.

"Ew, no." Kyle swats him away. "You smell like sweaty boy."

It feels weird to kiss on cue, but I stand up behind my desk, leaning forward and letting my mouth brush his.

"Hey," he says quietly so that only I can hear.

"Hey." I smile.

He pulls up a chair beside mine, and we unwrap our sandwiches. Kyle and Noah cross the room and join us and we spread our feast out across my desk. As I pop the last bite of my sandwich into my mouth, I crane my neck to see over Mannix's head and watch as Lottie's truck pulls into the parking lot.

"Man your stations," says Kyle, noticing exactly when I do.

"Should we go?" Mannix asks.

"No, she won't be mad about bringing us lunch," I reply.

"Hello, team." Lottie carries a large box. "Who wants to test out audio equipment on the water?"

"Us!" Kyle stands up quickly, raising their hand.

"And your friends?" Lottie suggests, slicing open the box and lifting out what appears to be pieces of a hydrophone.

"They were dropping off lunch for us," I explain.

Beside me, Mannix clears his throat. "I wouldn't mind going," he says, hands shoved in his pockets.

Kyle stands at the box with Lottie and Noah, unpacking all the equipment from its plastic and Styrofoam.

"It's going to be boring," I say, and a laugh escapes me, like I want to minimize this as much as possible. I don't know if letting Mannix in on this is too much, too soon. I don't know if I'm ready for him to be a part of this.

Kyle silently quirks an eyebrow at me, and I try to ignore what they're implying.

"Do *you* think it's boring?" Mannix asks.

Standing under the ribs of the right whale that hangs from the ceiling, Ella says, *Let him come. Show him why they matter. Show him what you love.*

I stare up at Mannix, who watches me, waiting for my reply. "No, not at all. It's like eavesdropping on a conversation that I was never meant to hear. Like I get to share their secrets."

He nods. "Then I want to do that, too."

My heart speeds up, and I smile at my feet. "Okay. Then let's go listen in on some whales."

The ride out into the Stellwagen where the whales are all feeding and congregating is a long one. I venture a glance in Mannix's direction, but he stands at the bow of the boat, hands gripping the rail. I forget that he's probably spent a lot of time on the water, too. With his dad, on his boat.

"We're coming up on them," Lottie shouts over the roar of wind and water.

Spouts break the surface of the choppy sea, and soon the gaping mouths of the whales appear amid squawking gulls and even a few white-sided dolphins.

"I have never in my life been this close to a whale before," says Noah, his eyes wide and taking in the scene as our boat lobs silently on the water. "How do their mouths get so big?" He asks Kyle.

"Humpback whales are rorquals, which means they have a ribbed belly that expands in order to take in as much water and fish as possible. Once they have a mouthful, they strain the water out through their baleen." They point to the open mouth of one of the whales. "And the fish stay inside."

The boat dips and rises, the water draining along the sides from the scuppers, and two whales approach us, rolling almost as though they're trying to get a better view of their admirers.

"Let's talk to some whales," Lottie suggests.

I stand at her side, handing her whatever she needs as she readies the hydrophone, and then finally, she lowers it into the water. There are only three headphones, and Kyle graciously gestures that Mannix and I should have the first go at them.

There's a rush of the sea in my ears at first, and it's hard to pick out specific sounds. But once I hear them, I can't ignore them. The whales call out in squeals, squeaks, grunts, and groans. Anyone who didn't know any better might assume they were listening in on the calls of aliens, creatures that couldn't possibly inhabit this world.

I steal a glance at Mannix, and he watches the whales break the surface of the water, grinning.

"Our turn," Noah says, swatting Mannix in the arm.

Mannix lifts the headphones from his ears and hands them to Noah as I pass mine to Kyle. While the other three members of our crew are listening to whales, I stand beside Mannix at the rail, watching.

Quietly, I tell him, "When I was little, I used to have the same dream over and over again about the whales."

"Oh yeah? What's that?"

I run my hand through my knotty hair, pulling it back in a

sloppy bun. "I'd be at the beach. Any beach. All the beaches. Cape Cod or California. New Jersey or Washington, and when I got to the edge of the water, the whales would be there. Right there. Like if I reached out, I'd be able to touch them. And I'd wake up feeling so honored that it was me they showed up for. I think that's when I decided I'd show up for them, too."

Mannix watches me, and suddenly I'm self-conscious again. Like I've overstepped that weirdness threshold Kyle was trying to help me identify earlier. And finally he says, "I really love when you talk about them."

I beam and cower into myself all at the same time.

"I love that you know what matters to you, and you know what you're good at, and what your purpose is." He shakes his head, almost in awe. "I love it, and I'm jealous of it, all at the same time."

"You're good at about a million things."

He laughs at this quietly.

"And I think you know what you want to do with your life, too," I add. "You might be a little scared of it, but you know."

A whale surfaces beside the boat, exhaling in a gust of spray that reeks of fish, and I instinctively step back and away from the railing before I'm showered in it. Mannix, however, isn't fast enough. He runs his hand down his face, his eyes squeezed close. "Nice. That was refreshing."

"You've been blessed with whale breath," Kyle says from behind us.

"I can die happy." He laughs it off but spares a glance in my direction. He reaches out and squeezes my hand.

Chapter Thirteen

While I wait for Mannix to pick me up for the fundraiser, I've been occupying my time by watching Uncle Jack's neighbor, Mrs. Mackenzie, curse about hornworms as she tends to her tomato garden. I sit on the cobblestone patio under one of the green umbrellas, my right leg crossed over my left and my foot nodding contentedly. Beside me, my phone sits idle, but I glance at it every so often in case Mannix sends me a text.

Uncle Jack and Chad left an hour ago to make sure things were ready for the Barnacles and Brunch fundraiser, but I didn't want to arrive with them. So I wait for Mannix, who assured me he'd be showered and dressed after his early shift at White Crest was over and would pick me up on time.

In the meantime, at least I have Mrs. Mackenzie.

"I have toiled with too much dedication to lose my tomatoes now," she says, and she must not realize that in addition to the hornworms, I, too, am witness to her struggle.

A warm morning breeze coasts up the sloping green hill of Uncle Jack's lawn, and it carries with it the scent of the bay and on its crest, the sharp tang of pine needles and the sweet scent of hydrangeas from the front of the house. I close my eyes.

I pushed a rickety wheelbarrow through the dormant weeds of the winter-gray main courtyard of my high school.

"We lucked out this week!" Mrs. Dabrowski called to us, her hands on her hips as she observed her eighth-period class prepping the ground for spring planting. "It has been an unseasonably warm January. Thanks, climate change." She rolled her eyes at this, as if climate change were standing among us, gloating.

The wheelbarrow and I stopped where Ella, clad in her winter coat and gardening gloves, dug mercilessly at the stubborn dead weeds.

"I can't believe we're gardening in the middle of winter," I muttered.

"Mrs. Dabrowski didn't get the go-ahead from the grounds people to use the courtyard until just before break. So we didn't have a chance to ready it for the spring back in the fall when we should have," Ella explained.

"Oh."

"You can help me."

"Sure." I got down on my knees, but my jeans were still new from Christmas, and I wasn't planning on getting mud on them yet. Plus they ran out of gardening gloves in my size, so I wore a huge pair made for a man, and my fingers swam in them. "What do you need me to do?"

Ella offered me an incredulous expression and then motioned at the raised garden bed loaded with weeds. "Dig. Pull."

She'd been snippy with me ever since the holiday concert three weeks ago. When I barged in on her solo, late, and couldn't stop giggling with Brent. We hadn't talked about it. Just maintained our usual level of company with the added charm of very little conversation.

She told me, though, that she wasn't taking chorus again next semester.

I lifted a garden trowel and pierced the ground. "I'm sorry," I said quietly.

Ella didn't respond right away. Then, "I said it was okay."

I still wasn't one hundred percent sure she knew what I was sorry about. "The concert and Brent. If I had known that he only went out with you because—"

She rocked back on her heels and brushed her hair out of her face with the back of her wrist. "So are you and Brent, like, a thing now?"

I scoffed like this was madness, but truthfully, I didn't know what we were. Over break, he'd invited me over to hang out, and we ended up in the dark, alone, making out in his finished basement. Then he took me to the movies with a whole group of his friends before New Year's, but no one really talked to me, not even him. The only thing that made me feel like he even liked me was that his hand was on my ass the whole time.

Ella watched me, waiting for more of a reply. Only I didn't have one. And I wish I'd told her that. I wish I'd told her about both of those scenarios, because I was so confused, and if it had been any other boy, I'd have told her everything, in detail, including how nervous he made me in a way that I simultaneously hated and wanted more of.

"Do you like him?" she tried again.

I swallowed hard. "He's okay." This was an untruth that I told a girl who'd liked Brent Tompkins since elementary school. She didn't buy it, but at least she pretended.

"Okay," said Ella. She got back on her hands and knees and kept digging at that poor, poor weed. What was left of its leaves was brown and almost slimy-looking, and they sagged and splayed out across the ground.

Across the courtyard, a few of the girls who'd gone out with me and Brent to the movies were watching us. I knew they wanted to do something on Friday, and I was keenly aware that I spent every Friday with Ella at a sleepover at either of our houses. I took a deep breath and closed my eyes.

"So I was thinking that maybe it might be fun if we invited Carleen and Angelica to our sleepover on Friday." I pressed my lips together and waited for her reaction.

"That's a joke, right?"

"No."

She dropped her hand shovel. "You want me to invite over two girls who have never had one nice thing to say to me? And, might I remind you, you have frequently been included in their vitriol."

"I hung out with them over break, and they're really—"

"Fake?"

"Fun."

"Wow, Cor."

I reached out and touched her wrist, but she wouldn't look me in the eyes. "I think we should give them a chance."

Ella's shoulders drooped and she leaned back on her heels. "Okay," she said. "For you."

"You're gonna like them, I swear."

"Again, this is for you."

Four days passed between my conversation with Ella and Friday night. Four days of quizzes and tests, four days of sneaking off to some secluded nook in the school to make out with Brent. Four days of eating lunch in the cafeteria with Carleen and Angelica instead of holing up in the library.

And by the time Friday arrived, I didn't even know what day it was. I was walking through the mall with Carleen and Angelica, heading to the food court for some terrible pizza, when my phone began to buzz in the back pocket of my jeans.

The moment I saw her face sipping a frappe on Cape Cod flash across my screen, I knew I had fucked up. I knew there was nothing I could say to make it right. So I did what cowards do and pretended like nothing was wrong.

"Hey, Ella."

"Where are you?" she asked.

I glanced around, like the mall was going to give me a hint as to what I should say. "Food court at the mall. Want to meet us here?"

"Food court?" She's quiet for a moment. "Who's us?"

"Um, Carleen and Angelica are here, and Cody and Brent are going to meet us in a little—"

"I thought the plan was inviting everyone over for a sleepover at my place."

"Oh," I said. My heart rammed against my lungs, and my breath came too quickly. "I didn't know we had decided. Um, maybe we can head over after the mall?"

"Cor, I went grocery shopping and cooked snacks all afternoon. I got stuff for pedicures."

"Ella, you didn't have to—"

"I know that." Her voice broke and she took a shaky breath. "I know I didn't have to. But I did. I did it for you, because it mattered to you, but like…Do I matter anymore, Cor?"

Carleen and Angelica stood beside the frothy fountain in the middle of the mall, and at the top of the escalators, Cody and Brent waved to us.

"That's a stupid question."

She laughed but it sounded more like a strangled sob. "And that's a telling response." She clicked off, and I dropped my phone back into my bag.

Even now, even when I'm sitting here on Uncle Jack's patio, my bottom lip trembles. I clutch my water bottle and take a long swig to wash away the guilt. No such luck. The crunch of tires on the shell driveway yanks me from the memory. Mannix's red-orange truck pulls up and stops behind the Land Rover.

He steps down from the driver's side, dressed in a white short-sleeve oxford and navy blue chinos that stop at his ankle, with gray dressy sneakers. I try to suppress a grin, but he's so handsome, and he tried so hard for my fundraiser, and my chest cinches at the sight of him.

"Hey," he says, crossing the lawn to the patio. He slows when he gets closer, and he has a little box in his hands. "Wow, you look…" He smiles. "You look so pretty."

I smile down at my sandals, running my hands over the skirt of my blue-and-white-striped dress. "You look really handsome," I tell him.

"Noah made me buy the pants. They're not too much, right?"

"They are exactly the right amount," I tell him when he's standing in front of me.

Bending down, he kisses me briefly, then pauses, and says against my mouth, "There's a lady holding a massive tomato watching us."

I tug at his collar, coaxing his attention back to me. "It's just Mrs. Mackenzie," I explain between kisses. "And she's probably thrilled that the hornworms didn't get all of her crop this year."

"Oh, good. Gazpacho for everyone."

I laugh, shaking my head.

"I got you something," he says, holding the box out to me. It's a cardboard jewelry box with a little turquoise ribbon wrapped around it. "Don't get excited, it's not a huge deal or anything, but I thought of you when I saw it in a window on Commercial Street."

I pull the ribbon and take off the cover to find a silver chain bracelet with a little blue piece of sea glass in the middle. "Mannix, this is so beautiful."

"You like it?" he asks.

"I love it. Can you help me put it on?"

"Yeah, of course." He takes the clasp and chain extender in each hand as I hold out my wrist. His fingers are clumsy, and he's shaking a little. "Sorry," he says, laughing at himself.

"It's okay."

"And I'm sorry I'm late. I had to drop my dad off down at the harbor. He was meeting his friend to do something on the boat, and we got into a fight."

"What about?"

"It's stupid." He tries again to attach the clasp to the chain, his eyes focused and brows knitted together. "He shouldn't be on the freaking boat," Mannix murmurs. "He should be resting and getting better, or doing his therapy exercises, but he doesn't listen to anyone." His eyes dart up. "What does your dad do for a living?"

"He's a musician," I say. "He has a music shop in the town we live in. He buys and sells all kinds of instruments and composes some of his own music."

"Oh yeah? Can I find him on Spotify?"

I clear my throat. "Yes, but please, if you care about me at all, you won't."

"Come on! I want to listen." Finally, he succeeds, his attention drawn away from my father's musical endeavors and down to my arm. "There we go."

I pull my wrist back and admire my new bracelet, the late-morning sunlight sifting through the leaves above us and glinting off the blue glass of the charm. "You didn't have to buy me anything," I say, a wave of guilt flooding me unexpectedly. He's already losing a shift at the Sea Ghost today, and now he's spending his hard-earned money on me.

"I wanted to," he says. "Come on, let's get going. Your uncle's probably wondering where we are."

We drive up Route 6 to Provincetown, Mannix taking a side road I've never been on before to avoid the hustle of Commercial Street and the summer crowds. I try to notice everything: the purple-painted Victorian house, the breaching whale carved from the trunk of a tree like it's exploding from the surface of the sea, something that I'll be sure to remember, so I can use this road when I go to work in the morning. He parks in the lot where we met last month, close to the spot he originally occupied, and when he exits the truck, he circles around the back and comes to my door, offering me his hand as I step out.

"You know," I say as he locks the passenger door with his key, "despite appearing the exact opposite, your truck is pretty comfortable."

"Right? She's a beauty." He takes my hand as we cross the parking lot to the street. "I'm still trying to fix it up. It was my uncle's truck, and he let it go for a while. It sat in his backyard until my aunt lost it and told him to get rid of it. He said giving it to me was only slightly better than getting rid of it. At least they could still visit whenever he wanted to."

"It's like you have co-custody."

"Something like that." He leads me up the street, and around the bend, the roof of the Sea Ghost comes into view.

"Here we go," I mutter under my breath.

"What's up?"

A few groups of guests congregate on the side lawn and under the canopy of an ancient tree, sipping from cocktails already. "I'm worried that my boss won't think this is enough. I feel like I'm constantly trying to prove to her that I'm doing this internship for the right reasons."

Mannix allows me to go ahead of him on the narrow sidewalk that leads to the main entrance. "I think she knows," he says.

Mannix grabs the handle and holds it open for me. Inside, we're led to the bar and the main dining room, and it's packed with people milling about, sipping mimosas and Bloody Marys, sampling appetizers from trays carried by waiters, and chatting in knots that loosen to welcome new participants.

On what's usually a blank wall, occupied only by a nautical mirror, there are black-and-white portraits of humpback whale flukes, each as unique as a fingerprint. My eyes scan their signatures until I find Fraction, right in the middle. What she lacks makes her stand out, gains her attention.

I glance around, searching for a face I know. Uncle Jack and Chad are greeting guests, and across the room, Kyle and Justin hover near the buffet, waiting for the go-ahead to begin eating. When Kyle sees us, they wave and motion for us to join them.

"Hey, group," I say. "Justin, this is my..." It occurs to me that I have no idea what Mannix is. Friend or boyfriend? It feels weird to label him at all when he's Mannix. That feels like enough.

He reaches out his right hand to shake Justin's. "I think I'm her date."

"Looks that way," says Justin.

Mannix's hand finds the small of my back. "I'm gonna go get a drink. You want anything?"

"Whatever you're having is good," I say.

"Be right back."

Mannix disappears into the thickening crowd of people, and I'm left with Justin and Kyle watching me with knowing smirks.

"Where's Lottie and Mia?" I ask casually, scanning the room to see if I missed them. I don't want Lottie to think I'm avoiding her. I want to guarantee she's having a good time.

"Out in Pamet Harbor trying to rescue a sunfish," says Justin, taking a sip of his drink. "People called in thinking it was a great white with the dorsal fin and all the thrashing it was doing, but when they went to investigate, it was just a lost mola."

Of course Lottie isn't here. Lottie isn't the kind of person who puts on a show so that people see her at a fundraiser. Fundraisers are for those who aren't going to get their hands dirty or wade into Pamet Harbor to rescue a wayward sunfish.

Across the room, Mannix stands at the bar in his outfit that makes him look like he belongs in a magazine, talking to his coworkers and laughing about something. When he notices me, he grins and holds up a finger to let me know it'll only be a moment.

"Did you get something to eat?" asks Uncle Jack, coming up beside me and kissing my cheek.

"Not yet," I say. "Mannix was getting us something to drink."

"Here you go. Diet Coke." Mannix hands me a glass with a paper straw, and I sip it gratefully as Justin and Kyle discuss what the procedure is for rescuing a mola. He must notice how distant I am, because his hand finds my back again, and he leans in so that only I can hear. "Everything okay?"

"I think so," I reply.

Before I can go into too much detail, Justin reaches into his back pocket to grab his ringing phone. It plays the theme song to *Gilligan's Island*. "How's the sunfish?" he asks.

I hold my breath. Lottie.

"Oh, hey, Mia, calm down."

Kyle and I exchange a glance; then they mouth to me, *What's going on?*

And I mouth back, *I don't know.*

"All right. I'll head down now and meet you there." Justin

clicks off the phone and his gaze shifts between Kyle's and mine. "The coast guard is bringing in the body of a dead humpback down at Sesuit Harbor. You wanna come take pictures?"

Kyle and I answer simultaneously, "Yes."

"Meet me at headquarters, and we'll pick up the camera."

I can't move fast enough, and I don't know what to do with my glass. "Where should I put this?" I ask Mannix.

"Here, on the table," he replies, touching the glossy wooden top of a dining table that lines the windows. "Hey, let me drive you."

I don't want to drive myself there, and driving with Justin and Kyle won't be at all comforting. Mannix will be, though. I want to get the camera ready. I want to prepare myself for being in the presence of a dead whale. I've seen dead whales before, in pictures and videos, snippets in newspaper articles or posts on Instagram where an appropriate response is as simple as a crying-face emoji. This won't be the same. This might extinguish me, and there won't be any avatar to hide behind. I'm terrified that I'll recognize it. I'm stunned with the fear that it could be Fraction, succumbed to her injuries and destroyed by a ship.

We speed down Route 6, avoiding the slow tourist-filled villages along the way, until we get to Dennis. We pass the restaurants and the shops of 6A, the marshes, and wind down a dusty road until we get to Sesuit Harbor. Justin and Kyle jump out of the SUV in front of us, and I follow them, fumbling with the camera, trying not to drop the expensive equipment. Mannix trails behind me, wanting to see, too, but letting us get there first.

We stand at the edge of the marina. Behind us, boats are

stacked high, and the smell of fried seafood wafts from the nearby restaurant, its cedared walls lined with buoys. A breeze far off on the bay lifts up from the harbor, and we wait. It's warm. All around, people are returning their boats from an afternoon on the water. They're having their meals at wooden picnic tables under colorful umbrellas. They're not ready for this.

The coast guard boat appears on the horizon, slowly cruising in past Harbor Beach, a gentle wake at its hull, and towed by its flukes is the almost-fifty-foot body of a humpback whale. Entangled in fishing gear, bleeding in several places where the rope bites into her flesh. But her flukes are in one piece. I begin to click the camera. I start taking pictures. I don't turn away.

"Shit," Justin murmurs beside me.

Behind us, people stand and gather. They take out their phones and record this, too. Because there's nothing sadder than the body of a creature so powerful, so miraculous, floating lifelessly behind a boat, upside down, its ribbed belly facing the sky, its beautiful white fins spread out like arms welcoming death.

Maybe she was. Maybe being caught up in that gear became too much, and death was something she was waiting for. I blink back tears.

"What do you think happened?" Mannix manages to ask. I don't know who he's asking, but it's Justin who finally replies.

"Can't be sure," he says. "We'll place her up on the flatbed and take her for a necropsy to find out, but if I were to wager a guess? The ropes slowed her down, and she couldn't get out of the way of a boat."

Members from the International Fund for Animal Welfare

meet us there. They weigh the whale, identify her as a twenty-three-year-old female. She had been spotted by a boat out of Duxbury last week, still alive, but tangled in rope. Now she's here, her body gently lifted by a crane, soaring high above us, dripping seawater, her flukes listless and limp. Then she's loaded onto a flatbed tractor trailer, to be dissected. Reduced to a science experiment. A statistic.

I try to picture her in the water, her massive body swimming thousands of miles from the Cape to the Caribbean, every single year. I wonder what storms she weathered. I wonder who her mother was. Who her calves might be. Who her mates were. I wonder what songs they sang to her.

As the sun begins to set, casting the sky in a lavender haze, Lottie finds us. We make our way through the crowd as the tractor trailer pulls out of Sesuit, the whale disappearing behind a wall of leafy green trees. People on the highway will see her, traveling with everyone else like a tank of orange juice or secured machinery. They'll record it without context. They'll post it for likes. I look down at my camera. My pictures will mean more than that.

"Rough day," says Justin, handing Lottie a bottle of water from the SUV.

"Atrocious," she says.

"How'd the mola do?" he asks her.

She's gulping down water, and when she finally stops for a breath, she closes her eyes. "It lives to see another day," she replies. "Which is more than I can say about most creatures this afternoon." Finally she turns to address me. "Did you get pictures?"

"Yeah," I reply. "I'll upload them to the drive when I get home."

"Maybe tomorrow you can write up a draft of what happened here today, so we can post to social media."

I blink, surprised by her willingness to put her trust in my words. "I'd love to do that," I tell her.

"Good," Justin says, and they start traipsing back to the parking lot. "Let's all get going. It's been a day. We could use some time to rest and recharge."

I follow Mannix back to his truck. He opens my door for me, and I climb in, numbly. When he comes around to his side, he starts the engine and we both sit there, staring out past the windshield at the long line that's forming around the restaurant. Mannix takes a deep breath and lets it out slowly.

I try not to cry because it seems silly to cry over an animal I didn't even know existed prior to this afternoon, but once I start, it's out of my control. My body quakes with my sobs, and I cover my face, like if I do, he won't see how violently this has shaken me. Mannix doesn't say anything as I draw in sharp breaths, like I've run a marathon, but I'm sitting painfully still. Minutes pass. I swipe at my face, my makeup sticky and seeping down my cheeks.

Slowly, Mannix's right hand inches across the bench seat of the truck, palm open, and once it's between us, he waits until I'm ready, his attention still focused on the long line of diners at the mouth of the harbor.

I thread my fingers through his, and he closes his hand around mine, his thumb caressing the inside of my wrist.

"I'm sorry," I say softly.

"There's nothing to be sorry about."

We sit like this for a while, and finally, he lets go, adjusts the gearshift at the steering column, and we pull out of Sesuit Harbor. Once we're on the road, he offers me his hand again, and I don't let go until we get back to Wellfleet.

Chapter Fourteen

I pull into Mannix's driveway, armed with two large cups of coffee and his favorite glazed sour cream doughnut. I like knowing what he likes. Knowing his order without having to ask him and then surprising him with it when he least expects it. And he could use a pleasant surprise today. His truck wouldn't start last night, so I offered to drive him to his CPR training so he can renew his certification. It's being run on the beach down the sandy road near the Nature Center, so it was convenient. Plus I get to spend the fifteen-minute car ride with him there and back.

Jumping out of the Jeep, I leave my breakfast surprise on the passenger seat and round the property to the back of the house. My pace slows as voices drift from the kitchen window.

"Well, if you didn't send for it, why is it here?"

"How the hell should I know?" Mannix replies. "Colleges send out pamphlets."

"This is a literal catalogue, Mannix, and you're not in high school anymore. You're not on any of their lists."

I duck behind a lilac bush, unsure how to proceed. I never know if I should pretend like I didn't hear anything or wait until the conversation comes to a lull. I can hear Mannix plod across the kitchen.

"Why do you even care?" he asks. "Throw it out." Another pause. "Let me help you with that."

His dad scoffs. "I don't need your help cooking breakfast, Mannix. I need your help on the boat, I need your help because I can't work right now. I need you out there with me, but you're too busy serving drinks, or splashing around at the beach, or—" He throws what sounds like a magazine down on the counter. "Planning on becoming some kind of goddamn chef!"

Mannix is silent.

"So that's it?" his dad asks. "That's the end of the conversation?"

"This hasn't been a conversation, Dad. A conversation implies that both parties have something to say, and I'm so fucking tired of telling you that I'm not taking over. I don't want the boat. I don't want the business."

I take a step out from behind the lilac bush and cough loudly, like a cloud of pollen's gotten wedged in my throat; then I make sure to take the crunchy seashell path to the back porch. "Hey," I say when I get to the slider. It's open, but the screen is closed.

"Hey," says Mannix, but he doesn't look me in the eyes. He opens the screen door to let me in.

"Hey, Mr. Reilly," I say. I've only met Mannix's parents

once, outside of the time Mr. Reilly attended the lecture in Provincetown.

"Morning, Coriander."

I scan the counter and find the mailing that's caused so much drama this morning. It looks like a course catalogue for the Culinary Institute of America.

"So how's your internship going?" Mr. Reilly asks as he grabs a mug from the cabinet next to the stove.

"It's going," I say, trying to make light of it. I don't want to talk about the dead whale at Sesuit, even though it was over a week ago. It's still raw in my memory.

Besides, this is glorified small talk, and he's being polite. The truth is, I don't know how to discuss my work with a lobsterman. It's awkward and uncomfortable. I want lobstermen to continue with their livelihood, and with success, but not at the risk of any more whale deaths. The balance is uneven, the cost too high. Mannix's dad might not want to hear this, though.

"I liked that lecture a few weeks ago," he says as he pours me a cup of coffee.

"Did you take one of the emergency contact cards?" I ask.

"No, what's that?"

I reach into my crossbody and pull out a card with important phone numbers to call when encountering needy wildlife. Reaching across the kitchen island, I hand it to Mr. Reilly. "If you're ever out on the water and you see a whale in distress, tangled up or something, you can call that bottom number to alert the Marine Research and Conservation Alliance. They'll send out the response team."

"Good to know," he says, taking it from me and reading it through.

Mannix hooks one of his fingers in the belt loop of my shorts and pulls me closer. "I made coffee cake, try some."

"Ooh," I say, as he retrieves two plates from the cabinet. I get us forks from the drawer at my hip. Since helping him clean up after his party, I have a pretty good idea of where everything goes in his kitchen.

From behind me, I think Mr. Reilly huffs. I disregard it because surely no one would huff over coffee cake.

"You want some, Dad?" Mannix asks.

"I'm not hungry."

Mannix lifts a plate and offers it to him. "It's still warm." But his dad doesn't say anything, so Mannix turns back to me. "Want a bigger piece?" he asks me, like we're the only two people in the room.

I shake my head and touch his back. "This is perfect, thank you." I take a bite, and it's almost magical. Soft, moist, gooey streaks of cinnamon and sugar.

"What time do you think you'll be back today?" his dad asks him, almost like he knows he's being ignored.

"It's an all-day training, so not till four." Mannix pinches my elbow gently. "That good for you?"

"Yeah, I'm in charge of nature camp today, and my last group leaves at three. So I'll find something to do around the Nature Center while I wait for you to finish up."

"Cool."

I lean against the counter, nibbling my cake while Mannix gets his lunch ready from the fridge. "You know, Mr. Reilly, when you feel better and you need someone to go out on the boat with you, I'd be a ready and willing volunteer."

"You like being out on the ocean, Coriander Cabot?"

"I would live there."

"You and me are of one mind," says his dad. "I love waking up before dawn and heading out, and then watching the sun rise on the water. Makes me feel the way sailors must have hundreds of years before me."

"I've never seen the sun rise on the ocean," I tell him. "At the beach a few times, but not actually out on the water."

"Well, then we have a goal, don't we? Maybe you'll be what motivates this kid over here."

Mannix raises his attention from his sandwich and plastic wrap, his eyes lingering on me for a moment. He smiles and looks down at his feet.

When Mannix's back is turned to me, I rest my fork on my plate, allowing my hand to inch freely across the countertop and filch the brochure before he notices that it's missing from his trash pile. Rolling it up, I stuff it into my back pocket and make sure my MRCA staff T-shirt covers any evidence of its presence.

"Okay," says Mannix, looking around the kitchen to make sure he hasn't forgotten anything. He has a cooler with his lunch and a huge water bottle, plus his cinch bag, which is probably filled with sunblock and his sunglasses. "You ready?"

I take my final bite of coffee cake, then rinse my plate in the sink and load it into the dishwasher. "All set."

"You didn't have to do that," says Mannix as I close the door to the dishwasher.

"You didn't have to make me coffee cake," I say. I turn to his dad. "It was nice to see you again, Mr. Reilly."

"You, too, my dear," he replies. "Mannix, invite her to dinner with the family tonight."

His shoulders slump. "Dad, give me a chance to do it first."

Sorry, his dad mouths, looking sheepish.

Mannix turns to me. "Hey, Cor, want to come out to dinner with us tonight?"

I shove him in the shoulder and try not to laugh. "Sure, where to?"

"The Quarter Deck," his dad replies.

"Dude," says Mannix, his eyes rolling up to the ceiling. He sighs and then tries again. "The Quarter Deck, and we have reservations at seven."

"That works for me."

"And I'd offer to pick you up, but as you know, I'm without a car."

"I can overlook your lack of transportation this once," I say. "Come on, we gotta go. Your sandwich-making put a crimp in our timeline." I wave to Mr. Reilly. "See you later tonight."

"Sure thing."

We exit out the back slider door and head around to where I parked in the driveway. "Left you something on the seat," I say casually.

Mannix opens the passenger door and stares at his treat, his eyes growing wide. "Is this a sour cream doughnut?"

"It is."

"With extra coffee?"

"You worked the late shift at the Sea Ghost last night."

"I've never been as attracted to you as I am this very moment."

"Well, you can thank me later," I say with an exaggerated wink as I climb into the Jeep. "But right now, we have to go."

We drive up Route 6 toward the Nature Center at a pretty

brisk clip, Mannix stuffing his face with his doughnut and asking me, mouth full, halfway through, if I'd like a bite. I decline, he keeps eating. It isn't until we reach the border of Truro that the traffic stops. It's a gorgeous day, and people are headed up to the beaches and to walk around Provincetown.

"Shit," I say, slapping my hand on the steering wheel.

"See that sign up ahead?" Mannix says, pointing. "Turn there."

"I don't know how to go from there," I tell him, craning my neck to see if I can spot the source of our holdup.

"I do. Make a right."

He takes us down a winding road that at times becomes so narrow that I'm scared the Jeep is going to end up in a ditch, and then I won't know what to tell my brother upon my return to New Jersey.

"Just tell me where to turn," I say.

Mannix nods, midsip.

It's only then that I'm reminded of the rolled-up brochure I nabbed from his kitchen. I lift my right butt cheek. "Hey, could you grab that out of my back pocket?"

The corner of his mouth pulls upward as he slides his hand into my pocket. "You're driving, though, so I'll enjoy this moment quickly before your want for me becomes too much and you swerve off the road."

"You know I can't resist those hands."

"You're only human." He retrieves the brochure and stares at it for a moment. "What's this?"

"I dunno, you tell me. It was on the counter."

"It's a brochure for the Culinary Institute." He says it like it's nothing, like it's a coupon from Burger King or something.

But the way he stares out the window says more than his mouth refuses to.

"Are you interested in going there?" I ask.

"Cor, you know I can't."

"I don't know that. *Know* is a pretty strong word. However, what I *do* know is that there is a glossy brochure from the Culinary Institute sitting on your kitchen counter, and it's not just for advertising. It's not like they randomly pulled your name and address out of a hat and decided to test the water and see if you were interested. This is full-fledged book of information. You had to have requested that. I *know* this because I'm in the middle of applying to schools, and I know what kind of mailers they send for free and which ones they save for requests."

"I might have. But shit's changed since then." He stares out the window as houses blur by us.

"But your love of food hasn't. Your skill in cooking hasn't."

"It doesn't matter, Cor."

I'm quiet now, because I recognize the fact that the ice I'm treading on is getting progressively thinner with every exchange. He won't look at me at all now, his attention fixed firmly out the window.

After about five minutes, I spot the roof of the Nature Center in the distance and Mannix sits up straighter, smiling.

"See?" he says.

"Why have you never showed me this way before?" I ask, pulling into a parking spot and shoving the Jeep into park.

Mannix opens his door and hops down. "Because Route 6 is faster and that road is weird and narrow. But in an emergency, it comes in handy." He circles around the back of the Jeep and ends up beside me. "And we're only, like, a minute late."

"Reilly, let's get your ass in gear!" calls a man from the top of the path that leads down to the beach.

"Gonna run, see you later."

I get up on my tiptoes and present my lips, but he gives me a quick and courtly peck on the cheek and dashes off to join his CPR class. That was not at all satisfying, and I hope it's not because of the brochure.

I can't do anything about it now, anyway. I sigh, turning and facing the Nature Center, where a line of parents' cars wait to drop their babies off and put them in my care for the day.

By the end of the afternoon, I'm exhausted and barely standing. I wave to the last kid as he rides away in his mom's SUV and breathe a sigh of relief, because I'm done, and I'm going to go lock myself in the office and sit and stare blankly at the wall until I have to drive Mannix home.

But he's coming across the parking lot now, not quite at the same brisk pace he had earlier today. He's a little red despite his adamant use of sunblock. When he gets to me, he wraps his arm around my waist and pulls me into a slow kiss. The scent of sweat and coconut wafts from his person.

"Done early?" I ask.

"Yup."

"Certified CPR giver once more?"

"Need a demonstration?"

I consider this, pursing my lips. "That's a weird thing to say."

He presses his forehead to mine and laughs at this, then

climbs the stairs up to the Nature Center. "Gonna run to the bathroom before we leave."

"I'll wait for you out here."

I stand on the steps, shoving my clipboard and pen into my tote bag and waiting for Mannix to come back outside. It's good that we're leaving early. There's a chance I'll get a nap in as well as a shower before we head out for dinner tonight with his family.

"Ready?" asks Mannix when he exits the Nature Center.

We set off for the parking lot, hand in hand, but before we can get too far, the MRCA Ford cruises past us, and in the passenger seat, Lottie waves to me and gives me the "one minute" signal.

"That your boss?" Mannix asks.

I groan. "Yes. Smile and don't act like we want to leave right away."

"Got it," says Mannix, watching as Justin and Lottie exit the truck, followed by two other people. A man I don't recognize looks up at the Nature Center, taking in his surroundings and jotting something down in a notebook he carries. His companion takes several pictures with a fancy camera. Lottie waves again as she approaches.

"Hey," I say with a halfhearted wave in return.

"Cor," says Lottie. "This is Dan Reynolds and Clarissa Hernandez. They're from the *New York Times*."

My spine straightens of its own accord.

"They're doing a feature on Cape Cod's coast, and they want to focus on human/whale interactions. I told them about the pictures you took last week of the humpback at Sesuit."

"Hi," I say, shaking each of their extended hands. "I'm Coriander, and this is Mannix."

Mannix smiles and shakes everyone's hands.

Lottie takes another step up the stairs, then turns to see if I'm following. "Come on, let's go."

"Who, me?" I ask, pointing to myself. I exchange a quick glance with Mannix, who shrugs.

"Lottie here says you're one of the interns working this summer, and I'd love to ask you a few questions," says Dan, shoving his pen behind his ear. "If you have time, of course."

"I'm Mannix's ride," I say.

"Hey, it's okay," says Mannix, touching my wrist and stepping down toward the parking lot. "I'll call Noah. He can spin back around and pick me up."

"Are you sure?" I ask.

"Positive." He watches as Lottie and Justin lead the two journalists into the Nature Center; then he raises his eyebrows. "It's the *New York Times*! Come on, you can't miss that just to drive me home. Get in there." He swats my butt playfully.

"Thank you," I say, and I lean into him, kissing him fully because he deserves that. "I'll text you when I'm on my way home."

"Cool."

I follow the group back into the Nature Center, and they stand, clustered, under the hanging skeleton of the right whale, under where her heart would be. Exactly where they should be. Lottie tells Mosaic's story, how she lived and how her life came to a prolonged, excruciating end.

When whales are caught in fishing lines, in nets, there's no easy way to die. It's slow, and it's painful. It's knowing you're dying and not being able to do anything about it. It's starvation, infection, attacks from predators. It's drowning. It's relying on someone outside yourself to care. It's relying on someone outside yourself to do something to keep it from happening again.

"I'm interested in the angle of young people out here with you," says Dan.

"We have two other interns, Mia and Kyle, and they'd love to talk with you, too," says Lottie.

There's part of me that knows this is a natural thing for her to say, because Mia and Kyle have worked just as hard as I have this summer. But there's another part of me that wonders if Lottie would prefer that he interviews them instead of me. Because she thinks I'm here for how it'll look on college applications. She thinks I'm here because, I don't know, I'm an overachiever or an ass-kisser, or something else that I used to be for a little while. But I'm trying. And I want her to know.

I want her to know that I'm here because I can't erase the expression on my best friend's face, the last one I saw before she slipped beneath the waves. I'm here because the ocean took something from me, and I'm not done searching for it yet. I'm here because when you love something as humbling and startling as a whale, you show up for them. I owe them that.

"So where are you from, Ms. Cabot?" Dan asks.

"New Jersey," I reply, my voice hoarse. Stepping under the right whale, I look up into her rib cage, allowing my eyes to roam her backbone to its end on the opposite side of the room. "But I've spent all my summers on Cape Cod. I'm staying with my uncle Jack, who lives here year-round."

"You were there when they brought in the humpback whale at Sesuit?"

I turn to the office where my laptop is. "I have pictures I can show you."

"You can use any of them you think you might want," Justin adds.

Dan nods, but he's still transfixed by the whale above us. "When was the first time you saw a whale, Coriander?"

The question catches me off guard, and I search my brain for the answer. As the memory unfurls itself, I reply, "It was in April at Herring Cove. We were spending Easter with my uncle Jack, and I saw two right whales skim feeding, and I could have swum out to them, they were so close." I shake my head in wonder. "I don't know if the passage of time makes them larger or closer than they actually were, but I'm okay if it does. And I felt so lucky, like I had witnessed something that people only read about or see on TV, and I felt so small and silly all at the same time."

Everyone is quiet. They watch me.

"That whale in Sesuit," I say, swallowing with some difficulty and fussing with my hair because I want to distract my audience, distract myself, from how this memory shakes me. "That whale made me feel the same way, only darker. And I don't want that to be the memory I take away from this summer. So I'm really glad you're giving them the spotlight."

Lottie looks down at her feet, and Justin nods his approval, his arms crossed over his chest.

"Well, let's see those pictures then," says Clarissa.

By the time I get back to the Jeep, the sun has set, casting the sky in a hazy gray with a streak of violet across the horizon. I blast the air conditioning and sit for a moment, silent and still, basking in my afternoon, until my phone buzzes.

"Mannix," I say out loud, glancing down at the screen. He's texted me three times. And the clock in my dashboard tells me it's 8:12 PM. "Shit."

> **Mannix (6:05 PM):** On your way home yet?
> **Mannix (6:28 PM):** We're leaving soon, so maybe you wanna meet us there?
> **Mannix (8:12 PM):** I'm hoping it's your phone that's dead and not you.

"Oh my god, I'm such a shit." I don't want to call him in the middle of dinner, so I settle for texting him back and begging his forgiveness.

> **Cor (8:13 PM):** I am SO sorry. I just got out, and I completely forgot to text you. Call me later?
> **Mannix (8:14 PM):** 👍
> **Mannix (8:15 PM):** Come to my house. Mom and Dad are having people over after dinner, and I want to see you.

I lean back in the driver's seat, my hands clutching the wheel in front of me, squeezing hard. I convinced him to give me a chance. I'm not proving that I was worth it.

> **Cor (8:16 PM):** Be over in a bit.

Chapter Fifteen

Mannix's yard is lit up with string lights and a fire roaring in the pit, surrounded by guests in lawn chairs. When I appear in the backyard, he grins and walks over. My whole body relaxes, and the rest of the group melts away.

"Hey," I say as he wraps an arm around my waist.

"Who's this, Mannix?" asks a man who's seated next to his mom.

"This is Cor," says Mannix. "She's spending the summer here interning at the Marine Research and Conservation Alliance."

"Hi," I say, offering the group a wave.

Mannix points out each and every person, most of them his uncles, a few cousins, and his dad's friends; then he offers me his seat and crouches down beside me. "You thirsty?" he asks.

"What do you have?"

"Water, beer, wine, iced tea, seltzer."

"Seltzer, please."

He leaves me to retrieve a seltzer from the cooler, and his mom stops him, asking him something I can't hear. She nods once and then disappears into the kitchen.

"Your seltzer," he says.

"Where'd your mom go?"

He takes a long swig from his own can. "Inside to get Uncle Jeff's birthday cake."

I whisper, "Did you make it?"

And he's so cute, he even blushes while trying to hide his grin, looking down at his sneakers. "Yeah, I made it."

I kiss his cheek.

When his mom comes back out carrying the cake, everyone breaks into song, and Uncle Jeff blows out his numerous candles.

"What are you implying, Tammy?" he asks, grinning and motioning at the cake.

"Don't look at me!" says Mrs. Reilly as she hands everyone a cake plate and fork. "Mannix made the cake and added the candles." Mannix's mom is petite, with short, neat blond hair and meticulous acrylic nails that she decorates appropriately for every season and holiday. Right now they're a beachy turquoise accented with coral stripes on her ring fingers.

I venture a hesitant glance at Mr. Reilly as he digs his fork into his slice. He shakes his head, still laughing.

"You made the cake?" Uncle Jeff asks, turning to Mannix in disbelief. "Hope you didn't get any on your apron."

The group all chuckles, and Mannix attempts to laugh it off as he hands me my plate.

"Mannix is an excellent cook," his mom says proudly.

"Really?" says another one of his uncles. "You like dusting things, too? Can I get you a maid's outfit for Christmas?"

"Trust me, his domestic skills are limited to cooking," says his dad.

"What kind of cake is this?" I ask, taking a bite and trying to distract him from everyone who thinks this is somehow funny.

"Lemon almond butter," he replies, refusing to look up from his plate.

"It's so good." This isn't a lie. Everything he makes is delicious, and if these people are going to make fun of him but still enjoy what he's made, then they should honestly get the fuck out of here. My skin prickles in defense of him.

"I think he's liked cooking for a lot longer than he lets on," says his dad. He has frosting on his mouth, so now he looks mean and dumb all at the same time. "Get a load of what I found in his room the other day."

Mannix looks up sharply, frowning.

"Wait, hold on," says his dad to his friends, laughing so hard that he's interrupting his own sentence. He gets to his feet slowly, grabbing his cane. "Let me go get it. I'll show you. You won't believe this shit."

"Dad," says Mannix, and there's no mistaking the edge in his voice.

"Relax, would you?" his dad calls over his shoulder. "Have a beer or something."

"Is this buttercream frosting?" I try again, but it's pointless. Mannix ignores me, completely focused on the slider door and waiting for his dad to come back out.

"Gary," his mom calls after him, but Mr. Reilly has already disappeared into the house.

When he returns, he's carrying a small trophy. It looks like a spray-painted whisk attached to a fake marble pedestal. "Look at this," says Mannix's dad, holding it up for all to see. "Look what I found in his closet when I went to get his laundry the other day. Apparently, I'm the proud father of the winner of the Golden Whisk."

In three strides, Mannix is across the lawn, and he snatches the trophy out of his dad's hand. "Thanks for finding this," he says tightly.

"Where the hell did that even come from?" His dad continues to guffaw and his friends offer multiple digs and one-liners.

"High school," Mannix replies.

"You've had it for that long?"

"Well, you get why I never shared it with you, right? That's pretty obvious." Mannix's shoulders are tense. "You're not exactly the most supportive person I've ever met." He grips the Golden Whisk and paces back to my chair. "Cor, it looks like we're almost out of ice. Want to come get more with me?"

I blink confusedly. "Yeah, of course."

"Oh, come on now, Mannix," says his dad. "You can take a joke."

"I'll be back in a bit," he replies. As he walks past me, he grabs my hand, clutching it, squishing my fingers between his, and we walk together to his truck.

"Mannix!" his dad calls, but he doesn't turn around.

I climb in the passenger side as Mannix silently starts my Jeep, then backs out of the driveway and heads toward Route 6.

Cars pass us, their headlights illuminating his clenched jaw, his knuckles gripping the wheel, in brief, articulate flashes.

My voice comes out soft. "I'm sorry your—"

"Nope," he says. "Nope, stop."

"Okay." I settle into my seat a little more, giving him the space he needs.

He pulls into the parking lot of Marshside Deli, and as we hop down from the Jeep, the lights behind the front wall of windows go out.

"You've gotta be kidding me." He steps into the parking lot, running his hand through his hair.

"Mannix...," I try.

From behind the building, a broad, bald man emerges, reaching into his pocket for his keys.

"Hey, Hank!" Mannix calls.

The man looks up, surprised, but then relaxes when he recognizes him. "What's up, Mannix?"

"I just need a bag of ice."

"Sorry, my dude, we're closed for the night."

"Come on, Hank. Just unlock the door, and I'll run in and grab some. You can even keep my twenty."

Hank unlocks his car and shakes his head. "I'd have to do the whole alarm again and open up the register. Surely you're not experiencing an ice emergency, right?" He ducks into the car with a chuckle. "See you in the morning, okay? Eggs and cheese at eight?"

"Yup," Mannix replies.

Hank backs out of his spot and cruises out onto Route 6.

Mannix stands in the middle of the parking lot, hands at

his side, shoulders slumped. Silently, slowly, he looks over his shoulder at me, then at the Jeep, and paces in our direction. Placing both hands on the hood, he drops his head and murmurs, "Fuck." And then loudly, "Fuck! Fuck it!" He kicks the tire, then stares out across the marsh behind the parking lot, slowly descending into a squat, his hands on his knees and his chest heaving.

"Hey," I say, kneeling beside him. I run my hand through his hair, rest my palm on his cheek. "Hey, look at me."

His face is red, and his eyes are wet.

I nod, suddenly understanding. This was it. This was the last straw. "You're right. Fuck them. All of them. Your dad. His friends. Your uncles. Hank with the ice."

"Cor." He reaches out an arm to steady himself on the side of the Jeep, and then sinks down next to it. He leans his head back, looking up into the night sky. "Cor, I'm so tired of it. Do you have any idea how exhausting it is to go through your life feeling like no one around you gets you or even wants to try? And then you get home, and your fucking dad is the worst out of all of them."

Truthfully, I don't. The first part, sure. I can't even count how many times I succumbed to the misunderstanding of my classmates, my friends, Brent....But when I got home, I was always safe from that. I had my mom and her embrace, and my dad with his guitar in the living room, and Peyton with her advice, and Rhett who threatened to beat people up who hurt me. And Ella. Always Ella. Who just *was*.

"I'm so tired. I'm so tired of being a joke to him," he says. "I'm so tired of having no place that's safe. That's mine."

"You're not a joke," I tell him, and my voice cracks. "That's why they laugh, because they don't know what to do with you. They get freaked out by people who know what they want, especially when they've spent their entire lives floundering, you know?"

He swipes at his tears with his knuckles and takes a deep breath.

"You are...," I say, but then I stop, wondering how to finish. I reach out and cradle his face between both my hands so he has no choice but to meet my eyes. "You're everything to me, okay? You're mine. Please don't do this. Please don't be upset. I'll be where you're safe. I'm here. I'm right here. I'll keep you safe."

He holds on to my wrists, his hands hanging there, and he nods, wordlessly.

I lean over and kiss him, slowly, so I can take him all in. His mouth, his tongue, the stubble on his upper lip, his fingers that dig through my hair.

He pulls away from me, his eyes darting across my face. "I know you are," he says hoarsely.

We sit like this, forehead to forehead, in the parking lot until the lights blink out.

Chapter Sixteen

I didn't know it was my last spring with Ella.

You never think that way, that you're going to lose someone. Until you do.

So when I chose to spend my remaining school lunches last year sitting with Carleen and Angelica, occasionally Brent and some other players on the basketball team, I forced myself to believe that Ella was sitting at that random table, basically alone, just to spite me. It was easier to believe that than to face my own cruelty, I guess. Blame her instead of me.

I stood up, cutting the main lunch line to get straight to the ice cream freezer, and on my way back to my table, I paused behind Ella. I sighed audibly.

"Out of breath from such a short walk?" she asked, hardly looking over her shoulder. "You need more cardio."

"I'm sighing because you're sitting here with a person who's reading a book, and another person who can't put their phone down."

"Still more riveting than your crew of winners." She crossed her arms over her chest and took a sip from her juice box. I didn't even bother asking why she had a juice box.

"You can come sit with me. Forget they're even there."

"Funny coming from you."

"Ella."

"You can come sit with me, too, you know," she said, finally turning. She stared at me and kicked the chair beside her to emphasize how empty it was. "There's a seat right here."

My whole table watched me, Carleen and Angelica whispering a few times to each other. "I can't just leave them, Ella."

"No, clearly."

"You're being stubborn to spite me."

"I'm trying to eat my lunch, Cor." She took a bite of her sandwich and turned away from me.

Back at my table, Carleen inched down to make room for me. "Why were you even talking to her? She's so awkward."

Angelica and her boyfriend laughed.

"She's nice," I tried. "And she's been my friend for so long...."

"Well, don't invite her over here. She'll make things uncomfortable."

Beside me, Brent lowered himself and his tray full of nachos. "Don't tell Cor what to do. She can invite whoever she wants to sit with us."

"She was going to invite Ella," said Angelica, leaning forward so she could see Brent more clearly.

"Oh." He rolled his eyes.

"Dude, didn't you go out with her once?" one of his friends asked.

"Only because I wanted to ask her about Cor. She's a fucking freak, why would I want to be seen with her?"

I sat up straight as the table around me laughed. Brent offered me one of his nachos, but I declined. I couldn't stop staring across the cafeteria at my friend, even as everyone else ripped her apart.

"I don't even get why you ever hung out with her," said Angelica.

Carleen leaned her head on my shoulder. "It's okay, we fixed her now. We made her normal."

I resented the idea that I needed to be fixed, or that Ella was some kind of freak, only useful if she could score Brent a date. The longer I sat there, the more complicated things became, and I wished so desperately to sit between the shelves of the library, shoulder to shoulder with Ella, ensconced in the silence of the ocean.

But things would never be that easy with Ella again.

When Lottie found out that Kyle, Mia, and I were planning on going to the food truck fest, she let us all leave headquarters early. We were finished with our paperwork anyway, and there was nothing pressing to do in the afternoon that couldn't wait until tomorrow. Once I climb into the Jeep, I text Mannix.

Cor (12:02 PM): On my way!

Mannix (12:09 PM): Meet me by the fire truck.

Things are easy with Mannix. For the first time in a long time, I'm with someone where the only expectation is to be me. No histories, no futures, only now.

The food truck fest is held in a church parking lot on one of the main roads off Route 6. It's not too difficult to find; swarms of famished lunchgoers mill around from truck to truck, trying to sample as much as their stomachs can manage. There's an artist drawing kid caricatures and another doing face paintings. Down at the opposite end of the parking lot, a huge cherry-red fire truck glistens in the sun, and Mannix and a few of his friends sit at the rear step, eating cheese fries from paper cups.

"Hot wings," says Kyle from behind us. They pause, assessing the length of the line. "Lemme just grab a few, okay? I'll be fast, I swear."

"Take your time," I tell them, standing off to the side with Mia so that no one thinks we're waiting in line, too. I study the different elaborate signs and menus posted around the hot-wings truck. They have eleven different sauces to choose from, plus dips. My eyes rove from one advertisement to the next and settle on a glossy poster for a sauce and dressing contest. Best sauce or dressing wins a grand prize of $5,000. I grab an entry form, fold it up, and stuff it into my crossbody. Mannix's salad dressing would obliterate the competition. But I'm not sure if he'd even be willing to enter. So I can be brave for him.

"Look at these delectable little wingettes!" cries Kyle when they have their order. "Let's go find Mannix so we can sit down and eat."

"He's over by the fire truck," I say, pointing to the massive vehicle.

219

"Hey," says Mia as we cross the lot. She tugs at the hem of my tank top.

"What's up?"

"Noah and I aren't a thing," she says quietly, glancing between me and Kyle. "Not like you and Mannix. So please don't tease me or anything, or make it weird if he's there."

"Of course not," says Kyle, looping their arm into the nook of Mia's. "We'll stare at his amazing hair and toned arms." They pause, sparing me a long look. "Well, maybe not Coriander over here."

"I will admire politely," I decide, my chin in the air, because there's something satisfying about not at all caring for Noah and his toned arms.

Mannix looks up from his cup of fries and then stands to greet us as we approach. "You got out early," he says, one hand wrapping around my waist and pulling me into a kiss.

"I convinced our boss that we should support local first responders by overindulging in fancy fast food."

"Good. Have a cheese fry."

I sift through what remains to find one that's good and coated. "Thank you."

Without being too obvious, I try to observe Mia and Noah's interactions, but they're still kind of nervous, a little shy. Mia more than Noah. I think Noah's trying to find his way in, and I hope he doesn't interpret Mia's shyness as lack of interest.

"Do I see fried avocado tacos?" Kyle asks, their sunglasses slipping down their nose as they try to see more clearly. All that's left of their basket of hot wings are thoroughly cleaned bones. "This way, Mia. We have our next stop." They march arm in arm down the row of food trucks and get in a rather long line of people who require deep-fried avocados on corn tortillas.

"You wanna go with them?" Mannix asks.

"Not yet," I tell him, and he drapes his arm over my shoulders. "Thought I'd follow you around for a while."

"Then follow me around to the barbecue truck."

He takes my hand and we wind through the crowds of people, followed by Noah. He casts an occasional glance over his shoulder to where Mia and Kyle wait in line for tacos, and I wish it didn't feel like betraying Mia to tell him to go over there and give it a shot.

When we get in line, Mannix points to the chalkboard menu posted on the side of the truck with scrolly handwriting in bright pinks and greens. "You've gotta try the pulled pork sandwich."

"You wanna split one with me?" I ask.

He frowns, confused. "No, I really, really don't. But I will absolutely buy you your own."

"You're going to fill me up too fast!" I cry in protest, play-punching him in the arm. "You have to have a plan when you go to one of these events. Like a buffet. You can't waste all your energy on filler, like those stupid fries. Rookie mistake. And you can't overindulge in one item and expect to still have room to sample the rest."

He's still frowning. "I literally don't have this problem, Cor."

I turn back to the truck, studying the menu. "I'm deciding," I tell him, crossing my arms over my chest and tapping my lower lip with my pointer finger. "I'm going with barbecue chicken and a side of cole slaw."

"Solid choice."

"Mannix!"

We both turn to find Jacob two food trucks down, his hands cupped around his mouth to make sure his voice travels far enough. When Mannix makes eye contact, Jacob waves him over.

"What do you want?" I ask him. "Tell me your order, and you can go and talk to Jacob."

"Pulled pork sandwich and potato salad," he replies, and before he trots off, he kisses my cheek.

Now that he's mentioned potato salad, I wonder if it's okay to break my filler rule just this once, because potato salad is worth it. As I contemplate this, Noah comes up beside me. "Are you gonna get potato salad, too?" I ask.

"I love potato salad," he replies.

"Then I guess that's that." I sigh.

"Hey," says Noah, and he nudges my arm with his elbow. "Ignore Jacob. He likes getting shit started."

I blink, trying to understand what Noah is trying to tell me. "What's he trying to get started?"

But before Noah can answer, Jacob trots over. "Hey, man," he says, greeting Noah with a fist bump. "Cor, what's up?"

I give him my usual half a hug, and he stands back, hands in his pockets, shoulders slouched, studying the chalkboard menu.

Tilting my head to the side, I finally ask, "I thought you were gonna talk to Mannix."

Jacob pauses for a moment, then acts as though my statement finally makes sense. "Oh, I did. But I was calling him over for Kayla." He points.

Mannix stands with a few of the other lifeguards, but the girl next to him is someone I don't recognize.

"He's mentioned Kayla, right?"

"Dude," says Noah quietly.

"Do you remember when they were together or whatever?" Jacob completely ignores Noah's plea. "He couldn't keep his hands off her. Not that I blame him, she's hot as hell."

"What can I get you?" asks the woman from the window of the barbecue truck.

My mind is suddenly blank, whatever Mannix wanted to order gone. I start with my own choices. "Hi, can I get one order of the barbecue chicken with potato salad, and, um..." I scan the menu one more time, trying to remind myself of what he asked for. "Oh, the, um, the pulled pork sandwich, also with potato salad."

"Name for the order?"

"Cor," I reply.

She holds out a ticket and gestures for me to join a collection of waiting patrons off to the side of the truck. I have a different view of Mannix from here, and even though she's hanging on him, he's not returning the action, and I'm not even mad.

I'm left wondering if I wanted something more from Mannix, when I should have ordered my priorities. Maybe he shouldn't have been so high on the list when I'm still trying to make it up to Ella. Maybe convincing myself he was a distraction was only distracting me from my real feelings for him, and now I'm left standing here on the outside.

"Ignore Jacob," says Noah again, coming up beside me and digging into a free sample of spicy barbecue chicken from a little paper cup. "Kayla's not you. I see how he looks at you. He's being polite with her, you know?"

"Noah, honestly. I've heard her mentioned before, but I don't even know who she is. It's not a big deal."

"Cool." He holds out his cup of chicken. "Want a bite?"

"No, thanks." My stomach roils, and I hope he can't hear the gurgling.

Mannix inches out of the girl's embrace and begins heading back over to us, followed by a trail of the people he was talking to, including the girl who was hanging on him. Of course Mannix has a past. That's okay, I tell myself. My feelings have to do with me, not him. It's not like he was a priest prior to meeting me.

"Cor," says Mannix. "I want you to meet my friend Kayla."

"Hi!" she says. She has on a hot-pink tank top, which glows against her olive skin, and she's toned in places I didn't realize one could be toned. Her deep brown eyes are warm and curious, and she has a thick ponytail of chestnut hair with golden highlights at the top of her head. "I'm Kayla." She reaches out to shake my hand.

"Hey, I'm Coriander."

"Mannix just told me all about you."

It's strange the way this makes me nervous, this shared conversation about me.

"Kayla used to lifeguard with us," Mannix says. "She's the one who got me into it."

"He was a natural."

Mannix looks humbly down at his feet.

Any knack I have for small talk is out the window, and I feel like my tongue doesn't know how to form words anymore. I want to slink away, to hide somewhere.

"Hey," says Mia, coming up beside me. "Check your phone." She shoves the rest of a half-eaten taco into her mouth as Kyle joins us.

I pull it out of my crossbody and shade the screen so I can read the text more clearly. Lottie sent us a group text about a seal caught with fishing line around its neck. They're about to disentangle and want to know if we'd like to be there.

"We can go," says Mia. "I don't think it's an emergency. You can stay here with Mannix."

He's standing close beside me, and the weight of my decision presses upon me.

"I have to go," I say quickly. I remember to pretend to be flustered, like I just received news that somewhat annoys me and is ruining my afternoon plans. Because that's what Mannix would expect, and maybe it won't hurt his feelings if he thinks it's out of my control.

"Right now?" He sulks, then looks down at his watch. "You just got here."

"Order for Cor!" calls the woman from the food truck.

"Do you wanna get that?" I ask, thumbing toward our plates of food. "We were called back to headquarters for a seal."

"You didn't even eat yet," he says, pacing over to the window and grabbing our order. "Do they need you specifically?" he asks when he gets back, glancing at Mia and Kyle. They both divert their attention quickly.

"She sent the text to all of us," I say, and I show him my screen, like he's actually going to read it, like he's going to care. "You know I'm still trying to impress Lottie. How would it look if Mia and Kyle showed up but I didn't?"

Mannix stands there, holding the food. "Do you want to eat before you go?"

"No, I should run." I turn to Noah. "You want my chicken? You liked your sample so much."

He looks more flustered than I do, and his attention darts between me and Jacob. Jacob babbles endlessly to Kayla, like nothing at all is going on. "Yeah, I'll eat the chicken."

"I'll talk to you later, okay?" I say quietly to Mannix.

"Yeah, whatever." He turns toward the picnic tables and brings his food with him. Noah sits down across from him.

"Oh, are you leaving, Coriander?" Kayla asks. But before I can answer, she waves. "It was nice to meet you."

"You, too." And I dash from the church parking lot.

"Cor, you okay?" Kyle calls from a few steps behind me.

"I'm good, just a little warm. I'll meet you up there."

Inside the Jeep, the hot air suffocates me, and I roll down the windows, rubbing at my eyes and grateful for the cool breeze that sifts through the stifling interior. I'm sorry I even came today. I put the Jeep into reverse, then slam on the brake when I almost hit a sedan coasting through the lot behind me. They stop and yell something obscene, throwing their hands in the air for effect.

"I didn't actually hit you, keep moving," I shout out the window with a roll of my eyes.

I drive for a little while with the windows down, not even bothering to turn on the AC. Cruising like this up to Provincetown is reaffirming and purposeful. It's not desperate or pathetic, and I can forget that I've allowed Mannix a place in my heart and a license to do damage if that's what he wants. Or even if he doesn't. Even if he wants to be a little reckless with it. Maybe I should pay more attention to my own priorities, anyway.

Chapter Seventeen

"This," says Noah, "is not going to be pleasant."

We stand in the parking lot of Newcomb Hollow Beach, next to the collection of random objects we're apparently going to use to erect a tent and a table. His hands on his hips, Noah stares down at the pile, then scratches his forehead.

"We should get started, though," I say. "It's going to be a big beach day, and I want to make sure we're up and running when people arrive."

I've been assigned as the Marine Research and Conservation Alliance shark expert for the day, talking to beachgoers about the biology of great white sharks and their growing numbers off Cape Cod's coast. Noah's their contact for shark safety and the rules for Wellfleet beaches. Kyle took on Head of the Meadow in Truro, and Mia's down in Eastham at Nauset Light.

"Okay, you hold this," says Noah, lifting a pole and handing it to me. "And I'll grab one of these...." He picks something up, but I don't know what its purpose is. "Maybe not. Maybe one of these."

I follow his directions because I'm a pretty decent helper when it comes to putting things together, but I don't read directions very well.

"You talk to Mannix recently?" Noah asks as casually as possible.

I haven't talked to him since I left the food truck fest two days ago. Maybe because I don't know what to say, or maybe I'm just embarrassed.

You're embarrassed? Ella asks me incredulously.

I try to shake her memory away. I don't want to think about her right now. I don't want to be reminded how much this is my typical method of operation. Avoid everyone when I've embarrassed myself. Pretend it's the other person's problem when someone is upset with me.

We stood in the driveway of her parents' house, me leaning on the door of Rhett's Jeep, and Ella holding the leash of her golden retriever, Charlie. "Embarrassed about what?" she asked, but it felt more like a dare. Like she was daring me to say it out loud, to acknowledge her.

"That you're sitting with those kids at lunch," I said. "Do you hang out with them outside of school, too?"

"I don't know, are *you* embarrassed by the kids you sit with at lunch?"

She knew I was embarrassed, and she wasn't going to let me off that easily. So I didn't reply.

I kicked an acorn that had fallen from the oak tree above me, unable to meet her glare.

"So you're not embarrassed that you never talk to me anymore? Or that you have this new group of seriously toxic friends?" She plugged an earbud into her ear but left the other hanging near her neck so she could hear my denial.

"I invited you to sit with us!" I cried.

"I didn't want to sit with them, Cor. I never wanted to sit with them. I don't want to pretend to like a group of people I have nothing in common with just because they suddenly take an interest in who I'm making out with between third and fourth period behind the junior/senior stairwell."

"That's not fair," I said in a low voice.

"No, it's not." She started walking down the driveway toward the one-way road that bypassed her parents' meticulous Dutch colonial in the woods. "You would rather be seen with them than confront and deal with what's really bothering you."

"How do you know what's really bothering me?"

She swerved, still amazed by how dense I pretended to be. "I've known you for almost ten years, Cor. I know how sensitive you are, and how much you want everyone to like you. How much shit those girls have put you through, making you feel absurdly smart or like a freak. Because they've made me feel the same way. You so desperately want them to think you're worthwhile, and you believe, you honestly believe, that hanging out with them is going to solve your problems. But how can anyone think you're worthwhile if you don't think it yourself?"

My chest heaved at this and tears brimmed in the corners of my eyes. "Then what's so worthwhile about me, Ella?"

She shook her head, popping in the other earbud. "Right

now? I don't know. Because someone worthwhile wouldn't abandon the people who want to be there for them." She jogged off and disappeared down the road, only the jangle of Charlie's collar and tags echoing behind her.

"Coriander?"

I snap my attention back to Noah. "Hm?"

"I asked if you've talked to Mannix recently, but you were watching the ocean."

I was. The waves crash along the shoreline below us, and I spot Mannix by the lifeguard stand. He's talking with two other guards, his arm resting against one of the rungs.

"No, actually," I say. "I think we've both been busy this week."

"That sucks," says Noah quietly. "Cor, I'm sorry if—"

"Noah," I say swiftly, smiling to soften his reaction. "It's okay. Not your fault. Also not a big deal. Shit gets in the way sometimes. I'll text him later."

After a solid half hour of trying to put this tent together, we're finally at the point where I'm organizing our table under the shade and Noah is greeting beachgoers, alerting them to our purpose here today.

"We're here to answer any questions you might have about our blossoming great white shark population," says Noah, handing out pamphlets to passersby.

"Blossoming," I say with an impressed nod. "Nice touch."

"I thought so."

Several families exit their cars, laden with folding beach chairs, tote bags and coolers filled with lunches, and buckets and shovels. A few of them pause at our great white display, especially the little kids.

Below the cliffs, Mannix climbs down from the lifeguard chair, pulling his white muscle tank up and over his head and throwing it back up to the girl at the top. He grabs one of the paddleboards, tucks it under his left arm, and strides out into the surf. No fear, no hesitation. He drops the paddleboard, launching it out in front of him, then hops on, sitting on his knees, his arms pumping through the waves. Once he's out past the breakers, he flattens out onto his belly and coasts across the surface.

"I'm not gonna lie to you, Cor," says Noah, flipping through the pages of the pamphlet. "And don't take this the wrong way." He grimaces at the image of a great white tossing a gray seal into the air. "But the only reason I volunteered to do this was because I thought Mia was going to be here today."

I wince. "I'm sorry. We were each assigned a beach without any input."

"I think Mannix wanted to work with you today, but he didn't say anything when he saw I already volunteered. Probably intimidated by the effect I have on women."

I plaster the most dedicated smile I can to my face and nod my head in agreement. "Yeah, that's for sure it."

But no matter how many times Noah attempts to reassure me that Mannix would have liked to spend the day talking sharks, it doesn't erase the fact that he's out in the ocean, and later, talking to different families as he patrols the beach, laughing with his coworkers, playing a game of paddle ball with some kids.

I return my attention to a group of older beachgoers who

intently study our great white handout. They've gathered in droves now because one of the tagged great whites recently pinged the buoy that drifts offshore. There won't be any swimming for another hour.

"But I want to see seals," says a sweet older lady with huge black sunglasses. She clutches a map of Cape Cod's outer beaches.

"If you travel a little bit farther north, you'll find a spot where they haul out in Truro," I reply.

I stare out over the cliffs, watching the people dip their feet in the frigid North Atlantic.

"Will we see any sharks there?" she asks. "I thought I'd see one here considering we can't get in the water for another fifty-two minutes."

"Maybe," I reply, trying to appease her. "But do you really want to see the sharks hunting the seals? It gets a little bloody...."

"Fascinating," says the woman. She turns away from me, her attention drawn by the howl of a siren careening up to the parking lot.

"I wonder what's wrong?" asks her husband.

Noah and I step out from under the tent, and he heads toward the top of the cliffs to assess the situation.

I follow him and the rest of the group, reluctantly, because I don't understand how something's possible suffering can be interesting to anyone. "Maybe we can talk a little more about the gray seal population?" I propose, only no one's listening. "We can talk about the..." My shoulders droop. "The seals."

Too late. Two of the lifeguards help an elderly woman up the path and place her on one of the benches near the restrooms. They speak gently to her as the EMTs get out of the ambulance.

And Mannix appears.

"Excuse me," I say, elbowing through my small crowd. "I know that person."

They probably assume that I think I know the ill woman, when in reality, I make my way toward the hot lifeguard in his new Oakley sunglasses.

"Mannix, hi," I say.

"Hey," he says, softly touching my elbow in greeting but swiftly moving past me.

I stand stupidly in place and watch him help the old woman into the ambulance. He stands at the door as they situate her, then edges away with the other lifeguards. They stand in a huddle, but I can't hear what they're talking about.

I take a step closer, like a needy puppy. "Are you, um, busy today?"

He turns back to me, pushing his sunglasses up into his hair, and he stares. "Cor, I'm at work."

It's funny that when he wanted to make out with me while he renovated the bathroom, it didn't matter that he was at work. I shake it off because I can feel some of the onlookers staring at me. Or maybe I try to shake the feeling because it's ugly. To want his attention when he won't give it, when he can't give it.

"Oh, okay. So maybe we'll talk later."

He nods, turning back to the group. Once the ambulance drives away, he returns to the lifeguard stand down at the bottom of the cliff. I spend the rest of the afternoon feigning interest in the buoy that's kept swimmers out of the water for most of the afternoon. Apparently our shark friend is patrolling the high seas for blubbery snacks.

At the end of the day, as the families abandon the beach for the trek home so that they can shower and get ready for dinner, I collect my shark paraphernalia and organize everything in the back of the Jeep. Maddie comes up and helps Noah and me disassemble the tent, and we tie everything up neatly and leave it near the porta-potty. Justin said he'd be around to collect everything with the big truck, which is good because I don't feel like driving all the way up to P-town before going home to Uncle Jack's. Especially because it's taco night.

Tired, salty, and feeling my skin tight and sticky from sweat, I climb into the Jeep, leaning back against the headrest and closing my eyes for a moment before I pull out of the parking lot.

A gentle tap on my driver's-side window rouses me from my daze. Mannix waits for me to roll it down.

"Hey," I say, my heart rate speeding up.

"Got a surprise for you," he says, reaching into the pocket of his board shorts and retrieving something he hides in his fist. Slowly, his fingers spread out, revealing a perfect gray pebble with a single white vein of marble crossing its center. Years being tumbled in the waves have left its surface smooth, almost silky.

I stare at it, my thoughts jumbling together so anything I might have said feels stupid and pointless even in my own brain.

"It's the pebble from the last beach. Race Point. For your collection." He allows the pebble to roll from his palm into mine.

I close my hand around it, feel its warmth against my skin. "Remember?"

Nodding, I finally reply, "Yes. Yes, I remember. Thank you. I..." I look him in the eyes. "I guess I didn't expect you to."

He grins. "Of course I did. I remember everything."

I lift from the driver's seat, my hands on the armrest of the car and my mouth finding his instantly. He's surprised at first, probably because no one would suspect that a pebble would warrant this kind of emotional response, but soon he relaxes, his right hand weaving itself into my hair.

"Thanks for that," he murmurs against my lips.

"Can we hang out tomorrow?" I ask him.

"Yeah, of course. I'm here until five, but I'll text you after."

"Okay," I say.

He kisses me again and then taps the door of the Jeep as he takes a step back. "See you tomorrow."

"Can't wait."

Chapter Eighteen

"Wow," says Mia. She sits in the passenger seat of the Jeep, reading through the entry form for the sauce contest I'm entering Mannix in. "Five thousand dollars is a big prize."

"He deserves it," I say, pulling into the parking lot of the post office. "And he'd never enter himself, so I'll do it for him."

"And he won't be upset?"

"Upset about what?"

Mia shrugs.

I take the form from her hands, checking to make sure I've filled everything out correctly. I gave them Mannix's name and address but included my email and phone number. When he wins, I want it to be a surprise. I want to be the person to give it to him. I fold the form in half and tuck it into the box with the carefully wrapped and sealed bottle of salad dressing.

There's no line in the post office, so I pace right to the counter, and send his dressing across the country to whoever's going to judge it. Back in the Jeep, Mia and I stop at Marshside Deli to pick up some sandwiches for lunch, and while she places the order, I browse for some snacks. I get the usual, and make sure to pick up some Gatorade for Mannix, as requested. But my gaze is quickly captured by the stack of newspapers for sale by the door.

Fraction's beautiful flukes, missing a section, raked by the scars of orca teeth, and pulling the heavy weight of nets and rope, grace the front page of the local Cape Cod paper. I grab a copy for myself and toss it on the counter with our sandwiches.

"Oh man," says Mia when she sees.

"This can't be the front page we leave her with this summer," I say, and I take a deep breath to steady the speed of my words. "I refuse to let this be how the world remembers her."

"Then that's that," says Mia. "You spoke your truth into the universe. Way to manifest."

When we get to White Crest, the lot is almost full, and the sun sparkles across the ocean before us.

"I don't even remember the last time I went to the beach just to go to the beach," says Mia with a contented sigh. "And, you know, not to save some sea fowl or clean up trash or disentangle a seal."

"It's been one hell of a summer, hasn't it?" I say, finding a parking spot in the back of the lot. We jump out and grab our beach bags. Mia makes sure to remember our cooler full of drinks and sandwiches, and I take responsibility for the awkward umbrella I hope doesn't impale any of the cars parked close to us.

At the bottom of the cliff, we inch along the outskirts of families on beach blankets and kids dashing through the sand and into the surf.

"Hey!" calls one of the lifeguards. "We need to confiscate that cooler!"

Mia immediately blushes as Noah jumps from the lifeguard stand and jogs over to us.

"I'm going to have to see a warrant," I tell him as he approaches.

"Fresh out, but I might be willing to find one for a snack." He turns and shouts over his shoulder. "Mannix! Lunch!"

"What makes you think we brought you lunch?" asks Mia, offering him a flirty little eyebrow wiggle, and I'm so proud of her right now.

"Well, let's see." Noah pops open the lid to the cooler as Mannix trots up beside me, leaning down for a quick kiss.

"Did you remember to bring me water?" he asks.

"Yup, plus a lime cucumber Gatorade."

Noah stands up straight. "Lime cucumber Gatorade? What the hell is that?"

"My beach beverage of choice," says Mannix, grabbing his green drink from the cooler and unscrewing the cap. He takes three long chugs and then sighs, wiping his mouth with the back of his hand.

I shade my eyes, scanning the beach and watching people dive in and out of the waves. My first order of business is a swim. "It's so hot out."

"You get freckles when you're out in the sun too long," he says quietly, then takes another sip of Gatorade.

"So do you."

"No, I don't."

"You do, too! All across your nose." I poke him in the cheek, and he swats my hand away.

"Guys, you're gonna make me lose my appetite," says Noah, staring.

"Take your sandwiches and get back to work." Mia hands them both their wrapped lunches.

"Thanks." Noah stares at his sandwich, then looks up at Mia. "That was nice of you to think of me."

This newly tense moment is a little too much for me to bear, so I chime in, "We're gonna go set up that way." I point to a clearing to the left of the lifeguard stand. "If you need us. We'll be eating our lunch, and I brought a riveting book to pass the time."

"What are you reading?" Mannix asks.

I whip out my copy of Hal Whitehead's *Sperm Whales: Social Evolution in the Ocean*.

Mannix nods, squinting. "Sperm whales, huh?"

"Sperm whales."

"Because…?"

"Not what you think."

"Okay, good. Don't forget to hydrate." He lingers for a little bit while Noah marches back to the lifeguard stand and Mia and I set up our beach blankets.

"What's up?" I ask, struggling to shove the umbrella into the sand deep enough to keep it upright.

"Here, lemme help you." Mannix takes the pole from me and somehow manages to accomplish what I could not. When it stands on its own, he opens it fully. "Ta-da."

"Thanks." I bend down, setting my book on the seat of my

folding chair, and pull my tank top over my head. Mannix still doesn't leave. "Are you okay?" I ask. "Or do you want to know more about sperm whales?"

He scratches the back of his head. "I wanted you to know that Kayla's here today."

I haven't thought about Kayla since the day at the beach when Mannix got me my last pebble, but she keeps surfacing when I least expect her.

"And you had kind of a weird reaction when I introduced you to her."

I crane my neck so I can see over Mannix's shoulder, and sure enough, Kayla's up by the lifeguard stand, chatting with the people there.

"Cor?"

I glance up at him, his face searching mine for some kind of sign that this isn't a big deal, and it shouldn't be, he's right.

"It's fine," I assure him.

"She wanted to talk to you about your internship, but she didn't want it to be awkward." He takes a deep breath. "It would mean a lot to me if you got to know the other people who matter to me."

I bite the inside of my cheek, his words making my insides flutter. I'm both flattered and terrified all at once, and I don't know what to say. I manage, "No, not awkward at all."

He relaxes, reaching for my hand. "Good."

Behind Mannix and out on one of the sandbars, his neighbor's nephew, Jackson, tosses a Nerf football back and forth with a few of his friends, boys that look to be a little older than he is. They splash through the shallow water, taking turns retrieving the ball. It's some version of Monkey in the Middle, and

Jackson is the monkey. They shout and scream at one another on the sandbar, blaming someone for losing the ball to the sea.

"Go and get it!" they cry, pointing for Jackson to go out into the waves and fetch the ball.

"Do you wanna come talk to her after lunch maybe?" Mannix asks.

"Do we have to make a plan or something?"

"No, we don't have to make a plan. It would mean a lot to me for you to get to know each other before she leaves to go back to California next week."

His words have roots, and I'm tangled in them. I don't want to get to know Kayla, especially when she's not even going to be here for the rest of the summer. This is exactly what I shouldn't have done. I shouldn't have let myself feel so much, get this involved, become a part of someone's life when I'm still flailing in my own. But I did, and it's too late to go back.

I should reply to Mannix, I know, but I'm still watching the boys playing. Jackson hesitantly steps off the sandbar to retrieve the ball, which is being sucked out to sea, and he loses his balance, drops down too quickly. My stomach lurches.

"Mannix," I say.

"What's up?" His arms are crossed over his chest.

"Mannix, behind you."

Jackson's little face fights to stay above the surface, and this isn't what I expected drowning to look like. He's struggling, I can tell, but it isn't loud, and he doesn't flail. He shouts up to the sky, his mouth laboring to avoid incoming waves.

Mannix turns to see what I'm pointing at. "Shit. Rip current." He jolts toward the lifeguard stand and grabs a torpedo buoy. I follow him, but keep my distance from the surf.

By now, a few of the other lifeguards have gathered around. People stand helplessly in the sand. "I've got him!" Mannix shouts at someone who looks like he could be Jackson's dad or uncle.

"Don't fight the current!" Kayla yells, cupping her hands around her mouth, but Jackson doesn't appear to hear her. "Swim along the shoreline!"

He continues to dip below the waves, his face appearing less and less frequently. Jackson's body bobs under and then pops back up, a gurgling cry erupting from his throat before the sea swallows him again.

I dash back to my blanket, rummaging through my stuff until I find my cell phone. I have to dial 911, I think. I have to tell someone, I have to do something. I have to do something because the last time this happened, I didn't. I wasted time, I thought too much.

"What's going on?" asks Mia, her voice high-pitched and panicked.

"Rip current," I say tersely. I keep trying to dial the phone, but my hands shake violently.

"Cor, stop," she says. "Put the phone down. The lifeguards can handle this."

I stare at the phone, something I use every day, but right now, I can't figure it out. I can't make it work when I need it or remember which button will unlock it. It's like I've never used it before. "I have to help. I have to do something."

"You don't!" she cries, grabbing me by my forearms and steadying me. "You can't do anything. That's not your job."

Mia grabs my hand, and we sprint to the water. Mannix emerges from the waves, carrying Jackson, and his body flops over Mannix's arms like he has no bones. His little arms flail at his sides, and Mannix drops him on the sand. He begins CPR, but the boy doesn't respond.

Time after time, Mannix compresses the boy's chest and then administers mouth-to-mouth, but Jackson still doesn't respond.

"Come on, come on," Mannix mutters as he works.

"Easy, Mannix," says Noah. The static buzz of voices on their walkie-talkies grates on my nerves, makes me jumpy.

Jackson's body lurches upward, and Mannix eases him onto his side. He spits up sand and water, choking and gurgling, but he's breathing. He starts to cry, and Mannix supports him, his hands on Jackson's back as he speaks softly to comfort him.

My breath comes out in a whoosh that's both a cry and relief. The crowd cheers and claps.

"We need to get him up to the parking lot," says Mannix.

Noah and Maddie appear with the stretcher, and they help Mannix secure him.

"I want to follow the ambulance to the hospital when it gets here," says Mannix. "Cor, come with me."

"Me?" I say.

"Yeah, come on."

I don't want to go to the hospital. I want so desperately to go home and hide from all of this. Because that's what I do. I walk away. I'm good at that. But I follow Mannix anyway, up the cliff to the parking lot, where he greets the EMTs and explains what happened. I wait in his truck with the windows down.

"Are you okay to drive?" I ask once he hops up into the driver's seat.

"Yes." He gets in, closes the door, but when he tries to turn on the engine, it falters a bit. "Jesus Christ," he mumbles, and slaps the steering wheel with his palm.

"It's okay," I say quietly.

"It's not fucking okay, so don't try to calm me down."

I press my lips together and give him a quick nod, swiping at an escaped tear running down my cheek.

He leans back in the driver's seat, rubbing his eyes and trying to slow his breath. "I'm sorry. I'm sorry I snapped. You didn't deserve that." He turns the key in the ignition one more time, and the engine roars to life.

I stare out the window as we follow the ambulance down to Hyannis.

We stay for hours at the hospital, until Mannix is positive Jackson is fine, leaving the boy with his family; then he drives me back to Uncle Jack's house. When we pull in the driveway, my Jeep is magically sitting there. I pull up my text messages.

> **Mia (3:39 PM):** I drove your Jeep back to your uncle's house. Noah dropped me off at home. Text me when you're back so I know you're ok.
>
> **Cor (4:01 PM):** We're back. Thanks for doing that, you're the best.

"Sorry," says Mannix, putting the truck into park. "I completely forgot about your car."

"It's fine," I say, quietly, unbuckling myself. "It's here now."

He sits motionless, his hands still on the steering wheel.

"Do you want to come in for a little bit?"

Taking a deep breath, he finally nods his head and turns the truck off.

The house is empty, and Uncle Jack left me a note on the kitchen island letting me know he's showing two houses and that we're ordering pizza for dinner tonight, and to text him the toppings I want.

"You wanna stay for pizza?" I ask, turning to see where Mannix has disappeared to.

"Sure," he says. His head is in the fridge as he rummages around for something. When he extricates himself from behind the door, he has one of Uncle Jack's fancy beers in his hand, the kind he saves for company to make it look like he knows beer and doesn't just stock his fridge with brands he's never heard of.

Mannix pops the cap and takes a long swig, then paces over to the living room and collapses on the sectional sofa in front of the big screen TV.

"What toppings do you want?" I lean against the frame of the door, phone in hand.

Mannix shrugs. "Sausage and pepper."

"K." I text this reply to Uncle Jack. "You wanna watch something on TV? The remote is on the coffee table."

Staring at the blank screen, he takes a sip of his beer and shrugs. "I'm good."

I cross the room and sit down next to him on the sofa, tuck my feet up under my knees, and lean against his side. I lay my head on his shoulder. It takes him about a minute, but finally, his cheek rests on the top of my head, and his right hand traces its way down my thigh and cups my knee.

"What happened today?" he asks quietly.

"You rescued Jackson from drowning. You saved his life."

I feel his head shake in my hair. "No, I mean with Kayla. What happened? Did I do something wrong?"

I close my eyes. I didn't even remember what had happened with Kayla. "No, you didn't do anything wrong."

"Then tell me what happened." He leans back, looking me in the eyes. "Because I feel like I almost pushed you into something you didn't want to do, and that wasn't the goal. I want you to be a part of things. The places that matter to me, the people who matter to me, or mattered, I guess." He shrugs.

My heart pinches at this. "I didn't want to talk to her," I say quietly. "I didn't want to get to know her or see what she was like or what she used to mean to you. Because then suddenly she'd be real, and I'd..."

He waits for more, but I don't know what to say right away.

"You know how you literally never let anyone down?"

Scoffing, he turns to the window and takes another sip of beer. "That's not true."

"Yes, it is."

"I let my dad down every damn day I don't take over his boat and spend the rest of my life fishing for lobster." He shakes his head. "I almost let Jackson down. I wasn't even paying attention. He could have died."

"Stop it. You saved his life." I touch his cheek, turning his attention back to me. "You don't let anyone down. Not your parents, not your coworkers, or your friends, or Jackson, or me. You don't even let my pebble collection down!"

He lets out a soft puff of laughter, then pauses before he asks, "So how are you any different?"

"I'm not you," I say quietly. "Not at all. I'm always terrified of letting everyone down. I never feel like I'm enough, and somehow I always manage to prove it. And I panicked the other day when Kayla showed up. I found out about her and then suddenly she appeared, and I had no time to process. I didn't want to meet her. If I never met her, then I wouldn't know how I compare or what I won't live up to."

He studies me. "I don't compare you to Kayla. I don't compare you to anyone. You shouldn't, either."

"I'm trying not to."

"Kayla and I..." He trails off. "I guess we dated. But I always knew she and I would never work out. Whatever we had hardly even began, and neither of us is upset about that."

I nod against his arm.

"Besides, who have you let down?" He adjusts so that he can wrap his pinned arm around me, and I rest against his chest, the beating of his heart thrumming in my ear. "Your parents?"

"No," I reply. "Not my parents. Lottie this summer, but I think I'm winning her back now."

"Mm-hmm."

"But definitely Ella," I add. I should have mentioned her first. "Ella on too many occasions to count."

"It couldn't have been that bad."

Bad enough, I think. Bad enough that she walked into the sea to escape my company, and she never stepped foot on dry land again.

"I started dating the guy she had a crush on since third grade, and I didn't even like him that much."

Mannix is quiet. "Okay, well that kind of sucks, I'll admit it."

I sit up straight, tucking my hair behind my ear and pulling my legs up so that I sit crisscross, facing him.

"Why'd you date him if you didn't like him?"

I shrug. "To prove that I could. Because I felt ignored for so long, and then suddenly everyone wanted to hang out with me, and everyone wanted to know what it was like to be with Brent Tompkins."

"I get that." He leans back against the sofa, his eyelids drooping and his smile lazy and soft. "So what was it like being with Brent Tompkins?"

I laugh down at my lap. "Um, he was a sloppy kisser. And honestly, anytime we were together, it never lasted long enough for me to find out."

"Oof." Mannix winces. "Wow."

"He was super selfish, we had nothing in common, and by the time we broke up, I had already lost Ella. Our friendship was too shattered to piece back together. Sometimes..." I allow myself to trail off, to think before I speak. "Sometimes I feel like I'm the one who drove her into the water, you know? Like the only place she could escape me was in the ocean."

His hand finds my knee again, and he traces circles with his thumb. "I'm sorry. Do you still feel that way?"

"I'm trying not to," I say, but my senses are overwhelmed by the endless circles. "I keep trying to find ways to make it up to her. To be the friend she deserved. The one she thought she had."

"I don't want to make you feel that way," he tells me quietly. "You don't have to prove yourself to me, okay? You just have to be here."

"I'm here," I promise.

He doesn't reply this time; instead, he runs his hand along my calf. Up and down. Slowly.

I can't remember what I was saying, and maybe more importantly, I can't remember what I was feeling. I can only feel his hand on my leg, and that's just what I want. Some weight is lifted, and the lightness of feeling is intoxicating.

I run my fingers through his hair, and he closes his eyes, though his lids flutter with every caress. I inch closer and kiss him, softly on the lips, to see how he'll respond. His mouth is cold and hoppy, and he watches me for a moment. Then his hand is in my hair, his mouth finding mine again, and he pushes his tongue past my lips. I rise up on my knees, straddle his lap, my hands on his shoulders. Biting his lip, I make him suck in a coarse breath, and suddenly he slows, his eyes opening, his fingers trailing down my arm. I kiss his wrist.

"Maybe not now, Cor."

I don't understand how his mouth can say one thing but his whole body begs to differ. "Don't you want to?"

He leans his head back on the sofa, and his eyes are soft and thoughtful. A slice of residual sunlight illuminates the stubble on his face. "Yeah, I want to," he whispers as I brush my lips against his. "But I'm not in the right place right now."

"We could go up to my room," I offer.

He laughs at this, his hand coming to rest below my breast on my rib. "I'm in a weird place, Cor."

Doesn't matter anyway. The latch on the back door slips open, and Uncle Jack clatters into the kitchen and drops his keys and a few grocery bags on the island. "Cor?" he calls.

I climb off Mannix. "Be right there," I reply.

"I have some groceries to put away."

Taking a deep breath, I glance over at Mannix. He sits up straight, then leans his elbows on his knees.

"I thought we were having pizza."

"We are tonight." Uncle Jack pops his head into the living room. "Oh, hey, Mannix. Glad you're staying for pizza."

"Thanks for inviting me, Mr. Sutton."

"But the groceries are for the storm they keep talking about. I wanted to stock up, and I grabbed a few items for Mrs. Mackenzie. Come on, up and at 'em. Help me unload, Mannix. Earn that pizza."

"On it." He stands and stretches, then holds out his hand to help me up.

"You okay?" I ask before we join Uncle Jack in the kitchen.

"Yeah, I'm fine. No worries." He saunters out of the living room and begins organizing vegetables on the kitchen counter.

Chapter Nineteen

Sometimes my guilt, my anxiety, my loneliness, manifest themselves in the hazy darkness of near morning and perch at the end of my bed. I'll wake in the middle of the night to see her sitting there, scrutinizing me as I sleep, I'm sure she was, her hands folded in her lap, in the white dress she wore to the Snow Ball in December of our sophomore year. She was cold the whole night, but she didn't bring a sweater.

I'm never afraid. My head remains on the pillow, and we silently observe each other. I drink in the sight of her, but I don't try to speak or tell her I'm sorry, nothing that might scare her away. Besides, I know she won't hear me. It's too late for that. Her nearness, though, is a comfort I never realize I need until it presents itself. Like if I stare at her long enough, she'll be real again.

But when I wake after dawn, when the searing light of day and reality pierces through the curtains, she's never there. I'm on my own, and whatever she's left for me, I have that to get me through. It's not a lot. It could have been more. But that's on me.

It's the perfect start to an August day. Commercial Street is still hushed, its morning demeanor in stark contrast with its nighttime antics, and my only companions are the pigeons that so patiently wait for me to drop a crumb of my breakfast as I walk into MRCA headquarters.

I spend the majority of my day in the office, answering the phone while most of the team is out on the water. I want to be here anyway, in case someone spots Fraction, in case they attempt another disentanglement. But she hasn't been seen for days, and my hope for her welfare is starting to disintegrate. I try not to think about her, try not to visualize the way her body would slip from the surface of the water, engulfed by the North Atlantic, nothing she can do but succumb to the weight that's pulling her down.

Last night, I took the newspaper with her flukes as the cover story and began cutting it up. Disassembling the truth to create my own quiet reality—a world where Fraction isn't something to be pitied, but a success, a creature to admire. A catalyst. By the time midnight appeared on the face of the clock on my nightstand, I had a scrapbook filled with words and images that showcased Fraction in her most beautiful light.

At the end of the afternoon, I journey to the souvenir shack on the pier to help Kyle clean up the displays. We finish just as the sky begins to darken and Justin and Lottie come in off the boat.

"Any sign of Fraction?" I ask hopefully.

"The seas were raging, Cor," says Justin, shaking his head. "The outer bands of this hurricane are killer. Even if we did find her, there was no way we were gonna be able to help."

"I understand."

As Lottie passes me, she squeezes my shoulder. "Don't lose hope yet."

"Trying not to."

"It's going to storm, group," says Lottie. "Justin and I are going to drive Dr. Mulroney back to his hotel in Orleans before it gets really bad, so why don't you both head home for the day?"

"Sounds good," Kyle says as they gather what remains on the sidewalk.

Once everything is cleaned up, I wave goodbye to Kyle and trot up the road toward the Jeep. A rumble of thunder overhead sends people off Commercial Street and into the nearest shop or restaurant. Raindrops splatter on my bare shoulders, and I quicken my pace.

I'm almost home free, at the door of the Jeep, riffling through my tote for my keys, when the sky opens up and drenches me. "Oh, come on." I dig deeper, checking the zipped side pockets, but no such luck. "Where the hell are my keys?"

The rain makes it more difficult to see, but I give up on the notion that they're hiding within my belongings. I drop to my knees, ducking under the car. I circle it, checking the back. I walk up the street a little, not that I was even there, and I check the sidewalk that leads to headquarters.

Nowhere.

I pull on the front door, but it's locked, of course, and when I peek through the window, cupping my hands around my eyes, I see my problem. I left my keys on my desk. My car keys and the keys to the building. Maybe Justin and Lottie will come back. I plop down on the chair beside the window, the rain streaming off the roof and into the potted plants beside me. I'm soaked, and I begin to shiver. The storm's brought in a cold front, and my clothes cling damply to me.

I pull out my cell phone, buried within the confines of my tote.

Cor (4:22 PM): Hey Lottie. Coming back to the office by any chance?

A long pause before a response flashes across the screen.

Lottie (4:26 PM): Already headed down 6. Dr. Mulroney needs to get back to Orleans by five. Why, what's up?
Cor (4:27 PM): Nothing, no big deal. It can wait till Monday.

Lies. I look at the time. Surveying the road, I see that no one is around. The soft glow from inside the Sea Ghost is more than inviting, and I know Mannix would drive me home. But there's no way I'm going in there now, looking like a drowned rat. I pull my feet up onto the chair, making myself into as small a shivering ball as possible, and wait until his shift is over.

"Jesus, Cor!"

His voice jostles me. I must have nodded off, and Mannix gallops down the sidewalk, his hoodie held up over his head as a makeshift umbrella.

"What are you doing here?" he asks once he's up on the porch and under the overhang.

"My keys are in there." I thumb toward the window. "Aren't you working?"

"My shift just ended. Come on, let's make a run for my truck."

He includes me under his hoodie, and I scrunch against his side. But it's pointless. The rain is coming down so hard, I'm soaked through, and now he is, too.

We scramble into his truck, breathing heavily as he turns the engine and jacks up the heat. The windows fog over as we wait for the warmth to permeate our clothes.

"Where are Lottie and Justin?"

I swallow. "They had to drive one of the other biologists back to Orleans. They were already gone by the time I even thought to text her."

"What about your uncle?"

"He's in Boston. Real estate convention." I close my eyes. "I'm so cold."

"Okay," he says, turning to me and rubbing his hands up and down my arms. "How about I take you home and make you dinner?"

"I don't know what's in the fridge." My lower jaw trembles uncontrollably.

"We can make a quick stop." We begin driving back down Route 6, toward home.

Even though the sun won't set for hours, it looks like the beginning of twilight. The sky is black, and when I check my weather app, it shows it's going to storm well into the night with some strong wind gusts. I hate spending the night alone in my uncle's big, ancient house. Now add thunder for the perfect cocktail of anxiety.

When we get to Marshside Deli, Mannix parks close to the entrance, but the rain hasn't let up at all. "Should we run for it?"

I push open the door, darting from the truck to the building entrance. Inside, fluorescent lights flicker above our heads, and the cashier stares at us from her roost behind the register.

Mannix gives a little wave.

"What should we have for dinner?" he asks, surveying the produce in a refrigerated bin. The vegetables are arranged in baskets, and they look a bit wilted. He picks up a zucchini, and I make a face. "Who doesn't like zucchini?" he asks.

"Me. It's gross."

"It's great when you know how to prepare it."

"I've never had a zucchini I like."

"So I'll change your mind."

I roll my eyes as I meander up another aisle. I decide to pick up some toothpaste while I'm here. Mannix follows me, and I see he's collected two zucchinis, a pound of spaghetti, and some cans of petite diced tomatoes in his basket. "You're gonna make me eat that?" I ask.

"I can't *make* you eat anything. But I am going to prepare some zucchini, if that's what you're asking." He pretends to be interested in something on the shelf. He picks it up and examines it. An enema. "Here, it sounds like you need one of these." Tossing it at me, he returns his attention to the neighboring toiletries.

It hits me in the shoulder and then ricochets to the floor,

the box breaking open as I try my best to suppress my peals of laughter. The girl behind the register gives me a look like I'm the biggest child to walk in the store all day, and then another one that obviously asks if I'm going to pick that up.

Two more customers peer down the aisle to see what the commotion is. Mannix squats down beside me, collecting the wrecked enema. "You didn't like my gift."

My laughter starts all over again, and I shove him in the shoulder. "Oh my god, I love you," I say, and continue to giggle. Until I realize how that might be interpreted.

Mannix pauses, smirking at the floor.

I cover my mouth with my hand, like that's going to retract my spastic verbiage.

"You ready?" he asks, standing and placing the enema back on the shelf. Our mood has shifted entirely. His voice is quiet and his face completely unreadable.

I place my toothpaste on the counter, and Mannix waits patiently beside me. Pulling my wallet from my crossbody, I try to control my shaking hands.

"And the enema, too?" asks the cashier, raising her eyebrow at me.

"Oh yeah. Yeah, you should put that on there. The box was kinda busted."

The man behind us snickers, and so does Mannix.

The cashier gives me my change, and she doesn't even wish me a nice night. It's like she knows I'm about to embark on the worst night. A night filled with awkward silences and rushed departures. There's no way Mannix is going to stick around for long after this blunder.

He opens the truck door for me, and I climb in as he places

our groceries at my feet. He starts to drive to Uncle Jack's and we're not talking, so I have plenty of time to stare out the window and dwell.

Not once. Not once the entire time that I was with Brent did I ever even suggest that I was in love with him. It wasn't even an option. So why did I say it to Mannix? The guy who I basically had to convince to go out with me. The guy who didn't want any strings attached. What a ridiculous thing. *I* am a ridiculous thing. What did I even mean by it, anyway?

Maybe I meant, I love you.

Mannix reaches to turn on the radio, gently tapping his finger on the steering wheel to the beat of whatever song plays.

Finally, Uncle Jack's house glides into view. The sheets of rain curtain almost everything. Mannix follows me into the house, our grocery bag in his hands. Upon opening the door, we're greeted by the rush of air conditioning that Uncle Jack insists on keeping at a steady sixty-eight degrees, but now it reminds me how soaked I am. My shivers come back with a vengeance, fully fortified by my anxiety.

"You should get out of those clothes," Mannix says from behind the fridge door. He drops something, picks it up and examines it, and then puts it back on the shelf.

When he closes the fridge, I can see he's just as drenched as I am.

"So should you. You must be freezing."

A chill causes a tremor through his body as I say it. "Yeah, a little," he admits. "But I don't have anything to change into."

"I'm sure Uncle Jack has something you can borrow."

Mannix arches an eyebrow in my direction. Uncle Jack is at least four inches shorter than he is, and, let's say, finer-figured.

"Well, we can at least look."

I ascend the creaky wooden stairs, a quake of thunder rattling the house. The lights dim and then regather their strength.

"It's getting bad out there," Mannix says from behind me.

"Not supposed to let up until tomorrow."

"Probably one of the first bands of that hurricane."

This conversation is mundane and perfect for after you blurt out that you love someone and they don't say anything in return. Maybe he really thought I was teasing. In jest.

"Uncle Jack's room is down that hall." I point in the opposite direction from the attic steps. "I'll just get changed and come back down."

"You want me to go through his things?"

"He won't mind. Besides, how would he even know?"

Mannix begrudgingly follows my advice, and I climb the stairs to my attic room. The little lamp beside my bed casts the room in a warm yellow glow. I go through my dry clothes and pick out a pair of black leggings and a long-sleeved T-shirt.

A bolt of lightning illuminates my dim room, and the crack of thunder that follows makes me yelp. I step away from the window, closing the curtains, like that's going to make the storm disappear.

The sound of Mannix's slow, burdened footsteps on the attic stairs draws my attention to the door, and with a quiet creak, he pokes his head in. He's found an oversize white T-shirt.

"I think that's Chad's," I say. "He's a little more your size."

Mannix doesn't say anything.

"I need to get changed," I tell him, reaching up to put my damp hair in a bun. "So I'll be down to help you with dinner once—"

"I love you."

I blink, my hands dropping to my sides, my hair splayed across my shoulders.

"I wasn't sure if you meant it back there, so I thought about it for a while, and I realized I didn't care if you meant it at all. But I do. I mean it."

My lungs can't seem to fill with enough air to sustain me.

"I just wanted you to know that. I thought it was important that you know that. I never want people to think I take them for granted. Especially you."

There are a thousand things running through my head, images of people I love, some people I thought I could love, only I didn't quite know what the word meant yet, and people who I've loved who probably didn't believe that it was true.

And then there's Mannix Reilly, standing right in front of me. Waiting for me.

"You're not saying anything," he says with a sad smile.

"You surprised me," I finally reply. "I thought I fucked up back in the deli, and it kind of spewed out of me before I could think about it, but I never have to think about it with you. I don't sit up at night wondering how I feel about you."

He takes a step closer to me, lifting my hand from my side and then frowning.

"What is it?" I ask.

"You don't have to say it if it's not true. Don't feel obligated because I did."

"Mannix, I'm not—"

"Because no girl's ever said that to me before. And I'm thankful if it's you. That matters to me."

I stand up on my tiptoes, my hands resting on his shoulders.

"Mannix," I try again. "I love you, too. I wouldn't say it if I didn't mean it." I press my mouth to his, my hands winding around his neck.

The tip of his tongue flicks my upper lip, then presses farther, and he tastes like peppermint gum. Taking a deep breath, he pulls me closer, tightly to his chest.

Another explosion of lightning and a crash of thunder steal what little light we had in the room. Something beeps three times: the fire alarm, protesting its lack of energy.

"Power's out," I say, but my lips hardly leave his mouth.

"I'm pretty sure I can find my way without the light." His hands clutch the hem of my shirt, but he waits, quietly asking, "Is this okay?" And when I nod, he peels my shirt off my body, his hands cold against my warm belly, then steps back and does the same for himself. He grasps me again, his skin chilled and damp, and I shiver against him.

"Are you just cold?" he asks. "Or nervous?"

"Maybe a little of both," I reply.

"It's okay if you don't want to do this," he says, and he pauses, holding me against him, his mouth so close to mine, and his warm breath playing with my hair.

"I know," I reply, tilting my head back and holding his face between my hands. "Only I want to. With you."

Smiling, he kisses me softly. "I never expected you, Coriander Cabot," he says. "When I saw you in that parking lot at the beginning of summer. I never expected you. I just wanted your attention."

"What about now?"

"I just want you."

Every feeling of drowning overwhelms me as he backs me

against the bed, lowers me onto the comforter, and covers my body with his. I know I'm drowning, but I'm not kicking or fighting the inevitable. All the fear has drained from me. He unfastens the buttons of my shorts, and I shift out of them, then help him do the same. His hands on either side of my body, supporting himself, he hovers over me, waiting. I grasp his hips and guide him to me.

And I let him pull me under into the inky blackness that's terrified me for too long.

Chapter Twenty

It's hard to tell how early it is, if I should push myself to get out of bed, or if it's acceptable to roll over and fall back to sleep. The storm still splutters against the window, trying its best to maintain its ferocity, but it's moving out now.

I twist in the sheets, lifting them and readjusting below, then tucking my hands under my pillow. My eyelids flutter, my gaze coming to rest upon a sleeping Mannix beside me. The power's been off since last night, and the room is chilly and damp.

Without opening his eyes, he murmurs, "Come here," and reaches his arm out to pull me into his chest. I share his pillow now, his warmth.

"Thank you."

"For what?" His chin rests on top of my head.

"This."

"Mm-hmm."

We're quiet for a while, just the rhythm of our breathing, the pulsing of our hearts synchronizing to each other, to the raindrops, filling the void between rumbles of thunder.

"I learned something the other day about humpback whales," Mannix says. His fingers trace up and down my spine.

"What's that?"

His voice is groggy and soft. "They sing songs."

It's sweet, what he's doing. Trying to learn more about something I love so much, but his newly learned fact makes me giggle into his chest.

"What?" he asks, laughing, but he's not sure why. "Is it not true?"

"No, it's true, but not something new."

"Well, I learned that in school when I was little, but I thought it was, like, a pretty phrase the teacher was using to describe the noises they made. Like she was being poetic. But the other day, I found out they sing actual songs. Like the definition of songs. Like people do."

"Only the males," I tell him. "And each song is distinct for each region of humpback whales. Humpbacks off Australia don't sing the same song as the humpbacks in the Caribbean."

"What do you think they're singing about?"

I inch back so that I can see his face, and he gazes down at me through his eyelashes. "Whale things."

"That's vague."

"I dunno."

"What if they're singing about us?"

I prop my head up on my hand, leaning into my elbow. "Us?"

"Like sea shanties. Sailors sang about whales all the time."

"Yeah, harpooning them. If whales are singing about us, I don't want to know what they think."

"Well," he says, reaching out and twirling a lock of my hair around his finger. "Maybe they know there are people out there who care about them. Maybe they forgive humankind."

"That would be very generous of them." I smile, leaning into his hand. "So do you want to sing me a whale song? They're used to attract mates."

"I already did that last night," he says, grinning. He leans in and kisses me, then rolls over to view the clock on the night-stand beside him. "I gotta get up," he says, rubbing his eyes. "I'm at Cahoon Hollow today."

"No, let's stay in bed all day." I lean over, kissing his shoulder.

"Tempting as that is right now, it's not gonna happen. But…" He kisses me softly, his hand cupping my jaw. "I'll make you an omelet before I go."

"That's an acceptable swap," I decide.

Downstairs, Mannix raids the fridge for all the supplies he needs to make me a French omelet with cheese and chives, and I sit at the kitchen island sipping from my mug of coffee.

"This coffee tastes so much better than when Uncle Jack makes it."

Mannix grins over his shoulder as he cracks the eggs. "It's a secret."

"Tell me."

"Then it wouldn't be a secret."

"But I don't count. I'll keep your secrets. Your secrets are my secrets."

He whisks the eggs in a speckled mixing bowl and replies,

"Cinnamon in the grounds." Then he adds, "I think I'd like to have a food truck of my own one day."

"Is this part of the secret?"

"You're the first person I've ever said that out loud to, so I think so."

"But why is that a secret? You would have the most amazing food truck."

Mannix shrugs, taking a pat of butter and dropping it into the heating skillet on the stove. "I dunno. I guess I've never thought of cooking as something you could make money doing. Maybe that's why I never really followed through with the CIA."

"Lots of people all over Cape Cod make money cooking. A whole lot of money. You can, too."

Another shrug.

"I'm glad you told me."

He glances up. "It's easy talking to you."

What he says makes me almost shy, exposed, and that doesn't make sense. I slept with him last night. He's seen all of me.

"It's easy when we're together. I don't feel like you expect something from me. Want me to be someone I'm not." He nods once, like he's still thinking about what he's said, and turns back to the stove, pouring the beaten eggs into the skillet.

"I know what you mean," I say softly.

"Do you have work today?"

I scratch my head, thinking about my actual responsibilities for the day. "I'm meeting the journalists from the *New York Times* at the Nature Center with Mia. They want to talk about Fraction and her entanglement. We're gonna go through some footage of other disentanglement efforts so that they can write about it for their feature."

"You don't have any footage of Fraction?" he asks, adding the cheese.

"There's some. I wish I had more. She hasn't been spotted for a while now, though." I slouch down on my stool and stir my coffee, even though the cream is already thoroughly blended. There's something soothing about the familiar clink of the metal spoon against the ceramic.

"Will the omelet make you feel better?" Mannix presents my eggs on a plate, sprinkled with sea salt and chives.

"It's worth a shot."

He seats himself next to me, the upper parts of our arms touching while we eat our breakfasts.

"Sorry I can't stay longer," he says. "But I need to go home and get my board shorts and stuff." He crosses the kitchen and places his dirty dishes in the sink, then turns back to me. "When does your uncle get home from Boston?"

"Not till tomorrow night."

He waggles his eyebrows. "That sounds like an invitation."

"It is."

Grabbing his keys from the hook on the wall, he stops at my stool and leans down to kiss me goodbye.

"I love you," I say, my forehead pressed to his.

"I love you, too." One last kiss, and he's out the kitchen door, rounding the side of the house until he gets to his pickup truck. The storm is moving out, a thin thread of brightness on the horizon, a promise of a day different than yesterday.

I cross into the front sitting room, mug of coffee in hand, and open the front door to watch as he pulls out of the driveway. When he gets to the end, he flicks his headlights at me, and I wave.

At the Nature Center, Mia sits with the journalists, showing them our archive of humpback flukes, explaining how each whale's pattern is unique.

I'm alone in the office, my door open so I can still hear the line of conversation. I'm supposed to be finding footage of disentanglements, but my mind keeps racing back to last night. Racing forward to tonight.

I think Ella would like Mannix. I think she'd like the me I am when I'm with Mannix, too. I try to refocus.

I do like him, Ella says. She stands at the door of my office, looking at the right whale hanging from the ceiling. *But it's never been about me liking him.*

It's strange that I forgot to remember. Strange that it's only right now, in this very moment, imagining what Ella would think of Mannix, of the me I've become in her absence, that I realize what today is.

It's been one year since Ella drowned.

I turn to the window behind me, and through the blinds, the sky is a brightening gray. I sit with this for a while, the way a year can feel as though it's dragging on, and at the same time, flit by so quickly that you hardly notice its passing.

I don't know if I should feel guilty or more sad than I usually do. If I should have prepared some way to honor her today.

From my crossbody hanging on the desk chair, my phone buzzes. There's a voice mail from Mannix. We don't really call each other, and if we do, we don't bother to leave a message. I listen, worried.

"Cor, I'm…and I'm not sure if…the boat hasn't been…

and now the coast guard...no sign of him. He's been gone... but we never thought...they said...his SOS call."

My thoughts are scrambled. I can't piece together what Mannix is trying to tell me. It sounds like something about a boat.

His dad. Somehow, his dad was out on the water during this storm, and he never made it back in. The major aspects of his message are obvious, but the finer details still elude me.

The phone rings, interrupting the half-finished message. My fingers fumble to answer. "Mannix?" I choke into the phone.

"Cor, it's bad. It's so bad—"

It sounds like he's in a tunnel. "Mannix, I can hardly hear you. The connection is terrible."

The sky trembles with thunder above me.

"They found his boat, but he wasn't..."

I click to put him on speaker, but now he sounds even farther away. "Mannix, can you hear me?"

"I should have gone with him like he asked me to," he says, his voice suddenly clear and uninhibited. "If I had gone with him, maybe he wouldn't have..."

"Mannix, you keep fading out. Can you hear me?"

"I can hear you. I'm on my...to the hospital. Can you... please?"

"What?"

"Will you...?"

He fades out.

"Cor, can you hear me?"

"Mannix, I can hardly hear you. He's at the hospital? Are you?"

"I'll be there soon. Please come, Cor—" The connection goes dead.

"Shit!" I throw my phone down onto the desk and then swiftly retrieve it.

I try to dial him back, but it goes straight to voice mail each time. I wait, but he's not calling back.

"Cor, you okay?" Mia appears in the door of the office, her eyes wide.

"No, I have to go. Can you tell Lottie I had an emergency if she comes back?"

"Yeah, of course. Can I do anything else?"

I grab my hoodie and throw it over my head, punching my arms through the sleeves but getting tangled in my rush anyway. "No, I have to go." I dash out the side door and down to the parking lot.

Shoving the Jeep into drive, I pull away from the Nature Center, headed for the hospital. I'll meet him there, and then he can explain everything to me. I cruise down Route 6, and the sky begins to lighten. Maybe the storm is finally passing.

My phone rings.

"Mannix!" I cry.

"Cor, it's Lottie."

I shake my head, like that's going to clear my thoughts. "Lottie, I'm sorry I had to go so quickly, but—"

"Can you get down to Chatham?"

I blink stupidly. Nothing makes sense today. "What?"

"Fraction got stuck this morning on the shoals just outside the harbor, and I wanted to call you first. She's weak from the entanglement, but still alive, and we need to get her back out to sea before we lose the tide. Get here as quick as you can." *Click.*

Despite how warm it is in the Jeep, my shaking is ridiculous. I clutch the wheel for stability. "Shit." I pull off to the side of the road.

Mannix thinks I'm on my way to the hospital. He's depending on me to be there.

My mind races, my thoughts encumbered by emotions, by the weight of this day pressing down on my shoulders.

Once, Ella and I were eating our lunches in her backyard. We were in sixth grade. She chewed her sandwich contemplatively. A little groundhog shuffled into view. And then she turned to me and asked, "Do you think animals give us signs? Signs they want us to interpret only we're too dumb to understand?"

"Maybe." I shrugged.

"I think maybe if we slowed down, we'd understand the signs."

I slow down now. I breathe, I stare at the tattoo on my wrist of Fraction. The noise of my own thoughts is drowned out by the rain, by the hum of the engine, by the air through my lungs. I slow down long enough to consider what Ella would think if she were sitting right next to me.

You're scared, she says. *That's all it is. It's easier to go to Mannix's dad in the hospital because there are other people there he depends on, and not just you. You can't fail there. But the whale. She needs you. She's always needed you, and you're afraid of failing. But if you don't show up at all, if you never even get there, then you failed no matter what.*

"I know," I say out loud, to no one. But maybe to Ella.

I know because she's why I'm here, thrashing and desperately trying to keep my head above water to prove to her that she mattered, that her friendship mattered. And the whale we cared about is within my reach. Her life dangles above me. And it feels like I can save her. Because I couldn't save Ella, and I failed to save our friendship. This feels real now, though. Some immediate way to make things right.

I make my decision.

I spin back onto the highway and head toward Chatham.

The sky is a strange concoction of fleeing black clouds and streams of sunlight, stronger than ever, breaking them apart, cracking through their once-ominous concealment. The sea is choppy and gray, but not nearly as threatening as I imagined. The tide flows back toward the land, but slowly. Perhaps even more slowly for Fraction, her huge body shaped like a J and stranded on a sandbar a few hundred feet from the shoreline.

I jump out of the car, transfixed by what I see before me. Before I lose myself completely, I stare at my phone. There's no signal. No way for me to let Mannix know that I won't be showing up anytime soon. I throw it back into the Jeep and head toward my whale.

She hardly has the gumption to flail or struggle, almost as though her proximity to the human world has drained that drive from her, slowly siphoning it from her being. She's weak and desperate, relying on the kindness of fellow animals.

And Ella is nowhere in sight.

Someone hands me protective gear, a helmet. I put them on in a trance, and I wade into the water.

People have gathered on the beach despite the occasional spit of rain the storm still produces. They hold their phones up, documenting every moment, because this is the closest they'll ever get to a whale, and they need evidence to prove it happened.

But not me. I won't need a phone to remember this. I won't need a picture to remind me how this whale makes me feel. That despite her circumstance, she still wields a power that makes me feel useless, makes me want to curl inside myself and weep. That this is what I've been searching for. This is what I came here for. This is something greater than me, and I'll work toward it for the rest of my life.

As the water deepens, I slosh through it, up to my stomach, pushing it out of the way with my arms, half walking, half swimming. And almost as quickly as it deepened, the water recedes as I climb the sandbar. There's hardly enough water here to cover Fraction.

"Keep her wet!" Lottie shouts over the sounds of working people.

Other rescuers haul buckets through the waves and then dump them over Fraction's back. They saw away at the lines of rope attached to her body. They haul the mesh out of the water and back to the shore where it won't harm anything again. The ropes have been weighing her down, keeping her from feeding with the other whales. They cover Fraction with blankets and then pour water over her to protect her sensitive skin.

I shouldn't be here, I know that. I wait for Lottie to tell me. But when she appears at my side, that's not what she says.

"Everything that's on her is totally legal." She swipes the salt water from her face. "This is what's been killing her." Lottie stands beside me, panting, her hands on her hips. "We've got to get her off this bank. The tide is coming back in. We need to take advantage of it. And we need to free her before she goes back out to sea with that shit all over her."

I nod, afraid if I open my mouth to speak, I'll break. I can't break now.

"Keep her damp and cool, Cor."

Lottie returns to her position at Fraction's flukes, severing the lines, but I stand here stupidly. I could join the procession of people who are taking turns dumping buckets of water over her body, but somehow, I can't move. Somehow, I'm stuck here in the sand, staring at her, painfully aware that despite my size compared to hers, I'm still capable of destroying her. If we wanted to, we could destroy her. People have in the past. People still do.

And almost as though she can read my thoughts, her massive flukes rise in the air, causing the workers trying to untangle her to scramble and shout. The tail falls back into the water with a sharp smack, sending spray and foam into the air. She cries. Like dogs cry, like bears cry, like humans cry, like we all cry. Because she's scared.

I fall to my knees, the sea swirling around my calves, and place both of my hands on either side of her eye. Her tail ceases its thrashing. She blinks, and then she returns my attention.

"It's going to be okay," I tell her, but then I regret my choice of words. "That's not true." I swallow. "It might not be okay, but I'm going to be here. And you can trust me. I'm not going to leave you. I'm not going to abandon you. We're doing everything we can for you."

Behind us, several workers call to one another, pulling the tangled lines and netting away from her flukes. Others begin the process of attaching her to boats that will attempt to pull her into deeper water.

Fraction lets out a hollow breath, weak and desperate.

"Not like this," I murmur, closing my eyes. "Not like this. It doesn't end like this." I lean my head against her cool, sleek skin.

But she takes another hoarse breath, and I'm back at the beach in Truro, standing in the sand and facing my friend for the last time. Except you never know when it's the last time, and that's what hurts the most.

"So you're willing to throw away an entire friendship because I hooked up with some guy you liked when you were eight?" I throw at her.

Ella's silent, staring at me for a long while, and when she finally speaks, her voice is soft. "Is that what you think this is about? You think this is about Brent?"

Of course it's not about Brent, but I cross my arms over my chest anyway, defiantly. It would be so much easier if this were about Brent. Then at least she'd be partially to blame, too.

"If you think I care that you liked Brent, or you dated Brent, or you slept with Brent, then I don't know what our friendship has been about. If you think I'm that shallow, or that I don't love you enough to accept who you like, even if it hurts me, then maybe you're not the person I thought you were."

"I'm the same person!" I cry.

The beach is empty, the setting sun casting the sky in cotton-candy pinks and Easter-egg purples.

"You're not! You threw away our friendship. You abandoned me."

"Well, maybe you need to branch out a little, Ella. Maybe you need more friends than just me. I can't be everything to you all the time."

She shakes her head adamantly. "When it came down to it, and you had to choose between showing up for me and getting to show off with a group of people you don't even like, I saw what you chose."

"It didn't have to be a decision," I try.

"No," says Ella. "It really didn't." The waves pelt her calves, and she steps deeper into the water.

"Ella," I whimper.

"God, Cor, what makes you think you're so singular? That you can just make choices and they won't have an effect on anyone else? That they won't hurt people? Leave me alone. I want to be alone." She strides out into the ocean, dives below a wave, and swims even deeper.

And I turn away one last time.

The wind whips my hair into my face, into my mouth, and I'm back again beside our whale. I rub at my tattoo of Fraction on my wrist.

"I'm here," I say to the whale in front of me. "I'll bring you back to the sea. I'll take you to the sea where you belong." I can't tell the difference between my own tears and the salt water, but they're really both the same. I press my forehead next to Fraction's eye, to be as close as I can to her, and I whisper, "I'm sorry, I'm sorry." I don't even know who I'm apologizing to. To Fraction, to Ella, to Mannix, to myself? But the words are out there, and they float along the water, rising with the tide.

We stay like this for some time, eye to eye. For how long, I don't know, but soon the water is up to my waist.

"Cor, move back!" Lottie shouts from somewhere down Fraction's body.

I stand, dripping, and Fraction's eye follows my movement.

"The tide's coming in. They're about to pull her out."

Lottie is beside me now, her arm around my shoulders, and she begins to usher me to the sandy coast where Justin, Mia, and Kyle wait. I keep peeking back, watching as the waves wash over Fraction's body. Two boats begin sputtering toward the open ocean as she writhes in the sand, lifting her huge, powerful flukes and slapping them back down. Wave after wave crashes across her back, but this gives her more control. The water is her element. She belongs there. And with every inch the tide rises, her body becomes buoyant, her pain recedes, her strength returns. The boats inch her slowly off the shoal.

"Do you think she can do it?" Justin asks from beside us.

The line of onlookers has grown, phones held high in the air. They whisper tensely back and forth to one another.

"I think she can," I say firmly. I don't know if I believe this but maybe saying it loud enough will make it true.

Minutes pass. Fraction contorts her long body in the shape of a C, then straightens again. She breathes, and though it still sounds hollow, there's a ring of determination I haven't heard before. I wade into the water, up to my knees, but no farther. The tide has brought rough seas.

I turn back just in time to catch Lottie's shoulders slouching.

The anger boils inside me and erupts into words. "You can't give up on her!" I shout back to them. "She can do it; we have to wait."

No one says anything.

The tide comes fast, coursing along Fraction. She pushes out a breath. Her right pectoral fin lifts a bit and then smacks the water, but she isn't thrashing anymore. She doesn't struggle. She waits.

She waits for a while.

Until the wave comes.

Almost as though the sea has gathered up its strength and concentrated its power into a singular, perfect form, the wave pulls from the shore, collects itself farther out at sea, and plows across the surface of the water, directly for Fraction.

It dislodges her from the sandbar, sending her body sideways and then sucking her back out with the gravel, and the sand, and some residual seaweed. Now Fraction moves, her powerful flukes pumping and pushing in the shallow water, her pectoral fins directing her body where it needs to go. She heads in the direction of deeper water, out toward the Atlantic, and the boats drop their hold of her. And for a second, I swear, for the briefest moment, I think I see Ella, each step she takes bringing her deeper into the ocean, until her almost-white blond hair is swallowed by a wave. Right where Fraction's flukes lift in their descent into the sea. Right where she belongs, forever riding in on the tides, and sailing back out with their recession.

The shore bursts into cheers and laughter, and for a few of us, tears. Justin and Lottie hold each other in a tight embrace.

I sob. I cover my face with my salty, sandy hands, and I cry. I cry until I'm completely silent and devoid of tears, my chest heaving. My friends appear beside me, both Mia and Kyle clutching me in shaking embraces.

"She's okay now," Kyle murmurs to me, gripping my shoulders and kissing the side of my head. "She's where she belongs."

"I know," I say. "I know."

They hold me against them for a while until my breathing steadies with theirs. We watch Fraction swim away. We watch her dive, her flukes proudly flashing one final time until she disappears into Nantucket Sound.

"You got some sick footage," says Justin.

He stands next to Dan Reynolds and Clarissa Hernandez, but Dan only nods, then finally says, "Holy hell, I can't believe we got all that."

"We still have a few more things we'd like to collect before we're through," says Clarissa, her camera in her hands. "But today was a gift on so many levels."

"So who let you know that Fraction was beached? Storm chasers?" Dan asks.

Staring out to sea, almost as though he's waiting for Fraction to show up again, Justin shakes his head. "Dude, no. We got a call about an entangled whale from a lobsterman yesterday. We asked him to stay with her, but I mean, who knows with this storm. Luckily she was spotted by the coast guard this morning."

I almost throw up. "Oh my god."

"What's the matter?" Lottie asks.

"I have to go." I wrench myself from her, peeling off all of my protective gear and dashing back up the sand.

"Is everything okay?" Lottie calls after me.

"I have to go!"

I climb into the Jeep, my body shivering and jumping. It's chilly, and I'm soaked with sweat and salt water.

I head down Route 6, cursing at drivers who are poking along. The ride is long enough without anyone deciding that forty is a reasonable speed at which to travel. I check the clock. Almost five hours since Mannix asked me to meet him at the hospital. It'll take me a while to get there, and the waiting makes me anxious. I pull at a few cuticles. I blast the radio to distract me, but nothing works.

Once I'm in Hyannis, the hospital looms in front of me, a modern brick building, and I find a visitor spot to park.

I zip up my hoodie and enter through the automatic doors, no hesitation.

"Hello," I say to the nurse behind the front desk. "I'm looking for a patient. Gary Reilly. Can you tell me what room he's in?"

She looks through the computer, her fingers pecking at the keyboard and then clicking the mouse. "Third floor. Room 317."

"Thank you."

My shaking becomes more acute as I press the button for the third floor in the elevator. I would practice what I'm going to say when I see Mannix, but I can't think of words for a scenario when I don't know how he'll react. I clench my hands in front of me.

The doors slide open, and I follow the signs for 317. The zig-zagging of the hallways disorients me, and I'm not sure how to get back. Hospitals are so quiet. My stomach begins to gurgle.

The hall opens to a small waiting room, and Mannix is the only one there. He's hunched over, elbows on knees, chin resting in his hands. He looks over at me and then returns his attention to the alternating blue and yellow tiles on the floor. He doesn't realize that it's me, and then he glances again, and his eyes widen. He stands.

"What happened to you?" he asks, stepping toward me.

My jaw trembles, and I wrap both arms around me for warmth. "I, uh..." Somehow the words won't form. The truth doesn't sit well. "Are you here alone?"

He shakes his head, pointing toward the room behind him. "No, my mom's in there with him now. Cor, you're soaked. You're covered in sand." He reaches for my hand, his warm fingers gently caressing my icy ones.

"We saved Fraction," I begin. "She's free. She beached herself this morning, and we were able to save her."

His brows crease together, and he tilts his head to one side. "The whale?" he asks.

"Yeah, the whale. My whale."

He lets go of my hand and turns away. "That's why you didn't come," he says to the floor.

"I know, but—"

"You went to the whale."

I swallow. "Mannix," I say, but it sounds more like a whimper than I'd like.

"Do you even know why he's here?" he asks, pointing to his father's room. "Because he saw your whale and remembered what you said. He remembered that you said to stick with the entangled whale until help can arrive. Even though the water was rough yesterday, and he should have come in. Even though he shouldn't have been out on a boat in the first place. He almost drowned, Cor."

"I didn't mean for that to happen," I say. "What can I do?"

Mannix turns away from me and begins walking down the hall.

"Mannix, what can I do?"

"Just go home, Cor," he says. "I don't need you here."

He disappears around the corner. And I don't even get to apologize.

Chapter Twenty-One

I've whisked the batter in this bowl for probably around two minutes, if I'm judging by the clock on the oven to my left. Behind me, Uncle Jack chops some dark chocolate for the cake we're making Chad to celebrate his new job.

"What'd that batter ever do to you?" he asks, peering over my shoulder.

I hardly hear him. I've called Mannix three times within the past two days. He's screening my calls. I've left him voice mails each time, but he doesn't call back.

"Uncle Jack," I say, staring out the window.

"Yes?"

"I screwed up."

He stands beside me. "Oh, I don't think so. The batter's still good, I'm sure."

"No, not the cake," I reply, letting the spoon fall into the brown mixture in front of me. "It's Mannix. I screwed up."

"What do you mean?" Uncle Jack leans against the counter, facing me.

Dropping my head, I close my eyes and take a breath. "That day when we rescued Fraction, Mannix called me right before I left. The connection was bad, I could hardly hear him, but his dad was in the hospital, and he wanted me to meet him there."

"All right," says Uncle Jack in such a way that I know he's prompting me to further explain.

I wipe my forehead with the back of my hand. "I made a choice, Uncle Jack. And I didn't choose Mannix."

He nods. "Does that mean you made the wrong choice?"

"No," I reply quickly. "No, it doesn't. I don't think I did. I needed to save Fraction. I promised I would—"

And that's when I realize that Ella is gone. And despite trying to avoid facing it this entire time, I still feel it. I still miss her. No promise I can make to her will bring her back.

Uncle Jack waits for me to gather my words.

"I know it wasn't the first time I didn't choose Mannix, but I think it's the last time. He's not really talking to me."

"If his dad is sick, maybe he's busy," Uncle Jack suggests.

I nod. "Maybe."

"In any case, you leave on Friday. What were your plans with Mannix once you left for home? What about when you go to college?"

"I dunno." I retrieve the spoon from the batter, carefully trying to avoid getting the mixture on my hands but failing miserably. "I want to go to Boston, and that's not so far."

"Not physically far, no."

I don't ask what he means, because I know.

"What's next? Chocolate chunks?"

"Yes." Uncle Jack twirls and produces the bowl full of chopped chocolate.

"I think I should go and talk to him."

"Yes, that would be fine." He sprinkles the chocolate into the batter, then takes the bowl from the counter, mixing it all together.

"Uncle Jack, you're not really giving me many answers." I moan a little.

"I'm not, am I?" He appears bemused by this as he pours the batter into a cake pan.

I arch my eyebrow, and he catches this.

"I don't have the answers, Cor." He smiles. "Even if I did, what if my answers weren't yours?"

"You're an adult, you're supposed to have all the right answers."

"I still learn something fairly new every day. Even if it's small. If you feel like you need to go and talk to Mannix about this, then you probably should." He holds up his pointer finger. "Just be back in time for cake."

"Wouldn't miss it."

I drive out of the town center, making a right down Mannix's road, the one that heads toward the bay. The sunlight streams through the green leaves and the needles of the pine trees, and finally falls on the red-orange paint of his pickup truck through the branches. The hood is up, and he leans over the engine, smudges of dirt and grease splattered across the skin of his arms and even a little on his face.

Mannix glances up when he hears the crunch of my tires

on the driveway, and my heart clenches. He doesn't make any expression that indicates he has feelings about my showing up at all. He goes back to work under the hood of his car.

I open the door of the Jeep and step out, inching my way around the front to where I can see him clearly. "Hey," I say.

He yanks on something in the engine, it doesn't go his way, and he curses under his breath. Then, "Hi."

I take a hesitant step forward. "I kept trying to call you, but you never picked up."

"Sucks, right? When you're hoping for someone to show up and they don't?"

"Yeah, it does." His head's still buried under the hood, making me work for it. "Is your dad doing okay?" I try.

Mannix reaches down at his feet for a wrench or something and goes back to working. "He'll be fine."

"Oh. Good." I trace a circle with my foot in the sandy dirt before me. "So, is he home now?"

"No." Something clunks inside the truck. "He's still at the hospital until tomorrow. Mom is spending the afternoon with him. My brother is driving up this weekend."

"That's good," I say hopefully.

But he doesn't reply this time, just keeps working on his car.

"Mannix," I say, and it comes out in a singsong sort of whine. I stand next to him, my hand on the side of the truck. "I'm sorry. I'm really sorry. I know you were counting on me, but you have to understand—"

"I always have to understand," he says.

"What?"

He pulls his head out from under the hood, cursing under his breath at something mechanical, I think, and then leans against the side of the truck. "I've always been the person who has to understand. Everyone else has pressing circumstances, but I can wait around, I guess."

"That's not what I'm trying to say."

"Listen, Cor, I don't know what you're trying to say, but at the beginning of all of this, at the beginning of whatever this was supposed to be"—he motions between us—"I tried to warn you. I tried to tell you that it'd be better if we didn't, and you convinced me. You convinced me, remember? You really had me believing...." He trails off, shaking his head and turning away from me.

"Believing what?" I ask.

"I told you not to say it if you didn't mean it. I told you it was okay."

I almost can't believe what he's insinuating. "What, that I loved you? I did mean it. I said I was in love with you, and it wasn't just talk, Mannix."

He pivots to face me again, his face washed in disbelief. "No, no, you're not in love with me. You're in love with the idea of me, and that's not the same thing."

"That's not fair. Don't throw that on me."

"At every opportunity, you've proven to me that you're too afraid to show up when it matters, and I don't have time for that shit, Cor. You need to figure yourself out."

"Show up? I came from rescuing a humpback whale. I came from a once-in-a-lifetime opportunity to show up for an animal that I based this whole summer around. Ella and I had—"

"That's what this is really about, isn't it?"

His interruption startles me, and I don't know how to reply to this accusation. I don't even know what he means. Everything that made sense this weekend is somehow unraveling, and I'm the one pulling the thread. "What is it about?" I ask.

"This is about Ella," he says quietly, stepping forward. "This is about showing up for Ella because you didn't do it while she was alive." Realization floods his expression. "That makes sense."

"What makes sense? Mannix—"

"Of course you had to show up for Ella. Of course you did that for her. It's easy to show up for a dead girl because you can't let her down anymore. But I'm right here, Cor. I'm right in front of you, and you were enough for me. You are enough for me."

His invocation of Ella's memory riles me, that he would even presume to understand the intricacies of our friendship, like he ever even knew her. Like he ever even knew the me I was when I was with her.

"I know you wanted me to come to the hospital, but it was impossible. It was my choice. I'm not sorry about the choice I made. I can't make every decision revolve around you."

He doesn't reply to this, just stares at the inner workings of his truck.

"I came when I was finished, Mannix. You can't have what you want, exactly when you want it. That's not how the world works, and you want too much."

His eyes widen. "I want too much?" he asks. "I want too much? Are you serious right now? Did you really say that?" His chest heaves. "I never ask anything of anyone! That's not me, Cor, so don't ever say that to me again."

I hate being told what to do. "The whale was dying. She needed me."

"I needed you, too."

"So I'm not allowed to have priorities, then, unless they involve you?"

"That's not what I'm saying."

"It's exactly what you're saying. You don't understand how that whale could have been a priority when *you* needed me. When something went wrong in *your* life. Well, guess what? She matters to me. She matters like hell to me, and the fact that I got to be a part of the effort that saved her, I achieved something I've always wanted, that means something to me. All I wanted was to research whales this summer, Mannix, and somehow I got sidetracked. Somehow there's always something in the way, and I guess I can't handle everything."

"I don't want to be everything, Cor, but it would matter to me if I were something."

"Then don't make *me* everything!" I throw my hands in the air. "Focus your attention somewhere else. Do something that matters to you. Do something meaningful. I'm leaving on Friday, and you're going to be stuck here!"

His face drops, and I immediately regret what I've said. I take a step back, trying to distance myself from the words I didn't think I'd ever say to him.

"Mannix," I say softly.

He shakes his head, bending back over the guts of his pickup truck. "No, I get it. I wasn't enough."

But he is.

"I think you should go, Cor. I have a lot I need to do this afternoon, and it doesn't feel like we have anything left to say."

Behind me, the front door whines open, and someone steps out onto the stoop.

Mannix stands up straight.

"How do you fold a fitted sheet, Mannix?" Kayla asks, struggling with the ends.

"I guess I see why you couldn't pick up the phone," I say, backing away.

"Cor," he says, his shoulders slumping and his head dropping.

"Just throw it in a pile and call it quits, Kayla," I call to her, head down, on my way back to the Jeep. "That's what I'm gonna do." I climb in and turn the engine on. In my rearview mirror, Mannix tosses his wrench to the ground, cursing. He runs his hands down his face and sighs deeply.

That's the last time I'll see him. That's the image I carry with me.

"And then the priest says..."

Everyone leans in toward Chad, waiting for the punch line.

"I thought you said a fishmonger!"

We laugh, wipe the tears from our eyes, and Uncle Jack refills glasses. It's my last night on Cape Cod. All my things are packed—souvenirs for my family. Specifically, an olive-wood cutting board decorated with deep blue waves for Mom, a clay baking dish for Dad, pretty handmade earrings for Peyton, and I even thought to pick up Rhett something for letting me borrow his Jeep. Tomorrow, I'll wake up early to beat the morning traffic over the Sagamore Bridge, and I'll head back to New Jersey. Return to my life.

But tonight, I'm surrounded by the people I've met up here. Justin and Lottie, Kyle, Mia, Chad, and a few of Uncle Jack's neighbors. It's a combination celebration of new beginnings for Chad and bittersweet departures for me. We sit around the fire pit and under a blanket of shimmering stars, and Uncle Jack has even lit the tiki torches. There's a hint of fall in the air, and I think of Mannix. I wish he were here, too.

Lottie sits down next to me, placing a champagne flute in front of me and holding up a bottle.

I shake my head. "I have to drive tomorrow."

"One glass of champagne won't hurt you. Besides, we have plenty to celebrate."

I let her pour me half a glass, and toast. I take a sip, but I don't feel like celebrating.

"I guess you didn't see," says Lottie. She hands me her phone, opened up to the home page of the *New York Times*.

"Is this…?" I begin, sitting up in my chair. My skin is tingling.

"Take a look."

I click on the link that reads, "The Tangled Web We Weave Beneath the Waves: The Ropes That Strangle Our Sea Life." Before me is not just Dan's article. It's his words, yes, but strewn together with my images, my photos, and my videos. There's pictures of the humpbacks of Stellwagen Bank, of Lottie, and Justin, and Captain Mike, and Kyle, and Mia, and me, even of Noah, Maddie, and Mannix. Pictures of the lifeless whale at Sesuit Harbor, a video of its body being lifted out of the water, underwater shots that Lottie supplied of Fraction's entanglement. And finally, the video of Fraction's freedom, taken by Clarissa. It's a long article, but I read every word.

Maybe it doesn't make up for how my friendship ended with

Ella, and it will never bring her back. But I was there for something even greater than me, and somehow the pain I'm experiencing now feels justified.

"This is really amazing," I say, and I feel tears pricking the corners of my eyes. "I'll be right back. Need anything from the kitchen?" I stand, starting to walk away before anyone can even answer me.

It's dark in the kitchen, only the soft light of a little lamp by the door illuminating my way down the counters. I grab my phone, plugged into the outlet near the fridge, and check my texts one more time. The last one I sent was to Mannix.

Cor (5:02 PM): Hey, we're having a BBQ at Uncle Jack's before I leave tomorrow. You should come.

But he never replied.

I should have told him I wanted him to come tonight. That he's the only person I really want to say goodbye to. I should have said all those things, but I'm too scared. My fingers won't type those words. Instead, they drop the phone back on the counter and turn away.

"Hey."

Lottie's voice at the kitchen door startles me, and I swipe at my eyes before she notices. "Hey."

"You keep coming in here to check your phone. Everything okay?"

I nod and try to smile, but that quickly disintegrates to crying into my own hands. Not a few tears, but violent sobbing that wracks my whole body. Lottie has me in her arms before I can even explain myself. She rests her chin on top of my hair and hushes me like a mother to her baby.

"What happened?" she asks me, her hand making circles in the middle of my back.

"I feel like I keep fucking up, and this must be me. This must be what I do."

She doesn't say anything, keeps rubbing my back, and I cry into her shoulder, soaking it in snot and tears, and I don't even care. "I'm sorry."

"Nothing to be sorry about."

"No, there is. I wasn't truthful with you at the beginning of the summer. I didn't represent myself authentically, and that wasn't right." I step back, rubbing at my eyes, trying to see clearly through my own tears. "I promise I didn't do this internship just because it would look good on college résumés. That's not me. I should have told you that I did it because it was something my best friend would have wanted to do if she hadn't died last year. But Lottie..."

She waits, listening.

"Lottie, I also did it because it made me feel useful. It made me feel like me. Working for something that was more important than me and all of my problems. That felt good."

"That's where we find our purpose," she says quietly. "And truthfully, Cor, you're right. I was annoyed with what you said on the first day, but then I noticed that little tattoo you have on your wrist."

I glance down at Fraction's flukes.

"You don't put something permanent on your body unless you really love it. I knew you loved her. And don't think for one minute that your work this summer hasn't proved your intentions to me. You don't have to explain yourself now."

I nod, unable to control the sob that escapes me again. "Okay," I say, covering my mouth.

"It's a tough lesson to learn," she says, leaning back against the counter. "It's something I'm still learning. I keep gathering new pieces of the puzzle each year, and I think that's what it means to be human."

"What does?"

She shrugs. "That we can't live in this world without affecting everything around us, for better or for worse. We just need to be a little more cognizant of the ramifications of our actions. Live a little more gently, you know?"

"I know," I say quietly.

She grabs a clean glass from the counter and fills it with water. "Does he know, though?" She gestures toward my phone, then rejoins the group outside.

I stare at the black screen of my phone. He knows. He knows better than anyone. I wish it hadn't taken me so long to figure out how much he mattered to me. I wish I had known before I hurt him.

Reaching into my back pocket, I take out my list, limp and soft from folding. I stare at our entries and grab a pen, crossing off what I've accomplished.

1. ~~Internship at Marine Research and Conservation Alliance on Cape Cod.~~
2. ~~Whale tattoos.~~
3. See Harry Styles in concert.
4. Wear elaborate ball gowns to prom.

5. ~~Real boyfriends. Not crushes.~~
6. ~~Complete the pebble collection.~~
7. ~~Save Fraction.~~

I stare for a moment. The important ones are complete.

I follow Lottie back out to the fire pit, where Kyle and Mia wait for me, their jackets on, their bags in hand.

"Are you leaving?" I ask.

"My parents want to leave before traffic tomorrow," says Mia.

"She's my ride," Kyle adds.

"I'll walk you to the car," I say, nodding toward the driveway.

The night grows cooler, the breeze whispering through the pine branches and oak leaves. The distant yip of coyotes floats over the yard, and somewhere, hidden among the trees, an owl offers an earnest hoot.

"It feels weird that tomorrow we're not all going to show up at headquarters and have our coffees together at eight."

"And Kyle isn't going to dash to the bathroom forty-three minutes later," I add.

"I'm very regular," Kyle says.

"And there won't be any whales until next summer," says Mia quietly.

"Next summer," I repeat. "That feels like forever away."

Mia reaches out for both of our hands and gives them a tight squeeze. It almost hurts, but I don't mind. It's the kind of hurt that lets you know you matter. You can withstand that kind of pain.

"But we're not going to let this fade, right?" she asks. "That's not possible. We didn't go through this summer together just to never talk again."

"That's why my parents pay for my expensive cell phone plan," says Kyle.

"I know this is sentimental," I say, my voice a little croaky still from before. "But I can't tell you in words what working with you this summer has meant to me. What it's meant to find friends who make me feel safe, who I feel like I've known forever. That's been something…" I sniff and turn away for a moment. "Something I've struggled with."

"Oh god, come here." Kyle extends their arms, enfolding Mia and me in a huge hug, and we cry and giggle all at once.

"Text me when you're both home tomorrow," I say as they climb into Mia's car. Before Mia lets go of my hand, I say, "Hey."

She glances up at me, waiting.

"What are you and Noah gonna do now that summer's over?"

Shrugging, she replies, "Nothing, I guess. I don't think I ever expected it to last more than the summer. But he was fun."

My heart drops. "Yeah, he was fun."

"Drive safe," calls Mia.

"I miss you already!" Kyle cries from the passenger window.

I wave to them as they disappear down Uncle Jack's street.

Chapter Twenty-Two

October

My sister sits in the passenger seat next to me, and we exit the rotary in Orleans and head north to Wellfleet. We took her Jetta this weekend, and it's my turn to drive. She's been asleep since we crossed over the border from Rhode Island to Massachusetts, and that's okay. Because Peyton is either talking incessantly or not at all, and the break is welcome at this point in our six-hour journey.

When she rouses at the sound of the blinker, she rubs her eyes awake. "Don't go over forty here," she says. "You'll get a ticket."

"I spent the whole summer here, Peyton. I know the rules."

She sighs, slumping against the console. "I'm hungry."

I glance at the clock. Almost one, and she finished all her veggie chips mid-Connecticut.

"Can we stop and get a sandwich?"

I stretch forward, trying to straighten my back. "Yeah, let's pick up lunch for Uncle Jack, too."

I drive to Marshside Deli, park the car, and take a minute to check my phone before getting out. Peyton stands beside her door, yawning and putting on her oversize cardigan. It's cooler here than at home, and the sky is bright but overcast.

My fingers automatically scroll to Mannix's Instagram. There's a picture of him and the other lifeguards standing at the lifeguard stand after hauling it up to the top of the cliff at the end of the season. There's a video of a humpback whale, just a few yards from shore, feeding on sand lances. People cheer and chase the whale along the line of breaking waves, like if they run fast enough, they'll keep up with her. She'll swim away, though. They don't stay the winter.

I wonder if Mannix thought of me when he saw the whale. When he went out of his way to take a video of it and then post it to his account.

Peeking into my crossbody, I touch the printed email I received from Sally's Sauces. The one that informed me Mannix won second prize in their contest and a thousand dollars. It was my goal to drive up here and show him what he won, to prove to him that it's not just me who saw all his talent. Because he deserves that. But now that we're here, it's feeling less and less realistic. I should have forwarded him the email.

"You coming?" asks Peyton, poking her head back into the car. Her long brown hair is pulled up into a messy bun.

I shove the email deeper into my bag. "Coming."

"What are you gonna get?" she asks, opening the glass door for me.

I consider this for a moment. "The chicken salad sandwich. We can get that for Uncle Jack, too. But he doesn't like any onions, so..."

Peyton meanders up to the deli counter, surveying the menu above the cash register, but I can't go any farther. Standing before us is a group of lifeguards in their turquoise long-sleeved T-shirts, and Mannix is right in the middle. I recognize the back of his head, the shape of his shoulders, his height, the way he carries himself, no matter how many weeks it's been since I last saw him. And I'm not ready.

I dart down one of the aisles, searching for something to preoccupy me, or at least make me appear uninterested.

"Cor?" Peyton calls from the counter. "Where'd you go?"

I screw my eyes shut, my heartbeat thundering in my ears. Glancing to my right, I see a little side door that has a NO EXIT sign above it, though clearly, this is an exit, and I'm going to take it.

Before I can even be sure if Mannix is paying attention, I'm out the door and sprinting across the parking lot to the Jetta. I hunch down in the driver's seat, hood up, arms crossed over my chest, and pretend I'm asleep until Peyton gets back.

"What the hell was that?" she asks, thrusting the sandwiches into my lap while she buckles in.

The group of lifeguards exits the deli, and Mannix glances around the parking lot.

"He's one of them, isn't he?" Peyton asks suddenly, a grin taking hold of her mouth. "Hot lifeguard. Which one? Can I guess? If I guess right, will you tell me?"

"Peyton, I can't do this right now."

"He's the tall one with sandy-brown hair, isn't he?"

I shove the Jetta into reverse and swerve out of the parking spot. "Yes, he is."

She turns in her seat to continue watching him, even as we leave and drive in the direction of Uncle Jack's house. "I can see you with him."

"I'm not with him."

"No, you're running away from him. Even though this is why we came up here, right? To give him his prize?"

"Not now, Peyton. Please."

When we get to Uncle Jack's, he's crunching down the driveway, about to load up the Land Rover with FOR SALE signs he plans on planting in people's lawns this afternoon.

"There are my beautiful girls!" he cries when he sees us. He gives us each a hug, but mine lasts a little bit longer. "I miss having my roommate around," he tells me like he doesn't want to make Peyton jealous.

"I miss you, too," I say against his shoulder.

"So what brings you up here this weekend? Skipping school for some quality Uncle Jack time?"

"I had today off, and Peyton skipped work for a well-deserved long weekend."

"We brought you lunch!" says Peyton, offering up our bag from Marshside.

"Oh, lovely," he says, circling his car to the driver's-side door. "But I have to run. Put it in the fridge and I'll have it when I get back. Give me twenty minutes." He kisses both our cheeks before he leaves.

Peyton and I lug our duffel bags into the house; then she

ducks into the powder room. I trudge up the stairs, throw my bag on my bed, and use my newly renovated bathroom. I lean against the frame of the door, taking in Mannix's work. Our navy blue paint job is so crisp and clean in contrast to the white trim. I admire the new vanity and its brushed-gold faucet and hardware. And in the corner, my jar of pebbles. A pebble from each beach. I reach in and retrieve my pebble from Race Point. Gray with the vein of white marble running through. Beside it is a little tray with tiny seashells. Carefully, I pick up a spiraled one, admiring the curve of the shell, the glossy pink interior, its random and strange perfection. I place it in my pocket.

Back downstairs, Peyton sits at the island with a lemon-lime seltzer, blissfully enjoying her lunch, and she pats the stool next to her, inviting me to sit down.

"You know what? I'm not hungry," I say. "I think I'm gonna go for a walk. I'll wait for Uncle Jack to eat."

"Okay," says Peyton, mouth full, eyes wide.

I pace down the driveway, out onto the sandy dirt road that skirts Uncle Jack's property, and I walk toward the bay, to the bridge that you can't cross once it's high tide. I still have a few hours before that's the case.

The green sea grass of the marsh pokes above the rising tide. At the edge, beside the bridge, I kick off my shoes and hop into the cold water. It hits just above my knees, but I wade over to the first pier holding up the structure, then reach for the beam closest to me. Withdrawing the shell from my pocket, I place it deep in the corner below the bridge. Something for me to find next summer; maybe it'll last.

Sloshing my way back to the sea grass, I steady myself with

one hand on the bridge, but I can't get a foothold in the steep bank. I keep sliding back into the marsh, my feet squelching in the muddy sand.

"Shit," I mutter. I keep trying, but it becomes more and more impossible the longer I'm standing here.

Until a hand appears in front of me, and when I look up, Mannix crouches at the top of the embankment. "I've got you."

I forgot him, I realize. Not literally, of course. How could I? But I forgot how he makes me feel when he's near me. I forgot the way he tilts his head to the side when he isn't sure what to say. The way his half smile tugs at the corner of his mouth. The way I want to reach out and touch him. Always.

I exhale, but my breath trembles. "Thank you."

With both hands, he hoists me out of the water and then walks me to where his truck waits on the side of the road. "What were you doing?"

I turn back to the bridge, pointing. "I wanted to...to put a shell. For next summer."

He nods, not needing me to explain any further. "That mean you're coming back next year?"

"I come back every year."

Opening the door of the truck, he retrieves a hoodie from the passenger seat and offers it to me. I take it gratefully, wrapping myself in his scent.

"How'd you know I was here?" I ask.

"I got a letter in the mail the other day," he says, leaning against his truck. "From Sally's Sauces telling me I won second place in their contest, and they've been trying to get in touch with me."

I wrap his hoodie tighter around me, nodding at the ground.

"And I never entered any contest. Then when I thought I saw you at the deli—"

"Yeah, that was me. I ran." I bow my head, embarrassed.

"I went over to your uncle's house and talked to your sister. Peyton?"

"Mm-hmm."

"And she told me you went for a walk."

"You knew to find me here?"

"I had one of those gut feelings." He smiles, but when he sees I don't return his expression, he looks back down at his feet.

"I entered you in the contest," I confess. "I did it over the summer, at the food truck fest."

"That was really thoughtful of you, but—"

I don't want to hear what comes after that. "I did it because I think you're wonderful," I say quietly, my voice quivering with the rest of my body. "I think everything you do is wonderful, and I'm not sure you see yourself that way. And I wanted to celebrate you. I wanted everyone to celebrate you. I'm sorry I didn't tell you, though. It was supposed to be a surprise, but then things between us just..."

"Yeah," he says, his expression soft.

"I'm sorry," I say, trying not to cry. "Please don't think you weren't enough for me. Please don't think that. *I* wasn't enough for me, and so how could I ever show up for you when I was still dealing with all this baggage?"

"Cor," he says quietly, reaching out and touching my arm, then letting his hand drop.

But I rush and tell him, "Everywhere I go, I find myself thinking of you. Everything I do, I find myself thinking of you.

Everyone I'm with, I find myself thinking of you. You're every-where, but you're not with me."

He takes a step closer. "I'm here now."

I laugh and cry all in one pathetically strangled yelp. "Yeah, you are."

"When you left in August, I...I thought about what you said. And I made some changes."

"With Kayla?"

He frowns. "What? No. I know that looked bad, but she found out what happened with my dad, and she came over to help get the house ready for him to come home. I wasn't going to say no; I needed the help. She's my friend."

I focus on the ground, a little ashamed. "So what changes are you talking about?"

He stands next to me. Close enough to touch me if he wanted to, but his hands remain in his pockets. "I, um. I signed up for some classes at the community college. Some culinary classes. I start spring semester. I thought if I liked them, if I was any good at them, maybe I'd apply to a real school in the fall."

I grab his arm automatically. "You *will* be good at them. You're amazing."

He stares at my hand. "I really missed you, Cor."

"I really missed you, too." Pulling me into a tight embrace, Mannix drops a kiss in my hair.

"You know," he says. "If you're going to Boston next year, it's not the worst drive from here."

"I guess not," I mumble into his shoulder.

"And if you pay for my gas, I might be willing to make the trip."

I punch him in the arm, but he laughs and backs away.

"What? No?"

"If paying for your gas was the only way to see you, I'd do it." I wipe my eyes with the sleeve of his hoodie.

"Nah." He waves it away and then takes both of my hands in his. "You just need to ask, and I'd be right there."

"I know." I lift my mouth up toward his, inviting him closer.

He tilts his face downward and his lips meet mine, hesitant, like we've never kissed before. But there are some things you can't forget. His mouth is soft and warm, and he pulls me closer, like this couldn't possibly be enough.

"Let me drive you home," he says, his fingers coaxing their way between mine. "You're shivering."

I agree, letting him open the truck door for me, but I peer over my shoulder at the bridge one last time.

"Think it'll last till June?" he asks, following my gaze.

"I do."

"You'll have to come back and check, I guess."

"We'll come back together?" I ask him hopefully.

"Of course." He kisses me again, his forehead against mine. "We always come back."

Author's Note

Whales have always been a part of my life, just as writing has. So I knew that when the opportunity arrived, I'd use whatever small influence I might have to write a story that shed light on the perils they face every day, why they matter, and why they're worth saving.

Many believe that the Save the Whales movement of the 1960s, considered the foundation for modern conservation efforts, is something from the past. And while we've made great progress in protecting whales, the harsh reality is that there's still a long way to go. Whales, along with dolphins, seals, sharks, sea turtles, and far too many other marine animals, are often the victims of bycatch. Nets and lines are set out to catch fish or crustaceans for human consumption but often end up ensnaring other unsuspecting animals.

I've always been aware of this, but the first time it really hit home for me was when I visited the Center for Coastal Studies in Provincetown, Massachusetts. There, much like my fictional

Marine Research and Conservation Alliance, they have the full skeleton of a humpback whale named Spinnaker. Spinnaker was born in 2004 and was found dead off Acadia National Park in Maine in 2015. During her brief life, she was entangled four times, the fourth causing her death. Lodged and preserved in the jaw of her skeleton is part of the rope that killed her. She was hogtied, mouth to flukes, unable to swim, unable to feed. She died a slow and excruciating death.

So I created Fraction, a whale with a similarly devastating story, but this one would have a happy ending. I'd rewrite Spinnaker's story because she deserved better than what she got.

Whales are incredibly sentient creatures. They have lives, emotions, rituals, culture, perhaps even language much like our own. Humpback whales, for example, have been known to perform acts of altruism—showing kindness and consideration for other animals with no benefit to themselves. This is a characteristic once believed to be found only in humans.

If you happen to visit the *Spinnaker* exhibition, you'll see her skeleton hanging from the ceiling, and you can watch the underwater footage taken during each effort to free her. It's difficult to witness, but don't turn away. Stand under her rib cage, look up, see where her heart used to dwell. Then make the promise to live your life a little more gently.

I encourage you to get involved and learn more about threats to whales, such as entanglements, ship strikes, ocean noise, and whaling. Whales suffer because of humans, and we are obligated to change that. The following organizations and links can be the start.

Center for Coastal Studies

https://coastalstudies.org

International Fund for Animal Welfare

https://ifaw.org

Atlantic White Shark Conservancy

https://atlanticwhiteshark.org

Natural Resources Defense Council

https://nrdc.org

Acknowledgments

This novel was truly a group effort by people who love books, whales, Cape Cod, and the sea. I am utterly humbled by the help I've received in researching and writing this book of my heart, my love letter to the whales of Cape Cod.

As always, to my agent, Liza Fleissig, whose help, support, and friendship always go above and beyond. I'm so thankful to have you as my agent and my friend. To my editor, Samantha Gentry: I can literally recall the exact moment Liza called me to say that you loved this book and you wanted it. I cannot believe the journey it's taken us on! I'm so grateful for your belief in this book, in Cor and Mannix, and of course, in Fraction. Thank you to Dion MBD, my cover illustrator, who created a stunning cover I had only ever dreamed of; Karina Granda; Jake Regier; Barbara Perris; and the entire team at Little, Brown Books for Young Readers/Poppy.

Thank you to my critique partners who worked with me through so many drafts of this book: Donna Galanti, Jess Rinker, and Joe McGee. I'm proud to be friends with such talented, generous authors. Thank you also to my friends, educators, and fellow authors who have had their eyes on this book in multiple capacities: Dr. Cherylann Schmidt, Elizabeth Keppel, Elizabeth Walls, Kerry Gans, Amanda Moore, and Anya Josephs.

Thank you so much to Kelsey Stone and Richard Dolan for giving me such detailed information about humpback whales and the ecosystems of Cape Cod. And especially to Cathrine Macort and the team at the Center for Coastal Studies in Provincetown, Massachusetts. There are no words to truly express my gratitude and awe for what you do. Your work is vital and selfless, and you've been so generous in answering my questions about Cape Cod and entanglements. Thank you to Suzy Blake of the Wellfleet Lifeguards for helping me bring Mannix to life. I hope he does you proud! And to Skott Daltonic, who has brought me out to Stellwagen Bank on countless whale watches: Your advocacy for animals and the environment is inspirational.

To my dear family and friends, without whose support no book would ever be possible: I love you.

Tyler Cranden

ERICA GEORGE

is the author of *Words Composed of Sea and Sky*. She is a graduate of The College of New Jersey, with degrees in both English and education, and is currently an MFA student at Vermont College of Fine Arts. She resides in northern New Jersey but spends her summers soaking up the salty sea air on Cape Cod. She invites you to follow her at ericageorgewrites.com or on Twitter @theericageorge.